D0341270

ALSO BY

FIONA SNYCKERS

Trinity On Track
Team Trinity
Trinity On Air
Trinity Rising
Spire
Now Following You

LACUNA

Fiona Snyckers

LACUNA

Europa
editions

Europa Editions
1 Penn Plaza, Suite 6282
New York, N.Y. 10019
www.europaeditions.com
info@europaeditions.com

Library of Congress Cataloging in Publication Data is available
ISBN 978-1-60945-725-9

Snyckers, Fiona
Lacuna

Book design by Emanuele Ragnisco
www.mekkanografici.com

Original cover design by publicide

Prepress by Grafica Punto Print – Rome

Printed in Italy

Author's Note

This book is not a retelling of J. M. Coetzee's *Disgrace*. It is also not a sequel to *Disgrace*. It establishes an intertextual conversation with *Disgrace*.

My character, Lucy Lurie, has two things in common with Coetzee's Lucy Lurie—her name, and the fact that she is a victim of gang rape. Everything else about her is original and fictional.

I use the character of Lucy to explore the phenomenon of white feminism in South Africa. My Lucy Lurie is a flawed character, trapped in her own racism and unconscious biases. She is solipsistic and selfish. She chooses racial solidarity with her father over gender solidarity with the victims of his sexual predation. In return for this loyalty, her father betrays her in a fundamental way.

My Lucy practises a shallow form of feminism that does not take into account intersectionality or the lived experiences of women from other backgrounds. She entertains wild thoughts and makes flawed life choices. She is the protagonist of this book, but not the heroine.

Some scenes in the novel take place in Lucy's imagination. This is not always clearly signposted.

The character "John Coetzee" in my novel is entirely fictional.

"It will be, after all, a child of this earth.
They will not be able to deny that."
—from *Disgrace* by J.M. COETZEE

LACUNA

LACUNA

PROLOGUE

J ohn Coetzee spent forty years writing a book.
It was to be a great novel of Dickensian scope and significance. An agent in London was very interested in the
book. As the years passed, that agent died and was replaced by
another agent, who was also very interested in it. At no time
was either agent interested enough to sign John Coetzee as a
client.

As retirement loomed, Coetzee realised it would be humil-
iating to leave the English Department before the book was
published. Especially since he had been using extracts from it
in his teaching for years. It had always been a question of when
it would be published, not whether. If he were to retire from
the department with the book still unpublished, there would
be sniggering—definite sniggering.

John Coetzee was on the horns of a dilemma, and there he
might have remained if something wonderful hadn't occurred.

A young woman, a junior lecturer in the department, went
to visit her father on his farm outside the Boland town of
Worcester. While she was there, she was raped by a gang of
intruders. The farmhouse was set alight, and everyone agreed
she was fortunate to escape with her life.

Something about the story struck a chord with John
Coetzee. He went home that night and began to write a novel
about the incident. Before he went to bed, five thousand words
had leaped from his brain onto his computer screen.

The Dickensian novel was never touched again. Instead,

Coetzee poured all his energies into the rape book. Eight, nine, ten thousand words a day were nothing to him. The story gushed out. The first draft was finished in record time. This time, the agent was interested enough to sign Coetzee on the spot and to take the book to auction. Twelve publishing houses joined the bidding war and a seven-figure sum was decided upon. The news was announced days before the Frankfurt Book Fair, and became the stuff of legend in the publishing world.

The book was the most buzzed-about publishing event of the year. Pre-publication copies were sent to selected reviewers and bloggers who wrote about it in laudatory—nay, worshipful—terms. It zoomed to the top of the bestseller lists. Commentators ran out of superlatives with which to describe it.

A year later, it had won most of the literary awards for which it was eligible, including the Man Booker Prize. John Coetzee went overnight from provincial academic obscurity to becoming one of the most celebrated authors of his age.

He shook the dust of the English Department from his feet and retired to his home to write his much-anticipated second book.

One of the most discussed aspects of John Coetzee's novel has been the complete absence of the raped woman's voice in the narrative. Indeed, the rape takes place off-stage in the manner of the ancient Greek tragedians. Critics have called this a deliberate "lacuna" in the novel—a gap more powerful in its absence than it would have been in its presence.

My name is Lucy Lurie, and I am that lacuna.

CHAPTER 1

A lacuna is an unfilled space or gap.

My vagina is a lacuna that my attackers filled with their penises. They saw the lack in me and chose to supply what I couldn't. Their penises were rough and dry and scraped my lacuna raw, bruising my cervix, and tearing my perineum.

Sometimes I dream that my rape is happening off-stage—in the manner of the ancient Greek tragedians. I am lying in another room and listening to it. I can hear my cries of pain—loud at first, then softening to whimpers. I can hear their grunts of frustration and triumph. One of them manages to ejaculate, which he does with a roar of victory.

I can't feel what is happening or even see it, except in my imagination. The soundtrack on the other side of the wall lets me know how far they have progressed. Now they are taking a break. Now they have got their second wind and are starting again.

It is less harrowing than being in that room myself. Experiencing something at one remove is a pale shadow of the real thing. The ancient Greek tragedians were wrong if they thought that leaving the rough stuff to the readers' imaginations was more effective than rubbing our noses in it.

But perhaps that wasn't their intention at all. Perhaps they simply thought it was more genteel to keep ugliness off the stage. No one wants to watch stomach-turning violence at the theatre, especially over dinner. It can be very upsetting.

Was that what Coetzee was doing? Was he being genteel—tiptoeing around the sensibilities of his readers? Or did he believe it would be more effective for the rape to take place off-stage in the arena of the reader's imagination? Coetzee apologists have suggested that he was making a feminist point by leaving that lacuna unfilled in the text—that he was illustrating how rape victims are stripped of agency and denied a voice.

I see it as a lacuna in his own literary imagination. He does not supply details on the page because his imagination failed him when it came to describing what happened to me.

You don't want to hear this, do you? There is nothing more tedious than a rageful harpy ranting about some cherished grievance. It's so 1981. So Andrea Dworkin. So Catharine MacKinnon.

Let me tell you what John Coetzee was like as a colleague instead.

I say colleague, but remember, he was the Rawlings Professor of Apolitical Close Reading while I was a junior lecturer on a one-year, non-renewable contract. In corporate terms, this would be the equivalent of the CEO of a multinational corporation being regarded as a colleague of the mould growing on the underside of the cleaner's bucket. It is impossible to overstate what a gap in status there was between us.

Furthermore, he was a man and I was a very young woman. You might think this is irrelevant, but that would prove how little you know about the generation of academics Coetzee represents.

Coetzee and I interacted face-to-face on three occasions. I should describe them for you. Show, not tell. That's Memoir Writing 101. Not easy for those of us trained in academic exegesis. We have been schooled to tell, with very little need to show.

The first occasion was at my thesis defence seminar, before I got the junior lectureship.

This is part of how PhDs are awarded at the University of Constantia: your thesis is read by a panel of your peers, before whom you appear in person to defend your work against such questions and comments as they might want to put to you. This is known as your thesis defence.

Mine went by in a blur, but some moments stand out. One is of Prof. Coetzee asking me whether I agreed that feminist literary theory had "run its course." This was in the middle of my animated discussion with a professor from the African Studies Department about whether the particular strand of Afrofuturistic feminist methodology I had chosen was the correct paradigm to apply to the texts in question.

He also asked whether I was married or intended to have children, without explaining why these points were relevant.

Later I heard that my thesis had been passed—provided I expanded two sections and corrected a few typos—by a majority of five panellists to one. I had no doubt who that one hold-out panellist was. At the time, it didn't trouble me. John Coetzee's questions about feminist methodology and my marital status became comic fodder for me to recycle among my friends at the Cap & Gown pub near campus.

Prof. Coetzee was an anachronism. His time was up. He and the generation he represented were history. Coetzee's failed literary ambitions were an open secret at the university. The unfinished manuscript was a running joke among undergraduates at the University of Constantia, who used to quote bits of its cringeworthy dialogue to each other.

Never did we imagine that he was a whisker away from writing the book that would scoop that year's major literary awards. He was about to become South Africa's next Booker Prize winner. First Nadine Gordimer, and now John Coetzee. We would have choked on our beers laughing if anyone had suggested such a thing.

The second time Coetzee and I came face-to-face was at my

interview for the one-year rotating post of junior lecturer. As is common in job interviews, there came a time when the panel asked me if I had any questions to put to them. I asked if there was a chance of the post being extended into something more long-term. Coetzee responded by asking whether I was happy with the maternity-leave provisions in the contract or whether I would wish to see them extended. The message was clear. He wasn't about to award a permanent post to a young woman who would be popping out babies at the first opportunity.

The third time was in the general office of the English Department. The main attraction of this office was its laser printer. Those members of staff who were too poor (like me) or too cheap (like Prof. Coetzee) to buy their own printers were allowed to send documents to the office printer. You had to be light on your feet when it came to collecting your document, or you might find it thrown into the recycling bin or scattered around the office.

On this day, I had sent a reading list to the printer. As soon as I pressed send, I jogged along the corridor to the office to pick it up. I found John Coetzee staring at the printer with an air of puzzlement as it spat out twenty-five copies of my second-year reading list.

I readied my politest smile as I walked up to the printer. This was the most senior member of the department, after all. He made no eye contact. Only when my print run was finished, and I reached into the tray to collect my reading list, did he speak.

"This printer is for the use of staff members only."

"That's right," I agreed.

"Staff members of the English Department."

"I know."

There was a pause as he stared at me.

"I'm a junior lecturer." My voice came out higher and younger than I wanted it to. "In this department." *You interviewed me*, I wanted to add, before self-respect stopped me.

The accusing stare didn't lift. The printer lurched into life again.

"Look!" I said. "Here comes your document now."

Up to that moment, I had been under the impression that I was making a mark on the department with my diligence and enthusiasm. The bigwigs were noticing. If I made myself indispensable, my contract might be renewed at the end of the year. The realisation that a senior professor was unaware of my existence put paid to that delusion.

Imagine my surprise to find myself, a year later, one of the central characters in Coetzee's novel. He even used my full name, Lucy Lurie. It was as though he were daring me to sue him, knowing I didn't have the means or the resolution to do so. Lucy means "light" in Greek. Scholars have made much of his use of nominative determinism in the book. Lucy is the moral centre of the novel—an unwavering source of light and goodness. She is an unflawed character, apart from some amusing mannerisms.

She has a way of walking with her toes turned out like a duck—a legacy of her early training as a dancer. She blinks her eyes and screws up her nose when she gets tired or when her contact lenses irritate her. When she is talking to someone who makes her uneasy, she twists a strand of hair around her forefinger until it hangs lankly by the side of her face. When she believes herself to be unobserved, she sucks on her baby finger until it becomes wrinkled and bloodless.

These are my mannerisms. Only one who has observed me closely would notice them. I want to shrink when I think of Coetzee observing my hank of over-fingered hair. Mortification slaps me on both cheeks when I realise he must have walked past my office and seen me sucking my finger.

The man who pretended not to recognise me when I ran into him in the general office had been watching me all that time, cataloguing my habits.

The critics ate it up. It was so perfectly Coetzee-ish (yes, that is now a word) to humanise an otherwise angelic character by giving her a laundry list of bathetic qualities.

* * *

I don't see many people from the English Department these days, but my friend Moira comes around sometimes. She asks whether I'm flattered to realise how carefully Coetzee had been watching me.

I tell her I'm not. Not at all.

But that's a lie.

Something within me blooms under the warm, acknowledging gaze of a clever older man. I feel worthy. Validated. I feel like I exist. Like I matter.

And I despise myself for feeling like that.

CHAPTER 2

I have a therapist. Of course, I do. Every middle-class white woman who gets raped has a therapist. It's only if you are poor and black that you don't need a therapist after being raped. You pick yourself up, dust yourself off, and get on with it. Your feelings aren't as tender as those of a middle-class white woman. Your scars don't run as deep. Your trauma isn't as real. You're a coper. A survivor. Your skin is thicker. You shrug these things off faster.

They say that going to therapy straight after a traumatic event is next to useless. The trauma is too raw for that kind of counselling to be of any help. So I did it right. Shortly after the rape, I went for crisis counselling—the first-aid of the counselling world. It gets you through the immediate aftermath of the event.

Then, after more than a year, I started going to proper long-term therapy. I committed myself to putting in the "work" I needed to recover. That's shrink-speak. When you go to therapy, you are doing "work."

My therapist is a woman. Naturally. You wouldn't consult a man after being raped. Her name is Lydia Bascombe, and she thinks I shouldn't be so flippant about needing her.

"Why do you feel the need to compare yourself to other rape survivors?" she asks.

"It's a natural impulse, isn't it? When you've been through something life-changing, you want to know how other people who have been through the same thing are coping."

"But you disparage yourself constantly. It's as if you believe you have no right to therapy just because not everyone can afford it."

"Do I, though?"

"Why do you feel that you don't?"

Shrinks always answer questions with questions. I am not the first to make this observation.

"It's a luxury," I say. "An indulgence. You can dress it up as something else by calling it 'work,' but it's an opportunity to talk about yourself for an hour. To someone who is paid to care."

"There are other luxuries that not everyone can afford. Like a roof over one's head and three meals a day. Do you feel unworthy of those too?"

"Perhaps I do."

"But you accept them. You don't put on sackcloth and ashes and start living in a shack. You don't choose to subsist on mealie-meal and tripe. You don't flirt with nutritional deficiency and hypothermia."

"Aren't you arguing with me now? You're trying to persuade me to see things your way. Therapists aren't meant to do that."

She goes quiet. She is struggling with what looks like irritation. She is annoyed with my refusal to see the light—to get better.

"Rational argument can be part of the therapeutic process." There is little conviction in her voice. She has overstepped the mark, and she knows it. I feel satisfaction at having rattled her. But now it is her turn to rattle me, and that won't be nearly as pleasant. It is all part of the give-and-take of what she likes to call "the therapeutic process."

"Perhaps you find it easier to focus on other rape survivors than on yourself?" The gentleness in her voice tells me she is moving in for the kill. She will make me cry today. She can sense my tears in the wind.

"No, actually, it's harder." Good. That came out steady as a rock.

"Why is that? Surely your own pain is the hardest to contemplate?"

"I can't think about anyone else's pain." Less steady now. "It's too much. I can't make sense of it." My voice is breaking on every second or third word. "Other women have been gang-raped. Other women have been through what I went through, only worse." I'm sobbing uncontrollably now—gasping out words between sobs. L. Bascombe leans forward to hear better. "Some of them were stabbed and strangled as well. They had their bellies cut open and their guts spilled out and coated in dirt. The doctors had to wash that mess before piling it back in again."

She nods to show she knows the case I am referring to. It was on the news a while ago. Astonishingly, the woman survived.

"It happens all the time to black women up and down the country. To impoverished women all over the world." It comes out as *impo-ho-ho-ho-vrisht*. "None of them gets to see a shrink afterwards. When they're patched up enough to walk, they're sent home—often to the bastard who hurt them in the first place." (*Ba-ha-ha-ha-stid.*) "And they have to get on with it—cooking, cleaning, looking after the kids, showing up for work. No fifty-minute hours for them. No sirree."

Lydia Bascombe's voice is soothing now that she is back in the driver's seat. Her patience is infinite. "Your capacity for empathy in the midst of your own pain is laudable."

I laugh. It comes out as a sob. "But that's it. I'm not empathetic. Every time I think about those other women, my brain tells me they're not really like me. They don't feel as deeply as I do. I'm more sensitive than they are. They're tougher, shallower. I mean, how can they possibly feel things as acutely as my precious white self? They're just living the life they're used to. Their trauma can't compare to mine."

L. Bascombe's eyes are shifty, darting from side to side. I

have made her uncomfortable. She swallows—a dry, clicking sound audible to both of us.

"How do you feel when it's a white woman who has been attacked?"

"The same. I find reasons why it wasn't as bad for her. She is probably not as bright as I am. Not as sensitive. She's more of a coper. She'll get over it." I draw a breath that shakes so much it sounds like three separate breaths. "There can't be that much pain in the world. It can't all be equal to mine. I can't stand it if it is."

She lets out her own breath in a thin stream. Her world has righted itself. I'm not racist after all—just traumatised.

"Total empathy is impossible to sustain. You must realise that. We cannot feel all the pain in the world all the time without going mad. It's a natural defence mechanism to find reasons for believing that someone else's pain is not as bad as ours. This is something we are trained as psychologists to recognise in ourselves."

"How do you cope?" I wail. "You specialise in counselling victims of sexual violence. How do you listen to these stories day in and day out without going crazy?"

"We're talking about you and your pain. Why do you think you feel the need to deflect the focus onto me?"

And we're back on familiar ground again. The classic shrink bait-and-switch.

Monday, 10.45, 17 May
Patient: Lucy Lurie
Diagnosis: bipolar, depression, schizoid delusions, border-line personality disorder, paranoia
Referred by: Dr. J. Coetzee

The patient is a twenty-eight-year-old well-nourished woman. She presents with a history of uncontrollable outbursts and delusions. She is trained as an academic and was working in this capacity until recently. She is not working at present.

She persists in her conviction that she was raped two years ago by a group of men who broke into her father's farmhouse where she was visiting for dinner. This seems to be loosely based on the celebrated novel *Disgrace* by John Coetzee.

Ms. Lurie identifies with the character "Lucy" in the novel and has become convinced that Coetzee based his book on her experiences. Ms. Lurie and John Coetzee worked in the same department at the University of Constantia for a time, and her fixation on him seems to have begun while they were still colleagues.

When Coetzee wrote his book, which instantly became a massive international success, Ms. Lurie was overcome by jealousy. She has repeatedly stated that she had novelistic ambitions herself.

There is evidence to suggest that Coetzee based the character of "Lucy" loosely on Ms. Lurie. Aside from sharing the same name, they are of a similar age and physical description. Coetzee appears to have drawn some of the details of his character's appearance and mannerisms from his observation of Ms. Lurie.

These few synchronicities persuaded Ms. Lurie that she suffered the same traumatic experience as Coetzee's character. This morbid eliding of truth and fiction is one of the most common symptoms of the true paranoid delusional personality.

We have here a classic case of an impressionable young woman who, achieving mediocre results in her own career, fixates on a powerful older man, and persuades herself that he returns her interest. Ms. Lurie has gone so far as to insert herself into the fictional world of Coetzee's brilliant novel in an effort to occupy the same psychological space as her idol. But, as is also typical in these cases, her love for Coetzee turned sour and may now more accurately be described as obsessive loathing.

A course of strong anti-hallucinogenic medication will be prescribed for this patient, along with behavioural rehabilitation. Serious consideration should be given to electroconvulsive therapy for its well-known calmative effects. I await your further instructions.

Kind regards,
Lydia Bascombe

That's not real.

I wrote it.

I am untrustworthy. But I'm the only access you have to this story. My lens is the only one through which you are permitted to peek. Does that make you feel unsafe?

I bet you'd prefer a calm, authoritative, third-person narrator to set the facts out for you. Neutrality is a man's job, after all. One needs an implied male narrator to cut through the hysteria of the feminine perspective and bring balance to the story. The testimony of women is not to be trusted. They are like children in that regard. And when you bring sexual assault into the mix—well, it makes the uncertainty worse.

Women regularly accuse men of rapes that never happened. It's a well-known fact. We used to have a law that took this into account. It was called the "cautionary rule." It didn't apply only in South Africa, although we were among the last countries to get rid of it. Most Common Law countries had some version of it. The idea was that judges and juries were required to take into account the fact that sexual complainants were inherently unreliable witnesses. This was particularly so where there were no corroborating witnesses to support the allegation.

And that's the pesky thing about sexual assault, isn't it? There often are no other witnesses besides the victim and the perpetrator. Defenders of the cautionary rule (and there were many) used to say that it wasn't specifically targeted at women. It applied to children, too. Children who claimed to have been sexually assaulted were assumed to be inherently untruthful. Female complainants could take comfort from the fact that the law regarded them in the same light as children when it came to their reliability and veracity.

South Africa got rid of the cautionary rule in 1998. Courts are no longer allowed to work from the presumption that sexual complainants are lying, but the legacy of that presumption lingers. "To cry rape" is a phrase that still exists in our lexicon. We feel automatic sympathy for the legions of men falsely accused of rape by their wives, girlfriends, colleagues, and random women on the street.

The #MeToo movement has caused this to run out of control. How are men expected to defend themselves when a single woman's testimony is enough to put them in jail? It is terrible the way all the world's legal and political institutions are skewed in favour of women.

Enough of that.

The thing is—I don't feel believed. Even with all the medical evidence supporting my claim: the photos of my vaginal tearing, the bruises on my thighs, the cervical trauma, the semen, the bites and contusions and saliva all over my body— I don't feel believed. I am the unreliable witness. I am the inherently untruthful complainant.

It's like quantum theory. If a tree falls in the forest and nobody is there to hear it, does it scream? If a woman gets raped in a farmhouse and nobody is there to witness it, did it happen?

My father witnessed it, but he doesn't count because he is my father.

Sometimes I see such scepticism in my therapist's eyes that I know she doubts my story. Yes, she has read the medical reports. Yes, she followed the media when the story was all over the news. Yes, she knew that Coetzee based his book on my experience. She had heard of me before I was ever referred to her.

But I was not what she expected. Sometimes I disgust her. Sometimes I irritate her. Sometimes I can see the words "pull yourself together" trembling on her lips.

And so, I write down my worst fears. My worst fear is not that I will be raped again one night when I am alone in my flat. My worst fear is that I will not be believed.

CHAPTER 3

M y friend Moira is a star-fucker. A literary star-fucker. She would walk past Idris Elba in the street without a second glance, but she would follow Jonathan Franzen to the ends of the earth.

Starfucker (Urban Dictionary)
A person who is obsessed with and seeks out personal interaction with celebrities. The desired interaction is often, but not necessarily, sexual in nature.

I don't like the compound word "starfucker" so I'm keeping it separate as "star-fucker," but the meaning is the same. Moira has always been in awe of John Coetzee. He was the official Great Man of Letters at the University of Constantia English Department, even before he produced any letters worth noting. After the book appeared and the literary plaudits poured in, her awe changed to worship.

It took little effort, therefore, to persuade her to accompany me to his house in the Bo-Kaap. Moira is hard at work on a Map of the Stars, showing where the most famous authors in Cape Town live. Coetzee's house is already on her radar. Number 15, Companie Street, Bo-Kaap.

Not for Coetzee the bright, Neapolitan-ice-cream colours of many Bo-Kaap houses. Neither cerulean blue nor fuschia pink have the power to tempt him. His house remains resolutely white—a lily among the colour-burst of roses.

"He bought the house in 1982, the year he got tenure," says Moira as I park my car pointing nose-first down Signal Hill and pull the handbrake up as far as it will go. We clamber out. I nod at a car guard who promises to keep an eye on my vehicle for me.

"How the hell do you know that?"

"The date he got tenure is on the university website, and the date he bought the house is a matter of public record. I put two and two together and figured that the financial stability of getting tenure enabled him to get a bond to buy the house. It must have been a very different place back then."

"You mean when the original residents could still afford to live here?"

"Well, yes. It was an odd choice for a white man during the height of apartheid. This place was basically a Cape Malay neighbourhood. I wonder how he was even allowed to buy property here."

"He was a white man. White men were allowed to do whatever the fuck they liked under apartheid."

"True. Mind you, he must be laughing all the way to the bank now. Property up here costs a bomb these days."

Coetzee's house shows no sign of the gentrification that has romped unchecked through the rest of the Bo-Kaap. Flyblown net curtains hang in the windows. The paint is weathered and dirty. Only the metal bars crisscrossing each windowpane and the old-fashioned security gate at the front door bear witness to Coetzee's days as the only white resident in the neighbourhood.

"Isn't it interesting that he bought a house here decades before it became fashionable to do so?" Moira clasps her hands. "Doesn't that make you feel kindlier towards him?"

I shrug. In the narrative looping through my head, Coetzee was a slumlord. He bought up dozens of these little houses and rented them out to poor families at punitive rates.

"Please, professor," a mother in rags begged him. *"My children are dying of cold. Please fix the broken windows and the holes in the door. The rain comes right into the house."*

"Begone, woman. And don't darken my doorstep again."

"So, what do you want to do? Shall we ring the bell?"

I'm not sure what I want to do. I want to confront Coetzee. I want to tell him that I'm nobody's lacuna, and that I won't be erased from my own story. But I also don't want to see him at all, and this is the more likely scenario.

The car guard has seen us looking at the house and wanders over.

"Is djulle hier ommie prifessa te visit?"

"Sort of."

"Djulle sal hom nie sien nie, merrem. He duzzin't answer da doorbell. Not for no one, merrem."

"We've heard that."

"Dja! Ou Prifessa Coetzee. Snaakse ou, daai. Djulle wiet hy't mos 'n boek geskryf, né?"

We nod. We know he wrote a book.

"Dja. Hy't a boek geskryf en alleranne pryse gewen mos . . . en dit was die laaste sien vannie blikkantien."

No. I can't write this in dialect. I feel like a minstrel dressed in blackface and suspenders. This is an act of piracy, and I can't participate in it. This man doesn't exist for my amusement or yours. His language is not "colourful" or "vibrant." I will not use this as an opportunity to demonstrate my facility as a writer of vernacular. I will tell you what he says in my own words.

It seems John Coetzee was once a well-known and recognisable member of this community. Then his book became famous and he vanished into thin air (*spoorloos in die niet in verdwyn*).

At first the locals thought he had merely become a hermit. He retired from his post at the university and from public life entirely. But he was still seen popping in and out of the local shops. He would buy groceries from the Seven-Eleven and coffee beans from the organic coffee roastery (see Bo-Kaap: gentrification of).

Then all sightings of him dried up. But the lights came on in his house at night and were switched off during the day. His wheelie bin appeared on the sidewalk on garbage collection days and was whisked back in again as soon as it had been emptied.

Now even those signs of life have stopped. John Coetzee has well and truly disappeared (*soos mis voor die môreson*). Rumour has it, the car guard informs us, that he has gone to Australia.

Moira and I exchange glances. This is one of the wildest and most out-there rumours we have heard. Or that she has heard. Moira, after all, is the one who still works in the English Department—the one who still has a job in academia and is in a position to keep her ear to the ground.

Hearing this repeated here in the rising sea mist—with lights popping on up and down the road, and the throat-catching smell of coriander seeds heating in a dry pan—gives it credence somehow. This is more than the booming of the departmental jungle drums. This might be true.

"He's not here?" I ask. "He is definitely not here?"

The car guard assures me he is not.

This emboldens me enough to walk up to the house with the peeling white paint, to insert my fist between the bars of the eighties-style Spanish grille, and to knock twice on the wooden door. There is no answer, so I knock again. Three loud raps this time.

There.

I will not be ignored. I have come to state my case. I am nobody's lacuna.

A scuffling sound next to me makes me jump like a cartoon character. I scrape my wrist on the rusting metal grille. It is only a pigeon scrabbling about in the dry leaves trapped in the gutter. I turn and hurry down the steps. My heart is beating so hard I can see the sides of my vision throbbing.

Moira is bent double from laughing.

* * *

"Australia." Moira settles in the passenger seat and fastens her seatbelt. "I wonder if that means the Twitter account is genuine."

"Twitter account?"

"There's a Twitter account in John Coetzee's name in which he describes himself as 'an Australian writer.' We thought it was fake. It might still be fake. It's not even verified."

"How did John Coetzee go from being a technophobic nobody to someone who has to be verified on Twitter?"

"He wrote a brilliant book."

"I don't think it was brilliant."

"That's because you aren't thinking clearly. You should try to be more like fiction-Lucy. She is nicer than you are. Fiction-Lucy would admit that the book is brilliant."

* * *

How can you live in a country your whole life and make no effort to learn any of its local languages? Most Swiss people can speak, or at least understand, both German and French. Most Americans who live close to the Mexican border have taken the trouble to learn basic Spanish.

What does it say about English-speaking South Africans that many of us don't understand a word of any African local languages apart from hello and goodbye? What kind of arrogance expects an entire country to conform to the language we speak? When we travel overseas, we acquaint ourselves with useful phrases, or use Google Translate to help us manage the language for the few weeks we are there. It is courteous to make an effort to speak the local language, even if your inter-locutor switches to English immediately.

Yet in three hundred and fifty years, we have never both-ered to learn any indigenous South African languages.

These were the thoughts that went through my mind as my assailants argued about whether they had time to rape me. At least, I think that is what they were saying. They were speaking isiXhosa. I had to infer what they were saying from the way they grabbed my breasts and mimed thrusting their hips. I didn't understand the words. I have never wanted to join a conversation more.

"No," I wanted to say. "Please don't. There is no time. You will be interrupted. Flee now while you have the chance."

I did say those things, but in English. Would it have made a difference if I had said them in isiXhosa? Would they have fallen back in wonder and declined to rape this woman who spoke their language? I doubt it. But the helplessness of not knowing what was being said, of being unable to take part in the negotiation, has stayed with me. I dream of a babel of voices around me. The only way I can escape the thing they are planning to do to me is by understanding what they are saying.

So I start to speak in tongues like a worshipper in some charismatic church. Perhaps if I open my mouth and let loose a stream of Xhosa-sounding words, it will turn out that I can speak it after all. But the stream slows to a trickle, and the trickle dribbles to a halt. And the rape begins.

Rape is the gift that keeps on giving. I was raped many times that evening at the farmhouse. Too many times to count. You'd think that would be something you would never lose track of. But I did—and I have also lost count of how many times I have been raped in my dreams. I don't always remem-ber the dreams, but I wake up with tears on my cheeks and pain between my legs, and I know it has happened again.

It used to be every night. Now it's not. Perhaps I am getting better.

* * *

Coetzee knew it was my father who interrupted the rape. It was widely reported in the media. A reporter for the campus newspaper, *The Constantia Reporter*, speculated about what it must have been like for a father to walk in on such a scene. She had a turn for the poetical. She was an English major with ambitions of joining John Coetzee's creative writing programme.

Her flight of fancy, lyrical as it was, did her no good. Coetzee retired as soon as the ink on his book deal was dry. He never took on another creative writing student, and now he has disappeared.

What was it like for my father to find me in that position? The father in Coetzee's book is a cold fish. He is undemonstrative and detached. His daughter discourages him from any of the mutual soul-searching he might want to undertake.

The moment my father's eyes locked with mine over the heaving shoulder of my assailant, they filled with pity.

As a parent, it is widely understood, you would do anything to spare your child pain. You would transfer that pain onto yourself if you could. You feel homicidal rage towards anyone who hurts your child.

My father was one of those traditional dads who joked about buying a shotgun when I grew up. He was suspicious of any boy who showed an interest in me. As I entered puberty and my body changed shape, he became awkward about physical contact between us. He would hug me sideways with one arm. If he knew I was menstruating, he wouldn't hug me at all.

My father has never been comfortable with me as a sexual being. If he could have kept me small and pre-pubescent forever, he would have done so. I know this doesn't reflect well on him. His attitudes were patriarchal and outdated. They denied my agency as an adult, and as a person with control over my sexual choices. But that's the way he was.

What must have been going through his mind when he walked into the sitting room of the farmhouse to find me in the middle of a gang rape? My clothes were in tatters, having been torn from my body. My face and neck were covered in blood from the nicks they'd given me with their knives to make me more cooperative. My legs were splayed open, numb from having been held in an unnatural position for so long.

The man rutting above me was finally finished, after sawing away for what seemed like an eternity. This was the moment my father walked in on.

The little girl he had taught to walk, and to swim, whose hand he had held while crossing the road, was undergoing the most profound violation a person could endure. He stood motionless, paralysed with shock. Then he flung himself forward and shouted. They fell back at once in the face of this paternal ire.

I rolled over and clutched the shreds of my T-shirt together, not to hide my breasts from my attackers, but to hide them from my father. I tried to raise myself onto all fours, but my legs were thick and stupid. They felt as though they belonged to someone else. All except my hips, where a distant, screaming ache was emerging.

My arms trembled too much to hold me up. I fell on my face twice, adding to the bleeding and bruising already there. By the time my father came back in, having scattered my assailants, I had given up on trying to rise without assistance. I lay on my side, tears leaking onto the floor, distressed at my father's distress, wishing I could have spared him this.

He walked past me without a word.

It's over, I thought. I have disgraced myself. But he was fetching a blanket, which he threw over me in silence.

After a long while, he said, "You must wash yourself, girl. You must get their stink off you. I will run you a bath."

"Yes, yes."

I wanted to scrub myself forever. I wanted to flay the skin from my bones. A clean skeleton, washed pristine by the tides, and brought forth onto the shore. *Those are pearls that were her eyes.*

He shuffled to the bathroom. I laid my cheek on the scratchy sisal carpet and watched his feet retreating down the passage. *Swish pof, swish pof* went his sandals. His ankles were thin and brittle, tendons jutting, bones stretching the skin thin. I saw age in my father. At sixty-eight, he wasn't all that old, but there was mortality in the papery skin and angle of bone.

He will never recover from this, I thought. I have tipped my father over middle age and sent him rolling towards death.

I heard the pounding of water filling the bath and saw steam billow into the passage. Good. The hotter the better. Let me boil myself. No trace must remain. The steam had an acrid smell that tickled my nostrils and caught at the back of my throat. It got thicker and thicker until I couldn't see down the passage. Yes, good. A cauldron to cleanse myself in.

The steam coalesced into a darker patch. My father burst out of the murk.

"Fire! Fire!"

Yes, fire. A cleansing fire.

"I thought there was time, but there isn't. We must go now." Go? Go where?

His hands scrabbled at my shoulders, plucked at my neck.

"Get up, child. Get up. The house is burning. We have to go."

I want to stay. He can't lift me. I'm too heavy. He will have to leave me here. The fire will cleanse me.

But a thousand red devils roared into the room and I was on my feet, clutching the blanket around me, running for the life I thought I no longer wanted.

othing is ever all bad, not even rape.

A few weeks later, I missed my period. I had always been irregular, so I didn't think much of it. Then coffee started to taste like metal and my sense of smell heightened to the point of pain. I could smell layers of odours everywhere, always with an underlying stink of rot. My stomach was unsettled most of the time. I didn't throw up, but I wanted to.

I missed another period. And another.

At four months, I went to have it confirmed. The obstetrician squirted jelly on my slightly protruding abdomen and slid his sensor over it. The monitor leaped into life. For a moment, it looked like a pot of thick marmalade boiling on the stove. Then the image resolved itself into a hydrocephalic baby.

Of course, the child of such a coupling would be a monster.

The obstetrician said nothing. He moved his sensor this way and that, freezing the image occasionally to take measurements. I wondered how bad the abnormality was. Was he steeling himself to tell me the truth, or had the delivery of bad news become routine to him?

"Everything looks fine. The four chambers of the heart are present and correct. The nuchal layer is within normal limits. The spine is well developed, with no signs of spina bifida."

"But the head. Is there anything that can be done?"

"The head is normal. What is troubling you about it?"

"It's so big."

"That's normal for Baby at this age. Their heads are quite large in relation to their bodies."

"Can you tell the sex?"

"Yes. I wasn't sure if you wanted to know."

"Tell me."

"It's a boy."

At the next scan, I was told that the bloodwork was normal. At the next, he was lying with his head up, but that could still change, right up until the last minute. At the seven-month scan, his head was down, and his buttocks were tucked under my diaphragm. At the eight-month scan, my placenta was looking good.

I was well throughout the pregnancy. Better than well. Everyone said I was glowing. I was the picture of health. My father said I had a self-absorbed, placid look. One day when I was picking vegetables for dinner at the farm, he said I looked like a peasant. He thought I belonged to the soil, and that my child would belong to the soil too. That made me feel peaceful and grounded, as though I had atoned for the sins of the white man in South Africa. I had taken the grievous act of colonialism upon my body and atoned for it with my rape. I had refused to name my attackers because I knew it was right to stay silent. The punishment was mine to endure alone, and now I was reaping the blessings that came after.

At nine months and two days, the baby was born after a ten-hour labour. He was a beautiful boy with wise, brown eyes. An old soul, everyone said. Something within me healed when I held him in my arms for the first time. Mother Nature saw to that.

It's you, I thought. Of course it is. Everything happens for a reason. Nothing is ever all bad.

He was a peaceful, joyful child. He slept well and fed well. I nourished him with my own body and he thrived. He slept in my bed, always content, never crying. Every time he smiled at me or reached up and touched my face, my wounds healed a little more.

At eight months, he crawled. At twelve months, he walked. At thirteen months, he started to talk. Mama. Mama. There was no one for him to call Dada. Which one of them had fathered him? I had no way of knowing. Sometimes it felt as though they all had. As though their sperm had fused inside me to create this child that was an amalgam of them all. He had been born out of that terrible night. We had created him together.

His skin was brown, and his hair was curly and soft. Strangers on the street came up to tell me how beautiful he was. A modelling agency tried to scout him. He could read before he started nursery school. The teachers told me he was a prodigy, that he belonged in a programme for gifted children. Their eyes lit up when he arrived for school each morning. He brought joy wherever he went.

Today, he is the light of my life. He is the reason I wake up in the morning. The reason I have the strength to go on. He has coalesced all the meaning in my life into one focal point.

More than that, he represents the future of South Africa. Born out of violent conflict, he represents peace and reconciliation. Black anger and resentment collided with smug white neocolonialism, and he was the result. The best of both cultures. A blending of everything that is good and hopeful in this country.

* * *

That didn't happen.

I took the morning-after pill. I took it so fast my hand was a blur of motion as I swallowed the tablets. The police were trying to take a statement and the doctor was trying to do a rape kit, but all I was interested in was how fast I could get my hands on Plan B. I didn't know I had up to seventy-two hours to take it. I thought it literally had to be taken the morning after.

I think even if I had known, I would still have wanted to take those pills straight away. The thought of anything taking root inside my body was an abomination to me. It would have felt like a cancer, not a baby. It was a demon and I was one of the Gadarene swine. I would have done anything, anything at all, to cast it from my body.

The pills did not agree with me, especially in combination with the antiretrovirals I had to take as well. Within two hours, I was vomiting violently. The doctor told me there was every chance I had vomited up the pills. She made me take them again to ensure their effectiveness. Then she thought I'd probably had a double dose as I ran the full gamut of side-effects, from the common to the virtually unheard of. Vomiting, diarrhoea, exhaustion, migraine and stomach cramps, spotting, severe abdominal pain, and vertigo: I had them all.

It was as though whatever was trying to implant in me was resisting being cast out.

Then there was a long, tense time during which I waited for my period to start. I knew it should start within three weeks of taking the pills—if I weren't pregnant. If anything, it should come a little earlier than normal. Mine made me wait the full three weeks. Just as I was about to phone the doctor, it started. I was safe.

If it hadn't started, I would have had an abortion. That was clear in my mind. I never for one second considered keeping any foetus that might have resulted.

Fiction-Lucy not only fell pregnant, she kept the baby.

In John Coetzee's book, her pregnancy was a blessing that made up for the rape. So convincingly did he describe her gravid state that many of my friends and family thought I must be pregnant, too. Total strangers agreed. When no baby came, they believed I must have had an abortion. They didn't approve. My almost-forgotten social media accounts were flooded with people condemning me for being a baby killer.

They flung Bible verses at me. They bombarded my time-lines with blood-soaked photos of abortions. I glimpsed pathetic little bodies in sterile buckets as I flicked through the images, deleting them one by one.

Then they moved on to what I deserved for having aborted my child. Images of women being gang-raped with my face Photoshopped over theirs became a daily sight—crime-scene photos of women having been brutally and bloodily murdered, now wearing my face.

Right about the time that John Coetzee was being nominated for his first major literary award, a man started taking photographs of me going about my daily life and posting them online, just to prove that he was watching me and knew where I lived. I went to the police. Thanks to their sensitivity training, they assigned a woman officer to take my statement. She gave me a lecture about how wrong it was to have aborted my baby.

I told her I hadn't aborted any baby. She wanted to know why I wasn't pregnant in that case. I said not all sexual encounters ended in pregnancy. She was sceptical. These were vigorous young men who had taken me, she said. Not the weak, pallid creatures I was accustomed to coupling with. This would definitely have caused pregnancy. I told her I had taken the morning-after pill, and she said that was just as bad as abortion.

* * *

Do I blame John Coetzee for creating a fictional child for me? One that I had to take the blame for aborting?

No, of course not. I am a doctoral candidate in English literature. Well, I was. I am now a deferred doctoral candidate. The external examiner wanted changes made that I have not got around to implementing.

The theoretical underpinnings of my thesis were predicated on the intertextual conversations between life and literature.

Not only is there no text in my classroom—and no Fish in my text—but there is nothing outside the text either. It makes no sense to talk about the author's intention, when the author, and his or her life, are merely texts feeding into the text that exists on the page.

My rape was nothing more than a text that John Coetzee chose to feed off for his novel. How could I blame him for that? A student of literature with my level of sophistication did not boggle for an instant at the dialectic involved. I could understand it and make peace with it for the simple reason that I was never at war with it.

* * *

Do I blame John Coetzee for creating a fictional child for me? One that I had to take the blame for aborting?

Of course I do. I blame him every day. The harassment I put up with would never have occurred if he hadn't written about me, and if his book hadn't become so ubiquitous. *Disgrace* is that rare thing—the literary novel that is also popular and widely read, even by people who don't usually read fiction. He turned my rape into a spectacle and me into a public figure.

People thought I was fair game. That I had somehow chosen to put myself in the public eye to be commented on and criticised. An astonishing number thought I must have been paid for my role in Coetzee's book. They still do. No amount of protesting or demurral can convince them that I haven't profited from the book. A disturbing number of these people are related to me. They ask for handouts at family gatherings. They send me emails asking me to help put their child through university now that I am rich.

I don't understand why Coetzee did what he did, and I will never be at peace with it.

CHAPTER 5

D id I benefit from Coetzee's book? Yes, I suppose I did. As South Africa's most famous rape victim, I get invited to speak on panels all the time. These aren't the kind of invitations you get when you are an impecunious graduate student. I've had enough of those to know the difference. Those invitations ask you to speak at a conference that stretches across two or three days. At most they might pay for your airfare, but often not. Your accommodation and board are never included, and there is no honorarium. In return for your intellectual capital, they will promise you "exposure." You will take up these offers again and again because you need to attend a certain number of conferences each year to fulfil the conditions of your bursary.

South Africa's number-one rape victim does not get treated so shabbily. These days my invitations to speak come complete with a return air ticket, accommodation at a three-star hotel, all meals provided, and a respectable honorarium. As a former colleague of mine remarked, it was almost worth getting raped for. He grinned as he said it, looking sideways at me, sure I would enjoy his edgy humour. I almost grinned back. My cheek muscles wanted to stretch into their reflexive man-pleasing smile. I stopped them just in time.

People say stupid things—things they don't necessarily mean. If they publish them on social media, it can cost them their jobs. My colleague would have been fired if he had tweeted that remark instead of saying it out loud. The public shaming would have ruined his life.

I am immune to that kind of disgrace. There is nothing I can say that is bad enough to cancel out the horror of what happened to me. My words and my behaviour can always be excused as a symptom of my PTSD.

I know this because I've tried. I've pushed the envelope so far it has fallen off the table. Take the last conference I went to. It was a colloquium on sexual violence convened by the well-meaning people of Rape Awareness South Africa (RASA). I was invited to take part in a panel discussion on victim blaming. It was called, *"She was wearing a short skirt*—seeking a discourse beyond patriarchy for rape survivors."

My fellow panellists included a medical doctor who had a lot of experience treating rape victims in state hospitals, an academic who wrote about sexual violence, and another rape victim like myself. The panel was facilitated by a member of RASA. We were all educated women, capable of speaking at the most sophisticated level about this topic. RASA hadn't wasted its time with your common or garden rape victims who don't know Derrida from a hole in the ground. We were talking the same language and we were fluent in it.

Well, most of us.

I caused a stir at the beginning of the session by refusing to call myself a rape survivor. I insisted on referring to myself as a victim instead.

"They didn't try to kill me," I explained, "I didn't do anything heroic. I couldn't escape or fight back. I was a victim. They made me into a victim and refusing to acknowledge that doesn't change the truth."

The survivor next to me shifted in her seat, and managed not to say anything. The facilitator nodded earnestly and spoke about the plurality of experience and the need to allow rape survivors to craft their own narratives. I got a pass. For the time being.

There was some general discussion about the way rape is

reported in the media, and the words that are chosen to describe the victim, her behaviour, and her clothing choices. I caused another awkward moment by asking why we don't call it "survivor blaming" instead of "victim blaming."

"If there are no victims any more, how can we speak meaningfully about victim blaming? We should call it survivor blaming for the sake of consistency. But it doesn't have quite the same ring, does it? For the sake of our agenda, we need to decide when to cast women as heroes and when to cast them as victims."

This led to a discussion about how to be more strategic in our activism without denying the subjectivity of lived experience. The subtext was that my words were seriously off-message, but that I was allowed to say them because I had earned my stripes in the trenches of sexual violence.

We came to the moment the audience had been waiting for. Each panellist was invited to describe what had happened to her in her own words. "Reclaiming our stories in a safe, non-judgemental space" was how it was billed. Am I wrong to suspect the audience of voyeurism? This was the most popular session of the entire conference. The venue was bursting with delegates who had come to watch us "reclaim our stories." No other session had attracted such numbers.

There were at least as many men present as women, and possibly more. The other sessions had been overwhelmingly attended by women. This didn't feel like a safe space at all, but what did I know?

We kicked off with the doctor who came right out and said she had never been raped. She was attending the colloquium for two reasons—to share her expertise as one who had treated, patched up, and counselled any number of rape survivors, and to learn more about the survivor's point of view with the intention of improving the service she offered. Her words were met with quiet respect, even from me. This was a woman who had seen horrors we couldn't contemplate. She had treated babies and toddlers. Her emotions were assaulted every day, and she kept going back for more.

The academic writer had a drearily familiar story. She was over fifty. Gravity had grabbed spitefully at the skin on her face. The pouches under her eyes drooped and the skin of her jawline hung in soft folds. Only her hair defied middle age with its mahogany resilience.

While she was at university, a boy had walked her home after a party. They were deep in conversation about the respective methodologies they had chosen for their Psychology Honours dissertations. He came in for coffee so they could continue their conversation. Her housemates were out, and they were alone in the flat.

After coffee, he tried to kiss her. She responded with surprise and indignation, having had no idea he was contemplating any such thing. She asked him to leave, but instead he held her down and raped her. When she screamed, he hit her hard in the face with a closed fist. He failed to achieve orgasm and blamed her for this, saying he would tell his friends she was a lousy fuck. Then he left.

She sat in class with him every day for the rest of the year.

"Why didn't you report him?" the facilitator asked.

She shrugged. "This was the eighties. Girls who made rape accusations on campus were systematically shamed, even by other women. They called it slut's remorse. They would have said I felt guilty for being easy, so I was 'crying rape.' They would have accused me of trying to ruin the poor boy's life."

"Where is he now?"

"He's married with three grown-up daughters. He has a successful psychology practice in Maine. He's even sent me a few friend requests on Facebook. We know a lot of the same people, so he pops up on my timeline all the time."

The facilitator made sympathetic noises about the secondary

victimisation of rape survivors, and how this can go on throughout their lives. I reflected on the fact that my rapists didn't appear in my social media feeds. We had no mutual acquaintances, no overlapping social circles.

I am that rare creature—a woman who was raped by strangers. This puts me in a tiny minority. Most women are raped by people they know.

As a case in point, the next survivor began to tell her story. It was also set on a university campus—that flashpoint for sexual abuse. This woman was much younger than the academic, but not quite as young as me. I guessed her to be in her early thirties. She was almost transparent with her milk-white skin and gingery-pink hair.

"He was my sister's ex-boyfriend. They only went out for three months, but I'd seen him at family functions and we had always got on well. I knew he was a cat lover like me and he was also studying Fine Art. I'd always liked him, but obviously he was off-limits. I would never consider hooking up with my sister's ex."

The facilitator nodded, and we nodded too. We knew the rules. One's sister's ex-boyfriend was off-limits. Naturally.

But sometimes, things happen. In fact, things happen quite frequently.

"I ran into him at the pub one evening. I didn't even know he was in town. We got talking, and soon the group of people he was with merged with the group I was with and we ended up chatting for hours. I told him about the two kittens I'd just got, and he said he'd love to see them. So at closing time, I invited him back to my place."

"Did you have any flatmates?" asked the academic. Like the rest of us, she was seeing the parallels between this story and hers.

"No, at that stage I was living alone. I was already a postgraduate and had enough bursary money that I could afford not to share. Anyway, we'd both been drinking all evening, but when we got back to my place, I opened a bottle of wine for us. He admired the kittens and we sat on the sofa together to let them climb all over us. I remember him saying something about being attracted to me, but I immediately said that nothing could ever happen because of my sister."

There was more nodding and murmurs of agreement.

"After that it gets fuzzy because I'd been drinking so much. I think the cats settled in their basket and went to sleep. We stayed on the sofa drinking and talking. I remember putting my feet in his lap, so he could rub them. My sister always said he gave the best foot rubs. Then we started kissing, but I said, 'This is wrong. We mustn't do this.' So, we broke apart. But then after a while we were kissing again."

There was silence in the venue. The delegates were leaning forward, straining to catch her words as her voice got softer and softer. She rubbed her hands over her face and took a deep breath.

"Then it gets really fuzzy. I remember us having sex. I remember saying my sister's name. Someone was laughing. For years, I thought it was me, but my therapist says it must have been him. We woke up in my bed the next morning. I don't even remember how we got there. There were two used condoms—one in the sitting room and one in the bedroom. I flushed them away without thinking. I flushed away the evidence. Things were awkward between us that morning. He had a cup of coffee and a bowl of cornflakes and left. I knew he was flying back to Johannesburg that afternoon.

"I spent most of the day lying on my sofa with the curtains closed. I felt terrible. My mouth was dry. I had a pounding headache and my eyeballs throbbed. I couldn't stomach any food. My therapist says this was my body's way of telling me I'd been violated."

"What happened next?" asked the facilitator.

"It was only years later when I was at a sexual violence rally that I realised what had happened. We were listening to testimonials from women who had been raped. They were so brave. They were like heroes. As I listened to their stories and heard the crowd applauding, I realised it had happened to me too! I had been raped. I was a survivor, just like them. I had been denying it all those years.

"I can still remember the chill of the floor through my shoes and the way the noise of the crowd sang in my ears as I got up from my seat and walked to the front of the hall to tell my story. Everyone gasped. They knew me as a sexual violence activist—a sympathiser and advocate—but none of them had suspected what I really was—a survivor, just like them. They roared in solidarity, and the love I felt in that hall gave me the strength to tell my story for the first time. After I'd finished speaking, I began to sob as years of pain came flooding out of me. I thought I'd released all my pain and anger. Little did I know that was just the beginning. For two years afterwards, I suffered from severe post-traumatic stress disorder and depression as I finally allowed myself to feel the violation of what had happened to me on that night."

She sank back into her seat as though exhausted and took a sip of water. Spontaneous applause broke out in the venue. Some delegates rose to their feet in recognition of her bravery and honesty.

"That's an incredible story, Marion. Thank you for sharing it with us." The facilitator smiled at her. "And now we have Lucy, who will also tell us about her journey."

I could tell from the start that I didn't have the audience's attention. They were still swept up by Marion's narrative. They couldn't keep their eyes off her. She sat next to me, glowing palely under the fluorescent lights.

Next to her, I was a creature of rude health and robust appearance. My hair was brown and my cheeks pink. My eyes shone with vitality. Sometimes I looked in the mirror and knew exactly why Coetzee chose me as his model for the bovine, unflappable fiction-Lucy. We were both sturdy of calf and thick of wrist.

I didn't have Marion's gift for storytelling.

"Six men broke into my father's farmhouse and raped me."

See? No narrative arc. No character development. Just ten words dropped into the auditorium where they sank without trace. Is it any wonder the audience were restless and whispering? The facilitator had promised them a journey, but this was more like a mid-air stall. I had no progress to report, no growth. I wasn't even able to refer to myself as a rape survivor. I was still a victim. It remained to be seen whether I survived this in any meaningful sense.

The facilitator nodded encouragingly, giving me every opportunity to develop my story. When it dawned on her that that was it, she smiled and turned back to the audience.

"Thank you, panellists, for sharing your stories with us. At this stage, I'm going to throw the discussion open to the floor. I'm sure the audience have many questions to put to our panellists."

A forest of hands shot up.

"I have a question for Marion. First of all, I want to say how inspiring I found your story and how incredibly brave I think you are. Then I wanted to ask if you have been the victim of any negativity from friends or family since you came out with your story? Or have they mostly been supportive?"

Marion shook her head. "I've encountered plenty of negativity, I'm afraid. Mostly in the form of victim-blaming, which, as we all know, is patriarchy's way of attempting to silence women. I've been asked why I let him into my home if I didn't want to have sex. What was I wearing at the time? Why did I drink that much? The usual questions women get asked when they report a rape."

"Yes, Lucy?"

I looked at the facilitator in surprise. Then I realised I had my hand in the air. This is not protocol. You don't have to raise a hand when you are one of the panellists. Some long-dormant classroom instinct had reared its head.

Why was my hand up anyway? What did I want to say?

Then I opened my mouth and my tirade came spewing out.

"Marion, do you really think you can claim rape victim status equal to mine? You think your experience is even one fraction as traumatic as mine? You think that because some vague question mark hangs over how meaningfully you were able to consent because you were drunk at the time, your experience was anything like mine? Your so-called rapist was drunk too. Maybe you were the one who raped him—have you ever thought of that?"

"Now just a minute . . ."

"You want to claim survivor status to give yourself legitimacy as an activist. But by putting yourself in the same category as me, you are denigrating my experience. You are trivialising it. You are dragging what happened to me down to the level of a drunken university bonk that you later regretted. I won't let you do that. If they gave marks for rape trauma, mine would get an A-plus and yours would get a D-minus."

* * *

My therapist stares at me. I have told her about the conference, and what I said to Marion the Pseudo-Rape-Survivor.

This isn't the first time I've felt her disgust. She tries to keep the non-judgemental facade intact, but I keep crumbling it.

L. BASCOMBE: You didn't really say that, did you?
ME: Okay, no, I didn't. I wanted to. I wanted to say it, and I've fantasised about saying it ever since.

L. BASCOMBE: Well, that's something at least. A while ago you were obsessed with rape survivors whom you perceived as having a harder time than you. Do you remember? Women who were poor and struggling and had no access to medical or psychiatric care?

ME: I remember.

L. BASCOMBE: Now you seem to be concerned with survivors who have an easier time than you do—women who weren't violently attacked, or who were raped by only one man, or whatever the case may be. Why do you think you have this need to compare yourself to others? To situate your own experience within a hierarchy of rapes?

ME: I've never been a high achiever. I never got the best marks or the highest praise, or the most prestigious scholarships. Why can't I be allowed to excel at this one thing? Why can't I be the most tragic rape victim?

L. BASCOMBE: I don't always know when you are being facetious. Your rape was appalling—you know that. It was in all the newspapers. It was turned into a bestselling book. You've said yourself that your friends and family are struck dumb by the awfulness of what happened to you. They don't have the words to begin to talk to you about it.

ME: Then I should have been the star of that panel. Not Marion Whatshername. She should have deferred to me. The audience should have been more interested in my story than in hers. Instead they fawned on her and ignored me. And she wasn't even raped. Not really.

L. BASCOMBE: She had her agency taken away from her at a moment when she was in no position to consent meaningfully to sexual intercourse. It is probably the very ambiguity of the situation that troubles her the most—and the fact that there are gaps in her memory.

ME: I'm sure there are gaps in his memory too. They were both drunk as skunks. Who's to say she wasn't the rapist and he the victim? He wasn't in any position to consent either.

L. BASCOMBE: By the very nature of sexual intercourse, the man is more likely to be the aggressor. You know that, Lucy. Your feminist studies must have shown you that.

ME: So, are you saying that every act of sexual intercourse with a drunk woman is rape?

L. BASCOMBE: If her consent was not fully or meaningfully given, then yes. No one should have sex with a woman whose judgement is impaired by alcohol or drugs or mental challenges. You know this.

ME: But still . . . my rape was worse than hers. Wasn't it?

L. BASCOMBE: This is pointless. It is meaningless to apportion degrees of terribleness to rape survivors. Trauma is a personal thing. One woman may process an event more quickly than another. PTSD can manifest itself immediately, or only years after the event. There is no correct or appropriate response to rape. There are as many responses as there are survivors.

* * *

And so, I am in the wrong again. My feelings are invalid and my responses inappropriate. I can't even get this right, this business of being a rape victim. I am the wrong kind of victim—the kind that goes off-brand.

People are particularly shocked by my wrongness because fiction-Lucy is so very right. She is a noble creature who harbours no bitterness. I, on the other hand, am a tightly wound ball of bitterness. I seethe with resentment. People expect me to be calm and forgiving. It is a great disappointment to them to discover that I am a rage-filled harpy.

I should take fiction-Lucy as my model. Whenever I don't know what to do, I should ask myself, WWFLD? What would fiction-Lucy do?

My friend Moira thinks this is a good idea. She thinks I could sort my whole life out like this.

"Fiction-Lucy wouldn't live in this chaos."

She has come to my place to help me track down John Coetzee. She has access to departmental websites and online bulletin boards that are now closed to me. My status at the university has been downgraded to "inactive." First, I was on leave. Then I was on sabbatical. Then I was on leave-of-absence. Now I am inactive.

I was just a few rewrites away from resubmitting my PhD— a hundred or so words at most. It might as well be a million words. I can no more finish it right now than I could finish an ultramarathon.

I can't think of a better way to describe myself than inactive. I don't know how to become active again, but Moira has some ideas.

"Right." She claps her hands. "We need to clean this place up. I've arranged for a char to come in twice a week, but first we have to make things tidy."

She has brought a bucket with her. It contains two pairs of rubber gloves, bottles of detergents, sponges, scrubbing brushes, and a mop. She plugs her iPod into my speakers and puts on a catchy tune to entertain us while we work. It is "Uptown Funk" by Mark Ronson. She describes it as an oldie but a goodie. We are wearing yoga pants and strappy tops. As we work, our tops ride up, revealing glimpses of our tanned midriffs.

Every now and then, one of us will pause to blow a sweaty curl of hair off her forehead. The hours seem to pass in a flash, and soon the two of us are sitting coltishly on the floor, our long legs folded under us. We are sharing a deep-dish pizza that we ordered to celebrate the sparkling new cleanliness of my rented house.

There are oversized glasses of red wine on the floorboards next to us. No, white wine. We raise them and clink glasses to toast the success of our hard work.

But Moira isn't done. She wants to clean me the same way as we have cleaned my house. She turns up at my door at six o'clock the next morning wearing workout gear and looking perky. I am wearing flannel pyjamas, bed-hair, and a grumpy expression. We go for a run around a sparkling lake. The morning mist curls around weeping willow trees as we run past. I spend a lot of time standing bent over with my hands on my knees, gasping for breath. I am wearing baggy tracksuit pants and a too-large top to make me appear slightly overweight.

As the weeks pass, my outfit metamorphosises into something more closely resembling Moira's. I ditch the baggy outfits for tight, bright Lululemon gym-wear. One morning, I surprise her by flinging open my front door before she even knocks. I am beaming with enthusiasm.

Such glimpses as one is afforded of my house reveal that it is now tastefully decorated with rugs, sofas and scatter cushions. The sun slants in through my clean windowpanes and warms the wooden floorboards.

Moira has me eating magical food and drinking magical water that cleans me from the inside out. I smile as I consume green juices that contain macerated spinach leaves. I laugh with a bowl of salad in my lap and a forkful of radicchio raised to my lips. In the movie reel of my life, you can see the numbers on the scale edging downwards as I move from being merely slim to model skinny.

When you run and eat salad, you don't have to worry about loneliness and unemployment. Happiness will find you. A woman I got to know through the gym offers me a job writing press releases for her company. Who knew that an unfinished

PhD in English Literature was good for something? This leads to comical scenes of me struggling to pull on a pair of tights in the morning and wobbling around my kitchen in heels. But I soon get used to my corporate battle-dress and can be seen striding briskly along the pavement in my sleeveless peplum top and knee-length pencil skirt, making my way in the world.

There is a cute delivery guy who pops up at work with IT equipment every few days. We exchange adorable banter, but of course I can't take him seriously. He's the delivery guy.

Then it turns out that he owns a start-up company that was floated on the stock exchange for millions. We fade out on the scene where we are looking at houses in the suburbs together because I have just a hint of the sweetest little baby bump.

That's how you get over a rape.

CHAPTER 6

Moira would love to motivate me back to health like the best friend in a romantic comedy, but she is starting to accept that this isn't going to happen. She became hopeful a few months ago when she noticed I was losing weight. It happened soon after the rape symposium.

The more I think about sturdy, corn-fed, fiction-Lucy, the more my own flesh seems to melt and thaw.

"Are you working out?" Moira asks when she first notices.

"Are you dieting?" she asks when she notices again.

A few weeks later, "Are you eating at all? You're almost transparent. I can see the skull beneath the skin."

I hold my hands up to the light. She is right. The webbing between my thumb and forefinger has become translucent. If I narrow my eyes, I can see the light squirming pink and blue and yellow and orange through my skin.

Fiction-Lucy has strong, bucolic calves. I had them myself once. My ankles were never dainty; they provided a strong base from which I supported myself. Now my ankle bones nudge against their surrounding flesh like whitened knuckles. I trip over my own feet and turn my ankles for no reason.

"There's nothing to you. A puff of wind could blow you away."

But I have things to do before I come apart and disperse like ash. I need to find John Coetzee. I need to stand in front of him and say, "You took something from me. Give it back."

"Word on the street is that he can't find a publisher for his second book," says Moira.

I find this hard to believe. "Surely he was offered a multi-book deal with his first contract?"

"He was, but his agent persuaded him not to take it. She thought he could do better. After the success of the first book, she was going to put the second one up for auction and make a killing. The big writers never accept multi-book contracts. They sell each new book to the highest bidder and flog the translation rights and foreign country rights as separate deals. No two-for-the-price-of-one for them."

I still find this hard to believe. It is impossible to overstate how big a splash Coetzee's book made when it first came out. Before he went into hiding, he was lionised by the literati in a way that made Salman Rushdie look like small fry.

Articles were written about him in *The New York Times*— in *Granta*, *The New Yorker*, *The Paris Review*, *The Times*, *The Guardian*, the *Independent*, *The Atlantic*, even *Rolling Stone*. People would pay good money to read his laundry list, never mind his next novel.

"It doesn't make sense," I say. "For someone of Coetzee's calibre, there is no such thing as an unsellable novel."

Moira shrugs. "I'm only telling you what I hear. His agent has screwed up big-time. When the offers for the second novel weren't as high as she hoped, she took it off the market and started writing to various publishers personally. But everyone knew it had failed to sell at auction, so they started low-balling her. And you know what publishing is like. Everybody knows everybody, and they all talk to each other. So, Publisher A heard that Publisher B had turned it down, and made an even lower offer."

I smile. Moira's assumption that she and I "know what publishing is like" is based on our experience of the minuscule world of South African academic publishing. Could we extrapolate from that and assume that the billion-dollar transatlantic publishing industry works in the same way?

Perhaps we could.

In academia, it is reputational death to have one's article turned down by too many journals. Word gets around and nobody wants to touch your piece, even if the original reason for turning it down was simply that it wasn't a good fit for a particular journal. Editors fear association with your untouchable article.

"Coetzee's new book has the cheese touch," Moira says. "He's the Greg Heffley of literary fiction."

Now I know she is exaggerating. Coetzee's reputation as the man who wrote the book of the century can't have died that quickly.

"What about the Australians? If he's living there now, aren't they eager to claim him as their own?"

"They are, but his agent won't let him look at their offers. It would be too much of a climb-down to give his second book to an Australian publisher. Besides, they pay peanuts compared to the Americans and the British."

This is smile-worthy too. As PhD candidates and junior lecturers, Moira and I were grateful to have our work picked up by journals that paid nothing, all for the sake of exposure. We would have given our right arms for the hundreds of thousands of Australian dollars no doubt being flung in Coetzee's direction.

"What else have you heard?"

Moira shakes her head. "You have squeezed the lemon of gossip until the pips squeak. I have nothing more for you."

"In that case, I must go. I have to visit my father."

* * *

Moira leaves at once. She thinks I mean right now—that I

am leaving to visit my father as soon as her car pulls out of the driveway. I pick up my car keys on the way out to strengthen this illusion. After she has driven away, I put them back and settle in my chair again. The visit to my father is only on Sunday.

This is what PTSD does. It concertinas time. Sunday's visit to my father presses up against me like an importunate lover. I can't leave too small a gap between Moira's visit and the visit to my father. That would be too much company in too little time. I can't tolerate that much socialising.

They say old age turns you into a caricature of yourself. This is what rape has done to me. It has stripped me of my youthful ability to tolerate people and things. I am no longer adaptable. I can't take life as it comes. I struggle to walk and talk at the same time. I need plenty of warning if something is going to happen. I hate spontaneity. I find refuge in routine.

When Sunday comes around, I wake up early to get ready. I put on my full-length knickers, my American tan tights, my bra and girdle, my long, thick skirt, the blouse that buttons all the way up to my chin, my cardigan. I lace my feet into flat leather shoes. I put on spectacles to shield my face.

I know what I am doing. I am making myself less rape-able. I'm falling for the old lie—that women are raped because of what they are wearing. But I can't help myself. It feels as though I am going into battle fully prepared.

If my father's house is the battleground, he and I are non-combatants. The ghosts of that night battle alongside us, unnoticed by my father and ignored by me.

This is not the house where it happened—the farmhouse. That was badly burned. The police say my father and I were lucky to get out alive. That was the first time I heard myself described as lucky after the rape, but it wasn't the last. I was lucky to be alive, lucky not to be more seriously injured, lucky not to be pregnant, lucky not to have contracted AIDS. I had never been so lucky in my life.

This is a new flat my father bought after the fire. It is convenient for his golf club and for the shops and the theatre. He employs a housekeeper who cooks and cleans for him. My father is sixty-nine years old. He was in his early forties when I was born. I am used to having the oldest father.

Today he looks young. His skin is plump and rosy. The thinning thatch of hair on his head appears thicker and more luxuriant. His shoulders have widened, and his waist has narrowed. The dressing gown and slippers he was so prone to wearing in the daytime are nowhere to be seen. Instead he is wearing cream trousers (he would call them slacks: slax) and a pale-pink golf shirt with a crocodile stitched over the pocket.

"Come in, child. Come in."

He holds the door open and stands back to let me pass. He presses a kiss onto my forehead, but his eyes don't hold mine. He hasn't looked me steadily in the eye since that night. My shame hangs between us like a carcass on a butcher's hook.

My father's flat doesn't have an old-man smell. My nose prickles with detergent and polish—smells that have become uncommon in my own home. My house is the one that smells as though it belongs to an elderly person. My father has furnished his new home with the bachelor trappings of a much younger man. One wall of the sitting room is entirely taken up by a flatscreen television. I can see a PlayStation console peeking out behind it.

"So! How are you?" His eyes flick towards me and skitter away again. "I mean, this week. How was your week?" Asking me how I am opens an existential maw neither of us wants to deal with. My week is much safer.

"My week was okay," I say. "I had quite a lot of proofreading work and even one editing job."

"So you're keeping your head above water?"

"Yes."

"That's good. That's very good."

My father has never urged me to finish the rewrites on my PhD, even knowing how close it was to completion. He never had one himself, although he was officially working on it when he took early retirement from the university after the misunderstanding with the female student. I think it is easier for him if I am perpetually working on mine too.

"And how was your week?" I ask.

"Sherry?"

I nod. My father has been pouring me sherry since I turned eighteen. It started when sherry was the only alcoholic drink he kept in the house. Now his stash has expanded and diversified to include gin, vodka, brandy, whisky (Scotch), whiskey (Irish), Sambuca, port, and rum. But he still offers me sherry. Not "Would you like a drink?" Just "Sherry?"

When I can focus my thoughts enough, I speculate that he genuinely believes sherry to be my favourite drink. Or perhaps sherry is the only drink he considers appropriate for a woman of my age. Or perhaps he wants to keep his stash to himself, and chooses not to share it with me. I think this is the most likely option. My father is not miserly, precisely. Misers take as much pleasure from denying themselves expensive treats as they do from denying others. My father enjoys spending money on himself, but not on anyone else. As human failings go, it is not the worst.

His biggest fear is that my editing and proofreading work will dry up, and I will no longer be "keeping my head above water." Then I might apply to him for funds, and common decency would force him to oblige. Every time I visit, I see him visibly relax when he confirms that my head is still above water.

He pours me a scant half-glass of sherry, and two fingers of Talisker malt for himself. The whisky makes a luxurious gurgling sound as it splashes into the crystal.

"So . . . my week. Very difficult. A real struggle. I tear my

hair out every time I have to deal with the insurance company."
He mimes grabbing the wisps of hair at the side of his head
and pulling them out by the roots.

I make a sympathetic noise. "Still? After all this time? What
excuse are they using now?"

"They are disputing the value of the furniture. Your mother
and I kept records of some of the antiques we bought, but not
all. And most of the records we had disappeared in the fire.
They are asking me to prove which tables were yellowwood,
which kists were stinkwood, and so on. But I can't."

"I thought you kept papers like that in a safe deposit box in
the bank?"

"Again, some, but not all. Some of the papers we kept in
the house."

He still sometimes says "we" as though my mother were
alive. She has been dead for eight years. Breast cancer. She
died two days after my twentieth birthday. Twenty is not the
worst age at which to lose your mother. You are an adult.
Independent. Making your own way in the world. (It felt like
the worst age.)

Sixty-one is not the worst age to lose your wife, either. Your
only child is grown up. You have no need to worry about who
will pick up the slack in terms of child-rearing. You are still
young enough to meet someone else. (I don't know if it felt like
the worst age.)

"It must be a worrying time for you."

He brushes the worry away. "It's fine. I'll get through it.
Just . . . if they phone and ask you about the contents of the
house, please say that the furniture was all antique, dating from
the days of the Colony."

"Okay."

"Thank you. You are a good child."

I happen to know that some of the furniture was flat-pack
modern, dating from the days of the OK Bazaars. But I agree

to the venal offence of lying to the insurance company. My father has been through a lot. A little extra insurance money is the least he deserves.

We eat a Sunday lunch of supermarket rotisserie chicken with vegetables and roast potatoes pre-prepared by his house-keeper. It is not a bad meal. There are individual crème caramels in plastic containers for dessert.

After coffee, I wait until a decent interval has passed and then I stand up, saying, "Well, I'd better be going. I want to finish some work this afternoon. Thank you very much for lunch."

"It's a pleasure."

I lean in for him to kiss me on the forehead. We say good-bye and I walk out of his flat, listening for the careful click of the door closing behind me. I try to unclench my stomach muscles as I reach the car. It doesn't work, so I try abdominal breathing—a relaxation exercise taught me by my therapist. It feels as though I am trying to inflate a balloon against the resistance of an iron band.

I put my key in the ignition and let my head fall back against the headrest. It is better to allow the images to come now rather than tonight when I am asleep.

My father's eyes jumping away from mine as though my gaze scalded him. Meeting his gaze over the shoulder of one of my attackers that night. His eyes didn't falter then, but held mine with a steady regard. His hand shaking my shoulder, try-ing to rouse me, telling me the house was on fire, and we had to go. The Minnie Mouse helium balloon he bought when he came to visit me in hospital. I slept for hours at a time. Every time I opened my eyes, the balloon had sunk a little lower, until one day it lolled drunkenly on the carpet and they told me it was time to go home.

CHAPTER 7

There is someone who might know where John Coetzee is. Dr. Essie September of the English Department at Constantia University. She is Prof. September now. When Coetzee left the department, they unfroze a chair that had been vacant for years and gave it to her. Essie September is now the Ruth First Professor of Women's Studies in Literature.

She was a student of Coetzee's thirty-five years ago when he joined the department as a junior lecturer. Apparently, she had a massive crush on him—adored every hair on his gingery head. She has never married, supposedly because of her unrequited passion for him.

He must have seemed impossibly grown up to her back when he was a twenty-five-year-old lecturer and she was a twenty-one-year-old third-year student. Now that gap has shrunk to insignificance. If he is sixty-two (and his Wikipedia page assures me he is), then she must be fifty-eight. From my late twenties vantage-point, they are the same age. I wonder if she still sees him as the wise mentor who remains as out-of-reach as a shooting star. She probably does. She probably feels this more than ever now that he has achieved international acclaim.

Coetzee used to give the impression of barely tolerating Essie September, but I suspect he liked having her around. She was the adoring acolyte, trotting at his heels, bringing him coffee, and talking up his unpublished manuscript to her students. If anyone knows where he is, it's her. She used to house-sit for him when he went to frolic in the warm Indian Ocean in KwaZulu-Natal every December. You don't leave someone alone with your secrets year after year unless you believe you can trust them.

So why do I think she will spill the beans to me?

Because I have something she wants.

Prof. September collects rape victims the way other people collect stamps. She runs something called the Survivor Project. It started out as a website—a kind of Tumblr for rape stories. Then she got funding from the government and published a couple of books based on the source material she had collected.

She has been after me for months to "tell my story." It bothers her that Cape Town's most famous rape victim doesn't have an entry on her website. And my connection to her beloved John makes it even more galling. I am the rare butterfly she is determined to capture. The thing is, I've looked at her website and the other contributions are beautiful and moving and inspirational. My story isn't beautiful. It is an infected boil I can't lance because its roots are too deep.

I have eluded Prof. September for months. The last time she wrote to me, she assured me that the stories on her website were as diverse as the women who wrote them (they aren't), and that she would wait for me. She believed I would come around in the end. I knew I wouldn't.

Today, I am going to meet her at her office in the English Department to tell her she was right.

It will be the first time I have been back on campus in two years. I dress with extra care. Girdle. Vest. Shirt buttoned to the throat. My thickest tights. (I found a pair at a dance shop that feel like canvas.) Bootleg jeans. Boots.

I start sweating immediately. Beads of moisture pop out on my forehead and upper lip. A stream trickles between my breasts and is soaked up by the latex of my bra. A blinding itch develops under my right breast. I claw at my clothes to relieve it, but nothing helps.

Moira is picking me up. I can't drive any more. Or rather, I don't drive any more, not for the past several weeks. Let me not participate in the obfuscatory psycho-babble that confuses an intense reluctance to do something with the inability to do it. Of course I can still drive. I passed my driver's test on my first try. In nine years, I've never had an accident. My car is still parked out there in the street.

Moira hoots. For a moment, I am unable to make my legs move. I am aghast at the prospect of going outside. Then I pick up my backpack and my keys, and walk like a marionette out the door, down the stairs, and get into Moira's car.

"You really think she'll let you through the door? Prof. September? You were never one of her favourites."

This is true. She used to have acolytes of her own. Skinny girls in long floral skirts and Doc Marten boots. Greasy hair and unmade-up faces. She'd hold court at the campus cafeteria, sharing snippets of Steinem, Dworkin, and Lorde with the select few who didn't argue or question.

"Not only will she let me through the door, she will roll out the red carpet for me. We have a confirmed appointment—one she's been begging for."

Moira's frown lasts only a second. "The Survivor Project. Of course. You'll be one of the biggest fish she has ever landed."

"Exactly."

Moira swings the car onto the highway hugging the mountain above the City Bowl and the air becomes thick in my chest. I used to love this view. I adored craning my neck to watch the boats in the harbour. I loved the icebreakers best. I used to imagine where they'd been—forging their way through the ice floes of the Antarctic, the crew bundled up in oilskins and rain slickers, their heavy-soled boots gripping the deck as it lurched and reeled with the movement of the waves.

Today there are no icebreakers in the harbour—only a couple of battered freighters and an obscenely top-heavy cruise ship. Anxiety is stealing up on me on Sandberg's little cat feet. It is getting harder to breathe. I want to beg Moira to take me home. If she won't listen, I will batter her with my fists, forcing her to pull over.

L. BASCOMBE: Why do you think you have this reaction to the university? The rape didn't happen there. It was your place of work. And, from what you've told me, you were happy there.

ME: I was hoping you could tell me.

L. BASCOMBE: Okay. Let's unpack this. You were last on campus before the rape, correct?

ME: Correct.

L. BASCOMBE: None of your attackers was associated with the university in any way?

ME: Not as far as I know.

L. BASCOMBE: You never saw them there, or anyone who looked like them?

ME: Nope.

L. BASCOMBE: You were attacked at your father's farm. He used to work at the university.

ME: He took early retirement years ago. There was some trouble with a female student. It was all blown out of proportion. And he never finished his PhD, so that was held against him too.

L. BASCOMBE: Does anything about the farmhouse remind you of the university? Are they built in the same style? Do they give you the same feeling when you look at them?

ME: Not at all. They couldn't be more different.

L. BASCOMBE: So what is the connection? Do you have any inkling?

ME: I think it had to do with the reason I was there.

L. BASCOMBE: Right . . . right . . . you were going to ask a colleague of John Coetzee's if she knew where to find him?

ME: That's right.

L. BASCOMBE: And he's the man who used your rape as fodder for his novel . . .

ME: Yes.

L. BASCOMBE: The university is a secondary site of trauma for you. You feel violated by what Coetzee wrote, so the whole campus has become associated in your mind with the rape. It is the scene of additional abuse that you experienced.

ME: I'm sure you must be right.

L. BASCOMBE: You sound sarcastic. Did you expect me to get it sooner? Wait, did you have it figured out all along?

ME: It's called the reverse Socratic method. Or if it isn't, it should be. Where the patient leads the therapist to the answer.

* * *

Moira parks in the little bay for which she pays an extortionate fee every month. It is close to the English Department, which is making my PTSD symptoms worse. I haven't screamed or beaten her yet, but I am considering the possibility that I won't be able to manage this.

"You know he's not there, right?" Moira says. "You know there is no chance you will run into him? He isn't even in the country. You need to chill. You look horrible."

Apparently, I'm not wearing as much of a poker face as I like to think.

"It feels as though he is here. Everything looks the same. It seems impossible that the building can be here without him in it. He was an institution. He practically lived here."

"Because he had no life. Now he has a life. It's the life of an internationally celebrated and fêted novelist. He's at a film premiere somewhere, Lucy, rubbing shoulders with other famous people. He's having cocktails with Jonathan Franzen. You can do this. You can come inside with me."

I go inside with her.

It all looks the same—crepuscular light, dust motes dancing. It smells the same—lavender furniture polish, dusty floorboards. It sounds the same—rubber-soled shoes squeaking down the corridor, a murmuration of students in the junior seminar room.

We turn the corner and see a tall man with stooped shoulders, a maroon cardigan, and a halo of silvery hair walking away from us.

"It's not him," Moira says as I grab her arm. "Look properly. That's Dr. Bentelstad."

She's right. This is the English Department of Constantia University. Old white men in cardigans are ten a penny.

Moira steers me toward Prof. September's office. "Do you want me to go in with you?"

"No, it's fine."

"Text me when you're done. I'll be in my office."

* * *

Prof. September is a little smaller and more faded than I remember. She looks like a photograph of herself that has been left out in the sun. Powder clings to the fine, post-menopausal hairs on her cheeks. Her hands are bonier, her plait paler. The pigment has leached from her skin. She was mahogany; now she is oak.

She is explaining to me why it is okay that my rape is the one part in Coetzee's book that goes undescribed.

"It's a lacuna, Lucy. You remember what that means?"

"An unfilled space. A gap." Ever the good student, I parrot the definition.

"Then you know the power of the lacuna in literary fiction. The absence of something can be more powerful than its presence."

"So, the absence of any meaningful discussion about rape in the public domain all these years is more powerful than its presence?"

She frowns at my obtuseness. "We're talking about literary fiction, not rhetoric. By omitting the actual assault, Coetzee creates a performative situation in which his text mimics the very tendency of Western society to turn a blind eye towards rape. It is a powerful critique of exactly what concerns you."

"Becoming the thing you are attempting to criticise is not the same as criticising it. It is an act of collaboration, not of censure. Besides, it is not as though mainstream culture has ever shied away from graphic descriptions of rape."

"Precisely!" She pounces. "Would you really have wanted your ordeal to become the next instalment of torture porn by an acclaimed male writer? John chose to spare you that. He didn't allow your assault to become a spectacle."

It occurs to me that she can't have it both ways. Either he was trying to make the violence of the rape extra powerful by turning it into a kind of howling black hole in the middle of the text, or he was being sensitive and sparing my feelings by toning the whole thing down. It also occurs to me that the blindness of her loyalty is of such an order that I'm not going to change her mind on this.

"And what about me?" I ask. "The Lucy character. The bearer of light in the text. I'm a bit of a lacuna too."

"What nonsense."

Prof. September reaches back to take a copy of the book down from her bookcase. As she flicks through it, I catch a glimpse of the title page. Coetzee's handwriting spiders across the recto page. He has signed it for her, and included a dedication:

Dear Essie,
Thank you for believing in me all these years. You knew I could do it, and you were right. I am indeed a very great man, as you realised all along.
Yours etc John Coetzee

No, it says:

Dear Essie,
I couldn't have done it without all your house-sitting over the years.
PS: Have you seen my Samsung charger anywhere? I swear it was in the house the last time you stayed over.
Regards,
John Coetzee

Actually, it says:

To my dearest Essie,
You have been such a comfort to me over the years, both in the bedroom and out of it. Your nurturing gave me the strength I needed to create this book.
Obviously, I couldn't mention you in the dedication, but I'm acknowledging you now. One day you can sell this at auction for a fortune.
With fondest wishes,
Your John

The truth is, I didn't see what he had written. She flicked past it too fast. Now I'll go to the grave wondering what it was. I'm not the only one who has speculated about their relationship. Plenty of people have wondered out loud if they were ever lovers. Perhaps they were, years ago when they were young and pulsing with desire. But not recently. Not since Coetzee joined the ranks of the literati. When men achieve celebrity overnight, they don't rush to sleep with women their own age.

"Look here." Prof. September stabs at the page with her forefinger. "'There is a snappishness to Lucy these days that he can see no justification for. There are times when they are like strangers occupying the same space.' And here: 'He knew he couldn't leave Lucy alone on the farm. She wouldn't be entirely safe.' Lucy, Lucy, Lucy. You're on practically every page."

"In the beginning, yes, but . . ."

"It's almost obsessive, the way he dwells on your every habit and mannerism. The way you screw up your eyes—you're doing it right now, by the way—your duck-footedness. *The New York Times* called it a fixation. I don't know if you saw that review?"

"Yes, but . . ."

"If there is a flaw in this book—which I am not prepared to admit—it is this compulsive attention to detail in his descriptions of you. It makes him seem a little silly when one considers how he must have been watching you all those months."

No, it is not yet Uhuru. We live in a world in which a notable feminist scholar, a black woman, shows pique at evidence that a white man has been paying attention to someone else.

"There is a double male gaze at play here," I say. "The male author has created a male character to observe a female character. He creates a fictional prism of maleness through which to filter his perceptions of me."

Prof. September has written about the layering of the male gaze in fiction. She was among the first academics to identify this prism. But she shakes her head.

"No, John Coetzee is a feminist ally. His consciousness is too acutely raised for him to fall prey to the traditional tropes of the male gaze."

I can't control the smirk that threatens to take over my face. John Coetzee loathed feminism. He thought Women's Studies shouldn't be recognised as an academic discipline. If he could hear himself described as a feminist ally, he would hoot with laughter. Or descend into a sullen rage. It is hard to believe that anyone could be this deluded.

"The point," Prof. September continues, "is that there is no lacuna in the text as far as your character is concerned. I'd call it an unnecessary wealth of description myself."

"It is only after the rape that my character truly disappears, but I would argue that she is a cypher to begin with because she lacks an interior life. She is described minutely from the outside only. After the rape, her vanishing is complete. It hulls her out as a character and leaves her empty."

"You have to recognise the performance in that!" Prof. September reaches forward to tug at my sleeve. "He is enacting the ways in which rape can erase the personhood of the survivor."

"For that to be true, there has to be some layer of awareness in the text—some nod to the reader, however subtle, that this is what the author is doing. Otherwise it simply is what it is— an erasure. And what's more . . ." My voice is getting louder and faster. I can hear it in my head. The gabbling of the unhinged. "All that stuff about Lucy not wanting to prosecute the rapists because she recognises the validity of their anger. She takes upon her body the sins of apartheid like some dungaree-wearing lamb of God. What utter, utter garbage."

"It's symbolic! It's a metaphor!"

"It's an insult."

"White women were complicit in apartheid, Lucy. You know that. And they continue to benefit from white privilege and institutionalised racism. Fictional Lucy chooses to make reparations by not identifying her rapists to the police and by continuing to maintain a cordial relationship with them."

"That just replaces one form of oppression with another. Patriarchy for racism. An eye for an eye. There aren't hierarchies of oppression. Patriarchy isn't better or worse than racism. By tolerating the misogynistic invasion of her body, Lucy isn't striking a blow for freedom. She is exchanging one jail cell for another."

Prof. September inhales deeply. She waits until the flush fades from her cheeks and the lines on her forehead smooth out.

"Lucy." She smiles at me. "The book is brilliant precisely because it stimulates such heated debate. I'm sure you can see that. No other book in recent times has been so fiercely discussed and disputed. It is a veritable conversation piece, as all the best novels are. I wouldn't give two cents for a book that generates no disagreement at all, would you?"

"This isn't a matter of opinion. It's not up for discussion. To paint a woman as admirable for acquiescing after the fact to her own rape is severely problematic."

She winces. "Such an American term—problematic. It is so overused as to be virtually meaningless."

By now, I want to tell her to stuff her website. I want to storm out of her office and never return. It takes an effort on my part to remember why I came here, and what I want from her. I do some deep breathing of my own. Her office has one small window with tiny cottage panes. I would like to open it and stick my head out, gulping the air. The window is smudged and grimy. My memories of working in this department are all of seeing dimly. Through a glass darkly. Moira and I used to joke about endarkening young minds.

I need to get out of here before a panic attack convinces me I can't breathe. I can feel it battering at my ribcage. Soon the walls will crumble, and it will emerge roaring.

I lift my hands to mime surrender. "You're right. In fact, you're the reason I've been doubting myself. If a feminist of Essie September's calibre admires this book, I asked myself, is it possible that my initial reading of it was too superficial? Am I not seeing it for the powerful critique of post-apartheid South Africa it is?"

Her face relaxes into an almost-smile. "I'm teaching a course on this book to Honours students next term. You'd be very welcome to sit in."

"That's kind of you. I'll . . . consider it. Of course, my dream is to discuss the book with the man himself."

"That's everyone's dream." Her tone is severe.

"Do you happen to know where he is these days? I've heard rumours of Australia." I shake my head and laugh. "Oh, what am I saying? Of course, you don't know any more than the rest of us. Judith at the front desk said you wouldn't."

There's a ringing silence. Bringing up Judith-at-the-front-desk was a master stroke. She is at least ten years younger than Prof. September, and dresses much better. She had an eyelash-batting flirtation with John Coetzee for years. Prof. September cannot stand her.

"As a matter of fact, I do know where he is. I'm the only one John took into his confidence—apart from his publishers. Judith wouldn't have a clue. There's no point in asking her. You shouldn't have bothered."

I cultivate a sceptical look. "It *is* Australia, isn't it? But that's an open secret by now. No one knows which city he's in. That's the real mystery."

"It's Adelaide!" Then, more quietly, "He lives in Adelaide. He wanted to get away from the attention and publicity, and he wanted somewhere quiet to work."

"Adelaide? That's in the middle of nowhere."

"It's the safest town in Australia. That was important to him. It was one of the main reasons he left."

"South Africa's security issues? Really? I never heard that he had any problems."

"I don't think he did particularly, but he got tired of looking over his shoulder all the time."

I'm not sure whether to feel disappointed or vindicated to hear that John Coetzee is as much a victim of white middle-class paranoia as anyone else.

"He does realise that crime in South Africa affects black people to a much greater extent than it does whites, right? White people tend to be disproportionately insulated from the effects of crime."

"It's not a question of objective fact. What matters is that he felt this way, and it took a psychological toll on him. I think it was courageous to up sticks like that and move across the world all on his own."

"Adelaide," I say. "I would never have guessed . . ."

CHAPTER 8

A h, Adelaide. Beautiful Adelaide.
It takes forty-eight hours of travel, but I get there at
last. The cheapest flight went via Dubai and
Singapore, with six-hour layovers in each airport. Then I had
to catch a flight from Sydney to Adelaide, but the next one left
only in the morning. So it is fully three days since I stood in
Prof. September's office, but already Adelaide is no longer just
a concept to me.

It's real and I'm here.

It is charming—every bit as beautiful as Cape Town, but
without the shacks and litter. It is also on the sea, with a river
bisecting the city like a mighty penis. Built on a grid, it shows
all the fruits of careful urban planning that Cape Town lacks.
There are parks and squares and boulevards, with ample park-
land on all sides. Everything that makes a city comfortable to
live in is right here.

And what a centre of culture it is, with arts festivals running
for most of the year, and a foodie Mecca stretching all the way
from the Riverbank Footbridge to North Terrace, taking in
Currie and Hindley streets.

How beguiling. How white.

If indigenous Australians ever lived here, there are precious
few of them left—just a few restaurant owners boasting a traditional Kaurna menu.

Is this why John Coetzee likes it so much? The well-
planned order of it all? The taming of the Australian bush into

parks and plazas? The corralling of the few remaining Kaurna people into a restaurant district? The mild whiteness of the faces on the streets?

He is on record as saying that there is no room for whites in Africa. Has he found room for himself here, in this place where the violent dispossession of the native population does not throb like a wound in his face every day? Has he found his lebensraum?

I have discovered where he lives. He has taken an apartment on the river on a five-year lease. He is not planning to return to his home in the Bo-Kaap, it seems. I asked at a coffee shop, where the staff confirmed that he was a regular. They were proud to have the Man Booker Prize-winning author patronising their establishment.

His apartment block is only two storeys high. Buildings aren't very tall in Adelaide. There is no doorman, but rather an intercom system with buzzers on the street side. I wait until a resident arrives with a key. Then I catch the door before it closes behind him and let myself in. The lift belongs to another era. It has a heavy wooden door that smells strongly of furniture polish. I have to brace my feet and lean backwards with all my strength to open it. The buttons protrude from the panel like chunky throat lozenges. I press the one marked 2 and the lift jerks into life. It jerks again when it reaches the second floor. The automatic door slides away and I shove hard against the wooden door to open it.

John Coetzee lives in flat 203. His name is on the cubbyhole in the lobby. It is empty, so he must have collected his post recently. I knock on the door, and he answers almost immediately. I can tell from the flare of surprise in his eyes that he recognises me. He rallies quickly and launches into a charade of not knowing who I am.

"Can I help you, young lady?"

Deliberate provocation. A few years ago, some of the women junior lecturers and graduate students raised a special item at a staff meeting asking that male staff members refrain from addressing them as "my dear" and "young lady" and so forth. The motion was carried, but Coetzee made a point of letting everyone know how risible he found it.

I don't rise to the bait. Instead I introduce myself, and ask if I may come in. He stands aside to allow me in. He offers me tea, and I accept.

While he is in the kitchen, I take the opportunity to look around. The furniture is new but utilitarian. There are William Kentridge prints on the wall. No plants. No scatter cushions. Pale round stains on the coffee table bear witness to the lack of coasters in his life. The room is dusty and smells faintly of ageing academic. It is a very particular smell—of shoes kicked off at night and feet left to air on the ottoman, of an infrequently washed body and sweat that has become deeply imbedded in the armpits of old shirts, of urine that has splashed onto the bathroom floor and not been wiped up, of flecks from ready meals that have sizzled and splattered in the microwave, turning diamond-hard over time.

The house in the Bo-Kaap had been lovingly tended by Maria, who also worked as an outsourced cleaner in the English Department. When students and workers protested against the outsourcing of labour at the university, John Coetzee ignored the controversy until it went away. People said he didn't even know Maria's surname, but that may have been a malicious rumour.

I bet he misses her quiet, efficient presence now.

I try to marshal my thoughts. This is it. This is the moment I've been dreaming of since I first read his book. This is my chance to state my case. I mustn't blow it.

When we each have a mug of tea in our hands, he sits down and inclines his head politely to show he is ready to listen.

"You must see how flawed it is to liken the restoration of black power in South Africa to a group of black men gang-raping a white woman," I begin. "At the best of times, rape analogies should be used with circumspection, if at all. If any people could justly be described as the rapists of South African history, it is the white colonists."

"You are assuming that the net effect of colonialism was bad for Africa. I would question your premise. History is still being made. It is too early to assess the overall impact of colonialism yet."

"I don't believe you would find many theorists from any disciplines who would agree with you."

"You'd be surprised. You see, we're allowed to talk about things like that here. It is so freeing, you can't imagine. Things that I would be lynched for saying in South Africa are calmly and openly discussed here in Australia. Like whether colonialism was good for Africa, and had the effect of drawing it into the global economy to the benefit of all its citizens."

"I think you'll find that the end of colonialism was good for Africa, and that the improvement in people's lives is a function of the postcolonial era."

"Where would Africa be if Europeans had never colonised it?"

I have to restrain myself from retorting. I have no idea whether he believes this white supremacist dogma or whether he is just spouting it to wind me up. It doesn't matter. I have to say what I want to say while I have the opportunity.

"Do you know what is just as flawed as casting black men as rapists? It is your decision to make Lucy accept the justice of her rape. She refuses to point a finger at her rapists because she chooses to take the sins of colonialism upon her own body, to accept her punishment as just. She welcomes the baby she is carrying as a messianic figure that will overcome the darkness of South Africa's past."

Coetzee smirks. "I know. It's what critics have particularly praised about my book."

"Have you ever heard of intersectionality, Professor?"

"Another buzzword? Just what we need."

"It's an acknowledgement that the struggles of all oppressed people are linked and that one cannot be free without all being free. It is recognising that different people face different challenges based on their race, class, gender, sexuality, culture, and so forth. The privileged white feminist who argues with her husband about whose turn it is to load the dishwasher does not face the same challenges as the black lesbian living in a rural village in the Transkei."

"I fail to see what that has to do with my book."

"You can't declare the country free and ready to move on from apartheid on the back of a woman who has been raped. Your analogy itself is oppressive. Can you see that?"

He thinks about this, staring into the mug of murky rooibos he has made for himself. I wonder where he got it from. Do the delis of Adelaide boast boxes of rooibos teabags? Did he bring a supply from South Africa with him? What will he do when it runs out?

"I see what you mean," he says. "Women have been the victims of violence long enough. It is deeply misogynistic to use the rape of a woman as an analogy for the just and necessary punishment white people have to endure to atone for their sins. I see where I went wrong."

Is he pulling my leg? Making fun of my earnestness?

There are tears in his eyes as he contemplates the injustice he has done to all South Africans with his book. He blinks, and a tear runs down the seams of his lined face.

"I'm so sorry. Forgive me."

Now I am crying too. He lurches to his feet and I am almost blinded by tears as I stand up. I fling myself into his arms and he strokes my hair, saying, "I'm sorry. I'm so sorry." For the first time since the rape, I feel at peace.

* * *

I don't have the money for a ticket to Adelaide. I can barely afford an Uber into the City Bowl. I am now so agoraphobic, I am about as likely to fly to Australia as I am to fly to the moon.

When you have an intense and vivid interaction with someone in your head, it is hard to believe that person remains untouched by it—that they can be unaware of the ferocity with which they have occupied your thoughts. Part of me believes that Coetzee knows I have been thinking about him.

I have settled back into my home after the expedition to visit Essie September. The air has subsided around me and the walls have ceased to vibrate. My feet sink into the thin carpets and the armchair sighs as it shifts to make way for my body. I don't want to leave it ever again. For a while I won't have to, because I have enough to sustain life. Powdered milk. Loaves of sliced bread in the freezer. A family-sized tub of margarine—it looks a little orange but still tastes okay. Tins of tuna. Tins of peaches. Water that comes out of the taps. I won't die.

(Sometimes I wonder if my house smells, the way I imagine John Coetzee's apartment in Adelaide to smell. I wouldn't notice it if it did. I sit in here day after day with the windows closed. My nose is too accustomed to this house to say whether it smells or not.)

(Sometimes I wonder if I smell. I try to shower most days, but sometimes I forget.)

I peck at my keyboard by day, whittling away at the little editing tasks that cover the bills. Just.

By night, I "listen to my stories on the wireless," just like my grandmother used to. I have let my Netflix subscription lapse because television is too vivid and absorbing these days. If I watch it, I don't sleep at night, consumed by anxiety for the characters and the cliff-hanger endings that beset them.

Reading is also off-limits. It stimulates my imagination. The literacy advocates are not wrong about that. And just now, my imagination needs quieting, not stimulating.

The radio is soothing. The presenters have learned to speak in soporific tones. I have found a channel that broadcasts *The Archers*.

I am sitting in my armchair one evening listening to the shipping forecast when there is a pounding on the front door. My heart tries to escape through my throat. Then it settles down to a pounding every bit as aggressive as the one on my door.

If I sit very quietly, the person will go away. The curtains are shut. No one can peek in and see me sitting in my chair with a crocheted blanket on my lap and the radio next to me.

"Dammit, Lucy. Open up! I know you're in there."

It's Moira. I feel besieged. She knows I want to be left in peace. Why must she persecute me like this?

The pounding continues.

BANG BANG BANG

"I can keep this up all night, bitch."

BANG BANG BANG

With a trembling sigh, I unwind the blanket from my legs and stand up.

"What do you want?" I open the door a crack and peer at her with one eye.

She shoves the door open, sending me stumbling backwards. "A drink. I want a drink."

"I don't have a drink. Not the kind you mean. There's water in the tap. Help yourself."

I got rid of all the alcohol in the house for the same reason I got rid of all the pills—even aspirin. I don't keep sharp knives either. I worry about the thoughts that strike in the wee hours of the morning. (As a child I used to think they were called that because that was when I got up to go for a wee.) No, strike is too strong a word. They creep up like mice. Nihilistic thoughts about how nice it would be to make the pain stop for good.

But I have nothing handy, and it seems like too much trouble to go out and buy something, and so I do nothing.

Moira pulls a bottle of Famous Grouse from her bag. "I came prepared."

I sit and pull the blanket back over my knees. "I don't want any whisky."

"Pooh, it stinks in here. Sardines and old farts. You should crack a window once in a while."

"It's tuna. And it doesn't worry me, so why should I bother?"

"Because it isn't healthy. I swear flies are starting to settle on you. You have moss growing on your leeward side. If you fiddle with your hair any more, it will fall out."

"What are you doing here, Moira?"

"I came to talk about sex. As in, when last did you have any?"

"Sex? Not that long ago, actually. It must be nearly two years now."

"That recently?" She walks into the kitchen and starts opening cupboard doors. Looking for glasses, probably. I make no effort to point her in the right direction. "Who was the lucky man?"

"There were six of them actually. All men. All lucky. They broke into my father's farmhouse. You can read all about it in the Booker Prize-winning novel by John Coetzee."

Moira flinches. "I'm not talking about the rape, Lucy. That wasn't sex, it was assault."

"That's funny, because it looked a lot like sex."

"Rape is a violent act, not a sexual one. I'm sure your therapist has said the same thing."

"She has. Repeatedly."

"You used to say it yourself, remember?"

"I did. But then I got raped, and realised rape and sex are the same thing. The only difference between them turns on that tiny, subjective question of consent. The absence of consent doesn't turn an otherwise sexual act into a non-sexual one. It's not alchemy."

Moira utters a crow of triumph as she finds glasses hidden behind stacked tins of peaches. Well, not glasses so much as plastic tumblers. Glasses can be smashed, and the resultant shards can be used to pierce skin. I switched to plastic crockery and glassware more than a year ago.

She pours whisky into two of the tumblers and brings one to me. "Here. This will put hair on your chest."

"That should repel any would-be rapists." A strange noise rumbles in my chest and breaks out of my mouth. A kind of belch. It sounds like amusement.

"There you go. Even the prospect of alcohol has cheered you up."

"I haven't had a drink in more than a year. It wasn't thought to be wise."

Moira tips a small measure of the amber fluid down her throat and smiles. "Wise shmise."

I lift the tumbler and feel the familiar heft of having a drink in my hand. I twirl it in my fingers to watch the light strike the whisky and catch fire. I hold it to my nose and inhale. The fumes make me recoil. I try again, more carefully this time. Petrol. Iodine. Plastic. For a moment, I wish I had a proper glass to drink this out of. I could ask Moira to go and fetch one for me from her house. She would probably do it. But now that the whisky is in my hand, I want to drink it. I don't want to wait.

I take a small sip. Too small. It evaporates on my tongue before I can swallow it. I take a bigger one that burns a fiery trail down my gullet, causing long shudders to wrack my body.

"You really are a lightweight, aren't you?" says Moira, watching this performance. "I didn't believe you when you said you hadn't had a drink in a year, but now I do."

I take another sip and my insides turn to gold. Lovely, lovely molten gold that warms my fingertips and heats my belly. Suddenly the blanket on my lap seems oppressive, so I toss it aside and pull my legs up to sit cross-legged on the chair.

"We need to get you back on the horse."

I try to make sense of this. "What horse?"

"The sex horse."

"There's a sex horse? Why did no one tell me?" I laugh again, and this time it sounds more natural and less like a long-suppressed eructation.

"The sex horse says you haven't had a ride in a very long time."

"The sex horse is right."

"Don't you ever get horny, Lucy?"

I drain my glass as I ponder this conundrum. Then I hold it out to Moira and she refills it from the bottle. *Do I?* I wonder. *Do I ever get horny?*

Yes, I conclude. *I do.* I dream about sex sometimes, and I wake up with my vagina contracting hard in orgasm. I dream about the rape, but in my dream, there is no pain. Just the feeling of being roughly penetrated, of my breasts being handled, of a hard, male pelvis pushing and pushing against my clitoris until I come. Sometimes one of the other men nudges his cock into my mouth while I'm being fucked, and I suck on it. Sometimes I'm not asleep and dreaming, but awake and fantasising. I masturbate to my own rape.

I haven't told anyone about this, not even L. Bascombe, my therapist. Not even when the urge to mess with her head is at its strongest.

I take another sip of whisky. Okay, a gulp. It no longer burns going down. My throat is numb, but my head is buzzing with the sound of angry insects.

"Lucy?"

"Sorry. I answered you in my mind, but not with my mouth."

"Well, could you repeat it with your mouth, please? I didn't quite get it the first time."

"Yes, I get horny. I think about sex all the time. I miss it." *I think about being raped and I masturbate until I come.*

"You what?"

The sharpness in her tone makes me look up. I realise I have said those words out loud.

"Dude, are you serious?"

"I'm a corrupt person. I'm evil. I deserved what happened to me."

"Wait." She fumbles with her phone. "I'm asking Google about this."

There's a solemn silence while she punches questions into Google, and I drink my whisky. The insects in my head are getting louder, and my eyelids feel heavy. I rest the back of my head against the armchair and slide into an uneasy doze. I jerk awake when the tumbler bumps against my leg.

Moira is still frowning at her phone.

"There's nothing there, is there?" I say. "I'm a freak. I knew it."

"You're not a freak. And there is some stuff here. Admittedly, a lot of it is porn. Turns out that when you type, 'I fantasise about my own rape' into Google you mostly get porn."

"Oh, joy."

"But wait. There's also a blog by a woman who was raped who says she used to fantasise about it for a couple of years afterwards. And there's an abstract in *Psychology Today* about a case study of a woman who eroticised her own rape in imaginative fantasy. It's behind a paywall. And there are quite a few articles about women who have reported experiencing orgasm during rape."

I seize at this straw. "That's worse, isn't it? At least I didn't actually come while I was being raped. I just fantasise about it after the fact."

"That's fallacious thinking, Lucy. There is no better or worse in this case. There are just individuals and their different responses to trauma. I don't know why you feel such a need to position yourself in competition with other rape survivors."

"Victims."

"Survivors is the word I choose when I'm the one who is speaking. When you are the one speaking, you're free to use the word 'victims.'"

There is a distinct snap to her tone, so I pour us more whisky. This girl needs to calm down.

"Getting back to sex . . ."

"Yes, getting back to sex. The fact that you're fantasising at all tells me you're ready to get back in the saddle."

"Of the sex horse."

"Precisely. You need to sign up to Cinder."

"How do you know I don't already have an account?"

"Do you?"

"No. But that's not the point. I could've had one. You assumed I didn't."

"Jesus, Lucy. Stop being fucking irritating. The first thing we're going to put on your profile is that you're mute. That way you won't be tempted to talk your partners to death. You can just have sex with them. Look at me!"

I glance up to find her taking multiple pictures of my face with her phone.

"Hey, wait. Let me just . . ."

"Put your hand down."

"But my hair! I'm not wearing makeup."

"Doesn't matter. These are good. Look."

She hands me her phone, and I flip through the dozen or so images she has taken. Surprisingly, they are not bad at all. The tight bun I've taken to wearing every day has come loose.

Strands of hair have fallen around my face, framing it in a fuzzy halo. The whisky has brightened my eyes and added a flush to my cheeks and lips. I don't look like the pale, pinched creature I see in the mirror every morning. The shapeless sweater I'm wearing has slipped down to reveal one shoulder. The glass of whisky I'm holding appears in some of the shots, tilted at a rakish angle.

I don't look like Lucy the Rape Victim. I look louche and fuckable.

"I look hot," I say in wonder.

"You do. Very Cinder-y. You're going to get a lot of swipe-rights. We could probably get someone over here this evening."

I am just drunk enough not to be completely horrified by this thought.

"What should I put on your profile?"

I wave my tumbler in the air. "Oh, you know. The usual crap. Likes long walks on the beach. Snuggling in front of log fires. Open-minded."

"That's code for being into anal."

"Really? Okay, make it broad-minded, then."

"That means you swing both ways."

"All right, nothing about my mind. Walks on the beach. Open fires. Sipping red wine. Theatre and opera."

"You sound like you're about forty-five years old."

"Fine. You write it then."

Moira smiles as though this is what she's wanted all along. I tell her to let me look at it before she posts anything, and pour myself more whisky.

Has this rape made me sexually disabled? I won't say I haven't considered that possibility. I've read enough blogs to know that most victims struggle to be comfortable in sexual situations. It takes years for some to get over their fear and anxiety. Some never do. It takes a special kind of partner to have the patience to negotiate the minefield that is sex with a rape victim. One step forward. Two steps back. I know what to expect. How even if you think you're fine, you're over it, your body will betray you with some physical manifestation of PTSD.

It all sounds too tedious for words. I want to skip ahead to the part where I'm okay again.

"Looking for adventurous man to break dry spell with," Moira reads. "City Bowl area. Must be single and under forty. Cultural background not important."

"Well, that's nothing if not frank. Woman seeks man for sex. Any man."

"Shall I post it?"

I try to give this the consideration it deserves. My mind feels like a radio that can't tune in to any station. It's all just loud static and occasional flickers of coherence. I feel entirely detached from the consequences of this decision. Nothing can affect me. I'm safe in my bubble of static.

"No."

That's odd. I meant to say yes.

"No? Really?" Moira sags.

"Write it again. Properly this time."

"You write it. I'm going to get us some chips."

She shoves the phone into my hand and heads for the front door, staggering slightly. I hope she isn't planning to drive. My mouth wants to warn her, but my brain isn't working properly. It'll be fine. There's a twenty-four-hour garage shop one block away.

I stare at the phone in my hand, willing it to come into focus. How would I present myself on a dating site? What aspects of myself would I choose to highlight in order to attract a potential mate?

John Coetzee's Lucy doesn't have this problem. When we leave her, she is happily pregnant, expecting the Messiah child that will be unburdened by the original sin of South Africa's grotesque past. She is farming the land with quiet, sturdy competence, working side by side with the men who raped her to create a better future for our country.

Her future as a sexual being isn't even hinted at. All we can assume is that, like everything else in her life, sex will be wholesome. Her father looks on with uncomprehending awe, aware that he is nowhere near as evolved as she is.

Fiction-Lucy would never sign up to Cinder. If sex were to appear in her life, she would probably develop an ongoing sexual relationship with one of her rapists or their associates. The sympathetic Petrus, perhaps. Apparently, they understand each other. In the absence of any other male protection in her life, Petrus is all she has. The possibility of her moving on without out a male presence is not even considered.

This book, I remind myself, won the Booker Prize. An entire panel of men and women read it and agreed that it was the best work of fiction published in English that year. The sky didn't fall. Twitter didn't explode in outrage. South Africa merely glowed with pride at another local-boy-makes-good story.

I wince as the front door opens and Moira comes back in. The whisky has relaxed me, but not enough to prevent me from reacting when someone walks into my house.

"Chips," she says, dropping an armful of packets on the table. "Popcorn, peanuts, trail-mix. Let's soak up some of that whisky."

She opens one of the bags and waves it at me. Vinegar-scented oil rushes at me, prickling my nose and prodding my stomach into life. After weeks of tuna and tinned peaches, I suddenly feel hungry. I reach into the bag and start mashing handfuls of chips into my mouth.

I try to hand the bag back to Moira, but she waves it away. "No need. I have my own."

The steady consumption of hydrogenated oil and carbohydrates sobers us both up. The salt makes us thirsty, so we drink water and that sobers us still more.

"So . . . Cinder." Moira opens the app on my phone and frowns in concentration. She taps at the keyboard, pausing occasionally to think. Once, she picks up her tumbler and almost takes a sip, but then puts it down again. No further alcohol will be consumed until a suitable profile has been set up for me.

"What do you think of this?"

I look at what she has written.

Still healing and processing after a bad experience, but ready to meet new people. Looking for Mr. Cute and Sensitive.

"That's better."

"Right? I have a good feeling about this. Should I post it?"

"It's too much information. I'll get no swipe-rights with that bit about the bad experience. No one wants to deal with that kind of baggage."

"Let's just post it and see. If you get no interest, we can always delete it and start over."

"Fine. Do it."

And she does, which means we can start drinking again.

Getting drunk all over again when you are already halfway sober is a very different experience to getting drunk from scratch. I'd forgotten that. It is a slow, golden build-up, like your second orgasm of the day. The first one might have been fast and urgent—nought to a hundred in ten seconds—but the second is more intense. The first is upon you so quickly, you're almost numb from the sensations slamming into you. The second is more satisfying.

I share this insight with Moira, and she tells me I really need to get laid.

At that exact moment, my phone starts buzzing with

replies. This strikes me as so apt as to be heaven-sent. I repeat "heaven-sent" to myself and guffaw.

These are the messages I get from men in response to my Cinder profile.

You look like a bad bitch. How much cock can you take? If you can take it, I can give it to you.

Aww . . . uv had a bad experince? Stop whining or I'll shut your rmouth with my dik

Do you like to take it in the ass? In ur profile pic you look like some1 is giving it to you in the ass. Wish it was me.

u whining cunts are all the same. Whine whine whine. Shut the fuck up bitch.

Do you know what will help you get over your bad experience? Riding my dick.

Did some man dump yo ugly ass? I don't blame him cos u ugly as fuck.

You need to be raped bitch. But noone wud rape you becos you so ugly.

Shut up, bitch. Noone wants to listen to your whining.
You're just a dumb bitch who deserved a bad experience.

Moira starts reading the replies out loud, but stops after a few words.

"Never mind. You don't want to hear this. I'll delete them."

"No, give it here. I want to know what they say."

"No." She lifts the phone above her head and pulls away from me.

I watch her for a moment, measuring the distance between us. I am drunker than she is, but I have the element of surprise on my side.

Lulled by my passivity, she lowers the phone.

I pounce.

"Jesus! Get off me."

I have the phone in my hand. I run into the bathroom and lock myself in, so I can read in peace.

CHAPTER 9

G ood news! The police have caught one of my rapists—the ringleader. They received a tip-off from a community leader in Khayelitsha. Apparently, someone had been going around the taverns boasting about how he was responsible for a high-profile rape that had been turned into a book. There were rumours that the book was going to be made into a movie with Jeremy Irons in the role of my father, and Rachel McAdams playing me.

I don't blame the guy for going public and seeking a little reflected glory for his actions, but it wasn't wise. The police went to his shack at the back of his mother's house and arrested him there. About a week later, they phoned and told me his DNA was a perfect match to the evidence collected in the rape kit.

I am so excited! After all this time, a solid arrest for my rape. I can't tell you what it means to me. It even made up for that awful evening with Moira. Any social occasion that ends with one person locked in the bathroom sobbing her eyes out while the other one hammers on the door and begs to be let in cannot be described as a success.

I'll admit I let those comments on my Cinder profile upset me even after I promised Moira I wouldn't. And, yes, I know that the internet is a deeply misogynistic place, and that the comments on Cinder are about as bad as you can get, and that I really shouldn't have let them get to me. But, what can I say? I'm weak. Being showered with hateful bile bothers me.

One way or another, the news about the arrest was just what I needed to pull me out of the misery I was wallowing in after the weekend.

I went to see my shrink, because that's what you do when you're a rape victim and something huge happens in your life.

L. BASCOMBE: They caught one of them? Really?

ME: Yes! It was even on the news. Didn't you see it?

L. BASCOMBE: I saw something about the arrest of a suspected rapist, but I didn't know it was your case they were talking about. Well, well, well.

ME: I didn't think this day would come.

L. BASCOMBE: Nor did I. So, this means it was all true then? You really were raped?

ME: I really was. You didn't believe me? I always felt that you doubted me.

L. BASCOMBE: It's not a likely story, is it? I thought you might have made up the bit about being raped to cover the fact that you had invited those men in to have sex. You were wearing a skimpy top, after all. You have to admit that's provocative.

ME: But now you know it was true.

L. BASCOMBE: Yes. The police wouldn't arrest someone for no reason. It must be true.

ME: So now I get to move on. I've been waiting two years for the chance to move on. It's very exciting.

L. BASCOMBE: But first you have to get through the trial. You are going to have to be very brave.

ME: Yes. I feel brave and empowered. I'm going to work with the criminal justice system to bring my rapist to book!

L. BASCOMBE: Perhaps he will tell the police who else he was working with. You know, if they offer him a deal.

ME: That would be great. Then all of my attackers will be behind bars, and I can move on even more.

L. BASCOMBE: This is a great day for therapy.

ME: I must confess I'm nervous about the trial, despite feeling so empowered. What if my rapist's lawyer tries to attack me personally while I am testifying?

L. BASCOMBE: You must understand that the man you consider to be your rapist is innocent before the law. The state has to prove its case beyond a reasonable doubt before anyone can refer to him as a guilty man. The duty of the defence counsel is to try to poke holes in your testimony—to submit it to the most rigorous scrutiny possible in the service of his client.

ME: You're right. And while still feeling brave and empowered, I am apprehensive about describing the rape itself in open court. Journalists will be present who will live-tweet this evidence to their thousands of followers on Twitter. It's one thing giving evidence in front of a hundred people in a public court. It's quite another having that evidence broadcast in two-hundred-and-eighty-character updates on Twitter.

L. BASCOMBE: It is the very essence of our court system that justice must be seen to be done, and that is why the majority of our trials are public. Anyone can go and listen. And this applies, obviously, to social media too. Public is public. Social media merely extends the reach of what it means to be public.

ME: Of course. That makes perfect sense.

* * *

"When you were in your first year at university, you had a relationship with a black African male, is that correct, Miss Lurie?"

"A black man. Yes, that is correct."

"A sexual relationship?"

"I suppose so, yes."

"You suppose so? You suppose so? Supposing is not good enough for this court, Miss Lurie. You either did or you didn't. Which is it?"

"I did."

"So, to clarify for the record, you had sexual intercourse—you had, in fact, full coitus—with this black African male on numerous occasions, is that correct? You admit that?"

"Yes."

"Yet you would have us believe that when my client, the defendant, arrived at your door and was invited in, you did not in fact intend to have sex with him?"

"That's correct. I did not."

"Do you find black African males repulsive, Miss Lurie?"

"No, of course not."

"So you admit you find them sexually attractive?"

"That's not what I said."

"Miss Lurie, are you so mired in the legacy of apartheid that you are not capable of feeling sexually attracted to a black African male?"

"Not at all. As you pointed out earlier, I once had a relationship with a black man."

"Then how can you expect us to believe you when you say that you did not invite my client in for sex?"

"But I didn't. Just because I'd previously had sex with men doesn't mean I wanted to have sex with a random group of men who broke into my father's house."

"With 'men,' you say? In the plural. Miss Lurie, would you agree that you were a promiscuous person?"

"No, I would not."

"You concede that you have had sex with 'men' in the plural. How many men?"

"I . . . I'm not sure . . ."

"Too many to count, eh? That sounds like the very definition of promiscuity to me."

"No, I just . . ."

"What about group sex? Have you ever had sex with more
than one other person present?"

"Uh . . . well, once at university . . . I mean, it wasn't group
sex, but there was somebody else in the . . . you know . . . in
the room."

"Again, that sounds like the very definition of group sex to
me."

"But I didn't . . ."

"So why wouldn't a daring young swinger like yourself welcome the advances of these men who came to your door on the
night of April the third? Your blood-alcohol level was over
0.05, so you'd obviously been partying."

"I'd had a glass of wine."

"You were all fired up, eh? You were ready to go."

* * *

The next day, the *Daily Mail* carries a story about the court
proceedings. It garners 3.5 million views in two days and is
shared more than fifty thousand times on Facebook.

Alleged rape victim was drinking, had history of group sex

JOHANNESBURG Lucy Lurie confessed in court yesterday that she had been drinking on the night of her alleged
rape, and that she had a history of group sex and of sleeping
with black men. Under cross-examination by Advocate Errol
van der Merwe, Lurie admitted that she was sexually attracted
to black African men.

Drinking, partying

Advocate van der Merwe described her blood-alcohol level as sky-high, and said the young woman was "all fired up and ready to go" when she let the group of men into her father's house.

Group sex

Under questioning, Lurie admitted that she had a history of participating in group sex and that she was sexually attracted, in particular, to "black African men." Lurie described to a shocked courtroom how she had practised group sex at university with other people "in the room." Constantia University, which Lurie attended as a student and then as a junior lecturer, has a history of scandal and licentiousness. Stan Loodts, leader of the civil rights organisation Afriforum, described Constantia University as "a hotbed of promiscuity where liberal parents send their children to smoke dagga and be taught lies about the white genocide."

Relationship with black man

Advocate Errol van der Merwe, nicknamed the Bulldog by his colleagues, was ruthless in picking apart Miss Lurie's testimony. As he went for the jugular, he reduced the previously confident young woman to tears, forcing her to admit that she had enjoyed a relationship with a "black African male." She confessed that they'd had sex on "numerous occasions" during the relationship. All of the alleged rapists Miss Lurie had sex with were black African males.

Advocate van der Merwe put it to her that she was now "crying rape" because she didn't want to admit her conduct to her father, who caught her in the act with the black men.

* * *

There is no suspect. There have been no arrests. I don't think there ever will be. After two years, the trail must be cold. But in the aftermath of the Cinder incident—Cindergate, if you will—I indulged myself by imagining what it would be like if there were.

It was lovely at first. Everyone believed me at last. I could see it in their eyes. Their doubts about my veracity had been banished. Of course, I don't know for sure that they had any doubts, but I've always suspected that they did. That is the nature of rape. Only those who were there know what really happened, and even then, they will have different versions of the truth in their own minds.

The only person whom I know for certain has never doubted that I was raped is my father. He was there. He saw it.

Once the glow of being believed had faded, I thought about what the trial would be like, and the glow disappeared for good.

I would rather browse my Cinder messages than imagine a rape trial with me as the star witness. The media frenzy would be extreme, thanks to the fame of Coetzee's book.

And so, I read my Cinder messages, while spooning peaches from the tin I have just opened for dinner. I luxuriate in the names I get called. It makes me feel better than thinking about being cross-examined under oath about what happened to me.

Today there are three new messages:

You need a real man to show you what sex is about. But you will cry rape and try to ruin my life like a typical cock tease bitch, Stay away from me.

I am sorry you've had a hard time. I like your photo. You have kind eyes. I think you would be interesting to talk to. PM me if you want to chat.

Who hurt you, bitch? Was it a man? He must have been blind. You're hella ugly. I wouldn't touch you if you were the last bitch on earth.

I read all three messages twice before I notice that the second one is different. And even then, I suspect a trap. A man who likes my photo and wants me to private-message him? He's gaslighting me. He wants to draw me in and get my hopes up only to turn around and vilify me for being such a dumb bitch as to think someone might like me.

But what do I have to lose? That is the advantage of hitting rock bottom. You're prepared to take chances because you have no expectations that anything will get better. I wipe peach juice from my mouth with my sleeve and click on the guy's profile.

His name is Eugene Huzain and he lives in Cape Town. His location-finder is active, so Cinder tells me he is one kilometre away from me right now. I double-check to make sure my location-finder is off. Of all the creepy and disconcerting functions of Cinder, this one—which sends you constant messages to let you know when someone whose profile you have viewed comes within a two-kilometre radius of you—is the worst.

He looks like he isn't thirty yet. He has dark-brown hair and light-brown skin. There is ironic stubble on his chin. A grey, oversized beanie cups the back of his head and droops onto his shoulder. His face is thin and ascetic and improbably beautiful. I suspect Photoshop.

I like craft beer and movies with subtitles. I am a feminist ally

and an animal-lover. Looking for an empowered woman to spend time with.

I wonder whether he is taking the piss. There are a few men who would be prepared to describe themselves as feminists (not many, but a few), but it takes a particular kind of aware-ness to describe yourself as a feminist ally. *I'm not trying to appropriate your struggle*, is what he seems to be saying, *but I want to support you in it.*

And he is actively looking for an empowered woman? Well, that lets me out. It's hard to imagine anyone less empowered than I am. But I aspire to empoweredness. Does that count?

I click on my profile picture to remind myself what I (or rather, Moira) posted. Kind eyes? I don't see it. More like haunted eyes. Perhaps it is the damage in me that attracts him. Do I really want to waste weeks of my life only to discover I'm feeding someone's saviour complex? No, I don't.

I put my phone down.

* * *

Two minutes later, I pick it up again.

I scroll through his Instagram account. There is a link to it on his Cinder profile. He is an architect. He posts pictures of animals. They are not stock photos, and nor are they photos of his own animals. They seem to be pictures of his friends' pets, and of animals he encounters during his peregrinations around Cape Town and the rest of the world. He captions them with loving observations of their beauty and just enough anthropo-morphism to be endearing without descending into sickliness.

Under a photo of an elderly, grey-muzzled mongrel: "I, Tiresias . . . perceived the scene, foretold the rest."

Under a photo of a fat black cat: "I just asked Nero here who ate all the pies and he gave me a Look."

Under a photo of a tiny lovebird nibbling his ear: "My heart belongs to this Tanzanian beauty."

It is hard not to be beguiled. He knows T.S. Eliot well enough to place the ellipsis correctly. He has a charming sense of humour. He has a warm and loving heart.

Scattered in among the animals are bottles of craft beer nestling next to tall glasses with foaming heads. They stand on battered wooden surfaces with platters of vegan sliders in the background.

There are stills from black-and-white European movies. There are photos with quotes from famous feminists—bell hooks, Maya Angelou, Ama Ata Aidoo, Toni Morrison. The number of likes and comments under his posts tell me he is well anchored in a network of family and friends. Some of them are people I know. That's right—we have mutual acquaintances. I realise I know his sister Lula slightly from university. She was in a different faculty, but we were in the same residence for a year.

This is no spambot or dummy profile set up to harass women. This is a living, breathing person who has expressed an interest in me. I remind myself why it wouldn't be a good idea to reply to him. I'm too fragile. I am nowhere near ready to be normal around a man. My issues will doom us from the start.

Then I remember that I initiated this process for a reason. I am lonely and sexually deprived. Yes, I was drunk at the time, but it was the vino that brought out the veritas, and the veritas in this situation is that I want to meet someone. The problem with this Eugene Huzain is that he is too perfect. He is relationship material while I am looking for a sex partner. I should put a pin in him for now and come back to him when I've had some one-night stands.

Of course, no one is queuing up to offer me a one-night stand. My Cinder profile has elicited nothing but abuse—

abuse and this one kind message from Eugene. Before I can think about it too much, I type a reply and hit send.

I like foreign movies too. Have you seen Delicatessen?

He must be online because his reply comes fast.

Only about a million times. I can quote whole scenes from it by heart.

I can't, so I decide not to pursue that line of chat.

A real fan! How about long walks on the beach?

He gets it immediately, which I like.

And sitting in front of a crackling log fire? Sure. I have a GSOH too.

An ironical reference to the pre-Cinder days of online dating. I like this too. I decide to invest more words in this conversation.

The trolls came out to play when I posted my profile. You were the only non-troll who responded. Unless you're a troll in disguise. (Now you have to tell me if you are because otherwise it's entrapment.)

He doesn't reply straightaway, but I can see a row of bouncing ellipses which indicate that he is typing. And not just a four-word response either.

I think there's a little bit of troll in all cis-het men. It's better to recognise and acknowledge that part of ourselves than to

distance ourselves from it. The more we isolate and drive out the trolls the less we are acknowledging our role in creating them. We are the supporting pillars of patriarchy, after all.

This is a deeper level of reflection than I was prepared for.

I guess I'm not used to cis-het men who choose to shoulder any share of responsibility. At least tell me you would make the choice not to participate in the kind of trolling that's been flooding my inbox since I posted my profile.

More bouncing ellipses.

I find misogyny abhorrent, so I would certainly do my best. I'm sorry you had to deal with that. Was this your first venture onto Cinder? Have you tried any other sites?

I decide to be honest rather than assuming a mantle of sophistication I can't live up to.

This is my first. I'm an online dating virgin. Haven't signed up anywhere else. This was my friend's idea. She thought it would be good for me to put myself out there.

The reply comes quickly.

Is Lucy Lurie your real name?

I know where this is going.

Yes.

The Lucy Lurie that John Coetzee based his book on?

Yes. I'm the girl who was raped.

That's the name of a book. I'm the Girl Who Was Raped.

That has a True Confessions ring to it. Like an article from *YOU* magazine. Whatever I was expecting him to say, this isn't it. I type back:

Sounds like something I should read.

It's completely relevant to you. The atypical South African rape. The stranger-danger rape. White girl gets attacked by black men she doesn't know. It's the least common rape there is in this country.

I know. Most women are raped by people in their community— often by friends and family.

Does the Coetzee book help or hinder? Is it good to have been immortalised in a work of genius—a modern classic?

No.

It's problematic. Coetzee's book, I mean. I've seen feminist critiques that take on his framing of gang-rape as a metaphor for decolonisation.

You're just a woke bae, aren't you?

This time there is a genuine pause in communication, without any bouncing ellipses. That was a catty remark, but I'm not sure he understood the cattiness. Perhaps the pause is due to his hasty Googling of this phrase. I could save him the trouble.

Woke bae (Urban Dictionary)
An attractive man who demonstrates a genuine awareness of the liberal agenda (*sometimes pejorative*).

And there's the rub. Because while the phrase is often used unironically to praise—nay, drool over—hot guys who are totally on-message with all race and gender issues, it is also used mockingly to skewer those who make a parade of their supposed enlightenment. Which camp does Eugene fall into? And does he even understand that there are camps to fall into?

It's not a pose. I care about gender issues. I want to participate in the dismantling of the patriarchy. I believe it oppresses men as well as women. We would all be better, freer people without it. I'm not saying I always get it right because I don't, but I am sincere.

I send him a meme. It's a gif of the words "woke" and "bae," each with a little empty box next to it. It is animated so that little blue ticks keep appearing and disappearing in the boxes, as though someone were ticking them over and over again. I can only be this brave because I'm not invested in him yet. If he were to disappear from my screen forever, I would feel no regret. I can be as jokey, mocking, and obnoxious as I like. I have the upper hand because I haven't started to care. As soon as I start to care, I will lose that. I will become anxious and clingy—a people-pleaser of the kind that displeases people the most.

He replies with a laughing face emoji.

Some of my swagger disappears. An emoji without text signals the end of a conversation. He started this interaction, and it seems as though he has ended it. If I try to keep it going, I will lose the upper hand.

Why do I care? Haven't we just established that I don't?

But this interaction has been pleasant. A part of me that has been dormant for two years is stirring into life. It's a shame it has to end so soon.

I look at my phone and see the bouncing ellipses again. He's typing. It's not over.

CHAPTER 10

I go to see my shrink. Eugene and I are meeting for coffee—our first face-to-face. I look forward to wise counsel from Lydia Bascombe.

L. BASCOMBE: How did you two meet?

ME: On Cinder. I set up a profile and he was the only respondent. Well, the only one that didn't respond with vicious, expletive-filled misogyny.

L. BASCOMBE: Cinder? Isn't that a hook-up site? Is that what you were you looking for, Lucy—someone to have sex with?

ME: At the time, yes.

L. BASCOMBE: Isn't that a little slutty of you?

ME: I prefer to think of it as taking care of my own needs. It's not easy living a celibate existence when you are twenty-eight.

L. BASCOMBE: But you've seen where sluttiness gets you, Lucy. You've already been raped. Do you want to go through that again?

ME: I hope it's not as inevitable as that. Not everyone who goes on Cinder gets raped.

L. BASCOMBE: You've arranged to meet up with a man you've never met before with the express intention of having sex with him. You're practically asking for it, aren't you?

ME: As I say, I went into this initially because I wanted to find a sex partner. But Eugene has the potential to be more than that. He is proper relationship material. Maybe even my future husband.

L. BASCOMBE: What do you like about him?

ME: He is intelligent and cultured and has good taste. He is a feminist ally. He has strong ties to the community and seems to be well loved by his friends and family. He is a vegan.

L. BASCOMBE: Are you a vegan, Lucy?

ME: No.

L. BASCOMBE: Are you planning to become one?

ME: No.

L. BASCOMBE: Are you even a vegetarian?

ME: No.

L. BASCOMBE: Then why is his veganism something that you like about him?

ME: I don't know. It sounds impressive. It makes him seem sensitive and committed and . . . and like a good person. To be so concerned about the welfare of animals that you won't even eat eggs.

L. BASCOMBE: But does he value human beings? Or does his sensitivity stop at animals?

ME: Like I said, he's a feminist ally. He posts quotes from Toni Morrison.

L. BASCOMBE: America's conscience. What about South Africa? Does he care about local issues too?

ME: Oh, yes. He reads *The Daily Vox*, and everything.

L. BASCOMBE: Then go forth and Godspeed. May fortune attend your wooing.

* * *

L. Bascombe didn't call me a slut to my face, but that's what she was thinking. How do I know? By the way she tightened her lips when I told her I'd signed up for Cinder. From the way she asked me whether I was sure I was "ready" for a relationship.

Is it possible I am misreading her cues, and that she doesn't judge me at all? Yes, I suppose it is. But I doubt it. I know her, you see. I've learned to read her face and to detect the unspoken words that lie between us like the casualties of war.

* * *

I'm sitting in a vegan café on Kloof Nek Road waiting for Eugene. It is one of only two strictly vegan establishments in Cape Town, although there are a number of restaurants that advertise themselves as vegetarian. Eugene suggested it, even though the plan is to have coffee only. It will be vegan coffee.

I've already lost the upper hand. I arrived first and now I'm sitting waiting for him. I should have made him wait for me so that I could make an entrance. All the women's magazines agree on this. But just getting here was stressful enough. I couldn't add being late to the requirements. And so, here I am, early.

I recognise this place from Eugene's Instagram photos. The furniture is made from scuffed railway sleepers. The smell of coffee and burnt onions hangs in the air, simultaneously appetising and stomach-turning. The walls have been stripped to expose the brickwork and the ceilings removed to reveal the roof beams. The effect is of a corpse that has had its flesh ripped away to lay bare the skeleton beneath.

A long refectory table runs down the middle of the room. I am perched at one end, sharing my space with clumps of talkative, tattooed people. I stand out for my lack of ink, of piercings, of shaven patches on my head. On the other hand, my thick tights, tweed skirt, Victorian blouse and jacket have a granny-ish sort of appeal. Rape Chic, I call it. Or Raped Chic.

I watch dust motes dancing in a beam of light that falls across my skirt. There are so many of them. Are they attracted to the light, or are they present all the time in the air we move around in—the air we breathe? How do our chests not get clogged with so many specks and spirals? I imagine them entering my lungs and getting caught up in a network of bronchioles—settling and accreting over time, building up into a sludge that all the coughing in the world can't dislodge.

Now I can't breathe at all. I try to draw air in through my nose, but an agonised wheeze is the best I can produce. I open my mouth, but my trachea has clamped down hard and refuses to open. My heart is banging like a barn door in a gale.

I look up and see Eugene walking into the restaurant. He looks around until his eyes stop on my face. He smiles, and suddenly I can breathe again. The vice has been released. I suck in air and smile back. From now on I will associate his face with relief, with a release from strain.

I stand as he approaches, keeping a close watch on his face and posture. Handshake or kiss? Handshake or kiss?

I don't know him. He's a stranger. We should shake hands. I've never met this man in my life.

I do know him. We have chatted online. We should kiss. I know things about him that his mother doesn't.

As he reaches me, he stretches out his hand. Handshake it is. But when I clasp his right hand, he brings his left in to enfold my hand, pulling me towards him for a double cheek kiss. A handshake *and* a kiss. I underestimated him.

I expect him to sit opposite me, with the broad planks of the refectory table between us. Instead he sits next to me, straddling the long bench so that he faces me.

"You don't have a drink yet. Can I get you a coffee? Or some tea? They do a great chai latte here."

"With soy milk?" I wrinkle my nose.

He misinterprets my expression. "With locally sourced

organic rice milk. Don't worry . . . it's grown on land that has been given over to farming for the last three hundred years. We're not talking rain forest here."

I ask for a double espresso and a glass of water. The server brings me a menu from their water bar and invites me to choose my preferred brand. I ask for tap water, thereby earning a smile of approbation from Eugene.

"I'm not saying the Patagonian Valley Stream isn't awesome, but the food miles on those bottles is appalling. Good for you!"

The server brings my espresso and Eugene's flat white, and a bowl of kale chips for us to share.

"So . . . John Coetzee." He gets straight to the point. "Your white whale."

"My white whale. Does that make me Ahab?"

"It does."

"And you are . . . Queequeg?"

"I haven't said I'll help you yet."

"Why wouldn't you?"

"I don't think Coetzee the man is relevant here. Your quarrel is with his book. Your engagement should be with his book only."

I put a sliver of kale into my mouth and feel it shatter. A strange brassican bitterness, overlaid with salt, is released onto my tongue.

"The intentional fallacy? That's a little high-school English, isn't it?"

"Doesn't make it less true."

"But it isn't true in this case. This book affects me because it is based on my life and because it was written by someone who knew me."

"The events of your life are a text. Coetzee's book is another text. There is an intertextual relationship between them, that's all. And Coetzee's life is yet another text that is intertextually related to the previous two. There is no point in viewing it any other way. You'll only upset yourself."

"That's my prerogative."

He smiles. He is extraordinarily gifted, this man—physically speaking. His eyes are dark and wide-set. His nose is a blade that bisects his face into symmetrical halves. His mouth is full but firm. I caught only a glimpse of his body before he sat down, but it seems tall and lean, with just the right amount of bulk across the shoulders. By all the tropes of romantic fiction, he is the hero of this story.

His benign influence will tip me out of suffering and into healing. He will awaken and satisfy my sexual appetite. He will guide me towards closure in my overwrought feelings towards John Coetzee. That's L. Bascombe's word—closure. I'm doing quite well without it.

"The white whale is the ultimate antagonist," I say, finishing my coffee. The caffeine is taking over my sympathetic nervous system. It is making my heart race and my hands tremble.

Eugene shakes his head. "The white whale is the victim. It exists as the antagonist only in Ahab's mind. The white whale is oblivious to Ahab except when Ahab forces himself upon its notice with harpoons and a running battle."

"That's not entirely true. The whale attacks the ship *Pequod* from time to time. Terrible, unprovoked attacks."

"The narrator is too unreliable for us to know that for sure."

"When an unreliable narrator is your only window into a story, you have to take some of what he says on trust."

Eugene smiles a peaceful smile and looks around the café. It seems the decor is to his liking. He runs a finger over a black rivet in the table. It has been worn smooth by time and weather. No rough edge remains, just this glassine, near-frictionless protrusion.

"The unreliable narrator is a tired old trope," he says. "It is probably the most hackneyed device in literary fiction today, wouldn't you agree? It's got to the point where I can't read those books any more. Even older books that date from before the unreliable narrator craze irritate me now."

"I'm going to go out on a limb here and guess that you didn't enjoy *Gone Girl*?"

He shakes his head. "Utter crap."

I am fascinated by the way his coal-black hair falls softly, Byronically, over his forehead. He is probably the most beautiful individual I have ever seen close up.

I don't agree that *Gone Girl* was utter crap, but I cannot argue with beauty.

"Even if John Coetzee is nothing more than a text that exists in intertextual opposition to the text that is my life, I still want to find him," I say. "I want to speak to him. Our conversation will be yet another text that can engage in dialogue with the other texts."

"You say he lives in Adelaide now?"

"Yes. I managed to worm that out of one of his colleagues in the English Department."

"And you can't afford to fly to Adelaide to beard him in his den."

Only in my daydreams.

I don't tell Eugene about the daydreams. They are more like hallucinations. I wonder if I go into a petit mal state when I have them. Time passes—time that I have no memory of. My only memory is of the dreams.

They have become as much a part of the warp and weft of me as my actual memories. The other day, I read an interview with a woman who had survived a shark attack. As she described the fear, the numbness, the bloom of blood in the water, I thought, *yes, that's how it was for me*. Then I remembered that I have never been attacked by a shark. I had a daydream about it once, and now it has been assimilated into my memories.

That's not something you share on a first date. I will edit myself until he can handle my unexpurgated self.

It is time for us to go our separate ways. This meeting went well, but not well enough for our coffee date to turn into a lunch date, despite strong hints from the restaurant. The smell of coffee and burnt onions has been replaced by coriander and roast pumpkin. The tables are filling up. The waiter has asked us twice if we'd like to see menus.

Eugene waves him away. We split the bill and walk out into the street. The wind has come up. The black southeaster. It blows us apart and we go our separate ways.

CHAPTER 11

There is no time for reflection. If I had the leisure, I would mull over every nuance of our date and online conversations. Not because I am a woman, but because I don't have enough to occupy myself. My mind runs along well-worn grooves. There is nothing to tempt it to jump the tracks and try something else. I don't have enough to think about.

Until today. Today I have plenty to think about. Too much, in fact, and none of it good. My father phoned last night while I was eating. He told me the insurance company was being difficult. This is a refrain I am accustomed to hearing, so I didn't give it my full attention. It seemed that it was the value of the furniture that was in dispute, so I made appropriate noises.

Only when he said, "So you'll go then? This weekend would be best," did I drag my mind out of the quicksand of introspection and pay attention.

"This weekend?" I asked.

"Yes. That would be best. The house is by no means gutted, you know. Well, I suppose you don't, because you've never shown an interest in it. The fire department got there quickly and saved a lot. The furniture came off worst. All that old wood and French polish. It must have gone up like a Roman candle. But the bones are there. The bones are definitely there."

"You said something about an inventory?" My mind rewound our conversation and dredged up keywords.

"That's right. I'd go myself, but the Masters golf tournament at the club is this weekend. I can't get away, and the insurance company isn't prepared to wait. It has to be now. They need a full inventory of the furniture that was in the house, as well as the appliances and electronics. When you see what's there, it will jog your memory."

Histrionics have never been encouraged in my family. You didn't make a show of yourself. Arguments were conducted in private and in a furious undertone. Emotions were never a reason for shirking your duty.

"You want me to go to the farmhouse and draw up an inventory of the contents?"

He sighed. "Yes. Haven't you been listening?"

"I have never gone back. Not in two years."

"I know. That's what I'm saying. You never ask about the house. You show no interest in its condition. It's time you made yourself useful, and it will be good for you to start driving again. This will benefit you too in the end—a good payout from the insurance company."

There was a pause while we listened to each other breathing. The air rushed into his lungs as he realised his mistake.

"When I'm dead, I mean. Obviously. When I'm dead and gone. It will all come to you in the end."

Daddy don't make me. I'm scared. Don't make me go back there. I haven't driven a car in weeks.

"Where are the keys? The house is locked, I assume?"

"The insurance company put up a temporary fence around the place. One of those unscalable security fences. I'll drop the keys off in your post box. You had better take a can of Q20 with you. The lock will be stiff."

If the English Department at the University of Constantia is a site of secondary trauma, what does that make the farmhouse where the attack occurred? Ground Zero? Omaha Beach?

L. Bascombe would want to hear about this. She would counsel caution. It is quite possible that she would urge me not to go. Or at least not to go alone. But I don't plan to ask her advice. Some things are too big, too weighty, to discuss with one's therapist.

I treasured up all these things and pondered them in my heart.

I am still pondering on Saturday morning as I drive out to Worcester. One hour and twenty-eight minutes of pondering time, the GPS promised me. That's just to get into the town of Worcester. The additional eight kilometres of travelling east on a gravel road wasn't factored in.

It dawns on me that my father had a formidable commute when he worked at the university. No wonder he chose to stay over with friends several nights of the week. I watched the distance between him and my mother grow during those years. Then there was the misunderstanding that led to his sacking. It makes more sense now from my adult perspective.

Worcester is beautiful in the way that a place once familiar and now strange can be. I never noticed its beauty before. It was just "town."

"I'm going into town. Do you need anything?" my father would say. And my mother would hand him a list. "Town" was a source of occasional treats like ice cream, and occasional woe, like trips to the dentist. It was never a place I drove through with my head swivelling from side to side, admiring the views.

I am struck by the width of the streets and the air of prosperity. I admire the steeples of the churches. To the north are the Hex River Mountains, and to the west (hulking, purple) the Du Toitskloof mountains through which I have travelled. This is one of the most beautiful places on earth, and I never realised.

I reduce my speed as I turn onto the gravel road that leads to my father's farm. I remember feeling as though all the teeth in my head would rattle loose when he took this road too fast.

Today it is eerily smooth. I pull over and open my door to look at the road. It has been resurfaced. The craterous potholes and bone-shaking runnels of my youth are gone. Everything has been smoothed over. Flaws have been erased.

Is it possible to choose not to be traumatised?

Today, it will be possible. I have a job to do and I will do it. I will not let my father down. I saw disappointment in his face once. I don't want to see it again.

When the road rises, and I spot the farmhouse in the distance, my breath does not clog. My chest does not heave. No racing heart. No crushing weight. I have chosen zero trauma. Perhaps I am growing closer to fiction-Lucy after all.

Fiction-Lucy never leaves the farm. She takes it over and makes it her own. She forms a partnership with the men who raped her. They work the farm together. It is no longer solely hers. And this—Coetzee suggests—is how it should be. A black man and a white woman work side-by-side to farm the land together. The rape of fiction-Lucy is a metaphor for the necessary phase of violent overthrow that has to be got through before a true post-apartheid era can begin.

South Africa never had a violent revolution. It had a negotiated settlement. The old regime grudgingly handed power over only once certain guarantees were in place. Those guarantees—"sunset clauses"—were not agreed upon in anything approaching a democratic fashion.

Coetzee's book has been praised as "unflinching," as holding a mirror up to the post-apartheid lie. But I refuse to accept it. I refuse to accept that my rape is the best metaphor for the overthrow of the old order.

As I pull up in front of the farmhouse, I can see her—Fiction-Lucy. She is coming in from the fields, walking shoulder-to-shoulder with her rapist. Her child is strapped to her back with two blankets tied at the corners. I can't tell if it's a boy or a girl. It is not an option for her to hand her child to a babysitter. She and the women who work here take it in turns to watch each other's children. She has no special status. She is not the madam. Her privilege has been stripped away, leaving behind a woman like any other—one who must work for her place in the world while raising her child.

A boy. It's a boy. I can see that now. He is the promised child born into modest circumstances, destined to lead his people to freedom. Perhaps he will become a carpenter.

Lucy and Petrus parent the child together. It is not important whether Petrus, who was not one of the rapists, is literally the father of the boy. It is not necessary for him to share DNA with the child to be its father. The boy is the child of everyone who participated in the rape, and their associates, and as such, he belongs to all of them.

He is the embodiment of the saying that it takes a village to raise a child.

Beyond the farmhouse, the fields are thriving. Wheat and barley nod in the wind, a rippling sea of green and brown. All is well with this new-new South Africa. It is a much better place than the old-new South Africa.

I smile as the palimpsest fades and the underlay reveals itself. I lift my fingers to my mouth and pinch the smile away until it is properly gone. Then I park outside the fence because the security gate is too narrow to admit a car. The lock resists the promptings of my key. There are scabs of rust on the metal, as always in this climate. I shake the can of oil my father reminded me to bring, and spray it directly into the opening. I am rewarded with rust-stained moisture oozing back out. The hole has been adequately lubricated. It is ready to receive the shaft of my key. I snigger at the trend of my thoughts.

The smell hits me as I step into the house. Ash. Damp wood.

Mildew. Cinders. They say it took a year for the smell of burning to clear from New York City after 9/11. This has been two years, but the house has been closed up. It has turned into a tomb for odours.

If the air smells like a funeral pyre, the house looks like one too. It is unrecognisable as the site of my attack, and therefore triggers no memories. This is a Salvador Dali painting of twisted, melting images and their mirrored shadows. I have to look long and hard to recognise the coffee table I grew up with. It is a Hieronymus Bosch parody of itself. Its legs are turned in on themselves and its top is a roller coaster.

The walls are blackened, and the artwork scorched or incinerated. The ceiling sags in a manner that makes me fear for my safety. I remind myself that it has stayed up for two years, and that the slight disturbance I am causing is unlikely to bring it down.

I wander from room to room, trying to discern my childhood in the wreckage. The bed that I slept in is a stranger to me. The view of the mountains I grew up with is bubbled and smudged through the damaged glass. My parents' bedroom is the least damaged of all. I still think of it as such although in recent years, it had become very much my father's room. He sold the bed when my mother died. He redecorated in a more masculine style—dark wood and studded leather, hunting trophies on the wall, an antique Mauser mounted above the window. The flocked wallpaper of my mother's day exists only in my memory.

I peer into the bathrooms, fascinated by this testimony to what severe heat can do to porcelain and plastic. I recognise the remodelled fixtures my father had installed a few years ago. In my mother's time, the fixtures were original or retrofitted to look original. We had wall-mounted cisterns that flushed by means of a long chain. They never gave a moment's trouble, but my father hated them. My mother was barely in the ground before he called Dream Bathrooms.

The new bathrooms disappointed him, I remember. Even

after they had been refitted to his specifications, he wasn't happy. The lock-up-and-go flat he has now is more to his liking.

I look at the clipboard my father left when he dropped off the keys. It has a spreadsheet attached to it, listing the furniture that was supposedly here before the fire. I think he would like me to believe it was drawn up by the insurance company, but I can see he compiled it himself on his computer.

1. Yellowwood tallboy, used as drinks cabinet, circa 1798, R23,000
2. Stinkwood kist, used for storing linen, circa 1801, R17,500
3. Cape oak dresser, circa 1857, R19,000
4. Stinkwood mirror frame with original bevelled mirror, circa 1870, R5,700

I am supposed to put ticks next to the items I find in this house. The total value of the contents of the house is set at a staggering figure. I know it's not right. I know we never owned some of the items listed. I think he got the idea for them from my late grandparents' house—my mother's parents. Their place was a treasure trove of antiques from the Cape Colony. Some of those items came with my mother when she got married, but most remained in her parents' house.

Other bits of furniture sound like things we owned years ago, before my mother died. My father couldn't abide them. He traded them in for flat-pack, assemble-it-yourself items a while ago. But some—yes, some—are still here.

My father is not interested in what is still here. He wants me to pick through this twisted landscape and confirm that everything on his fake spreadsheet was once here—even the items that were never here. He wants me to help him defraud the insurance company.

How can I?

How can I not?

How can I choose to side with a faceless corporation—one that has been pocketing his premiums all these years, and which would screw him over without a moment's hesitation—rather than my own father? It is a small thing he is asking me to do. The merest nothing. A few strokes of my pen and it is done.

Has my father not suffered enough? He lost his wife a few years ago. He watched his daughter being raped. He saw his house torched and all his possessions go up in flames. Of course he wants to make some of the awfulness go away. Money has the power to do that. The insurance company won't even notice the difference, but it will make all the difference in the world to my father.

The clipboard shakes as I grip it.

I owe it to my father. I owe him this small favour. No father should have to see what he saw.

I grab the pen with slippery fingers and start ticking boxes. Yes, an oak dresser. Yes, a yellowwood tallboy. Yes, a stinkwood coffee table crafted by Huguenot hands in 1726. I tick and I tick and I tick. Then, when there are no boxes left to tick, I add my own items. The box used by Jan van Riebeeck to store his shaving brushes. A wooden chest with original iron clasps used to store the Governor's smallclothes. A fragment of the True Cross.

I stop before I have furnished the entire *Drommedaris*. I scratch out some of my wilder fictions, but there is enough here for a hefty claim. My father will be pleased.

My phone buzzes against my hip. I take it out and see that my good deed has already been rewarded. It is a text from Eugene. Karma is delivering promptly these days.

Eugene: Hey. I have tickets for the Laugh Barrel on Saturday night. Would you like to go with me?

The Laugh Barrel is a comedy club in the City Bowl. They feature new and established stand-ups, improvs, and other comedy acts. They have open mic nights on Wednesdays. I haven't been in years. I can't think of a reason not to go now.

Lucy: Sure. That sounds like fun. Meet you there at 7?

I lock up when I leave the house. If I look down when I walk, I notice my duck-footed gait—the one Coetzee made so much of. So I look up and see Fiction-Lucy and her family again. Her daughter is older now. (The baby is a girl, not a boy.) She is running around the yard barefoot in a white smocked dress. Her hair is braided into two plaits tied with white ribbons. Her face glows with health and joy. There are other children running with her. They are the babies of the collective of labourers now running this farm. I saw them earlier, but they are older now.

The little girl runs up to me and lifts her shining face to mine. "I belong here," she tells me. "This is my place."

* * *

"You should write an op-ed for *The New York Times*."

I stare at Moira. "Why would *The New York Times* be interested in anything I have to say?"

"Because you have a tale to tell that piggybacks on the tale of a famous man. The stories of unknown women become interesting when they are linked to the stories of well-known men. No one cares if you were sexually harassed. They only care if you were sexually harassed by a famous Hollywood producer."

"That's depressing."

"But true. John Coetzee's book is still huge."

"Correct."

"Everyone is talking about it. The *NYT* devoted two major reviews to it—one before it started winning awards, and one after."

"Correct again." I have copies of both reviews.

"The *NYT* would be interested in a piece from your perspective about how Coetzee processed your personal pain into fiction, and how that made you feel. They publish that stuff all the time. Think of the Angelina Jolie piece. And Jodie Foster. And Salma Hayek. And . . . and Bono."

"I can think of several ways in which I am not like those people."

"No, but listen. You're not nobody. You are the girl who was raped. You are the real-life inspiration behind Lucy. She is one of the most important female figures in literature today, and she was based on you."

Pride expands in my chest like a gas leak. I am somebody. I matter. Hubris yawns and stretches inside me, waking up for the first time in two years. But the doubts won't be banished.

"Coetzee is the darling of the literary world. No one will be interested in a piece that challenges him."

"The media built him up, and they can bring him down again. He is perfectly poised at the apex of his fame. If you brought him down, the schadenfreude would be immense. It would be delicious."

I am dazzled by this vision of myself as the woman who brought down John Coetzee. No—The Girl Who Brought Down John Coetzee. That's better.

"How do I do it?"

"First, write the piece. Make it punchy and heartfelt. Serious, but not too serious. Tap into the #MeToo hype. Check the submissions guidelines on their website. Clean up your piece and hit send. It will be published by the end of the month. I guarantee it."

* * *

Lucy: I am writing an op-ed for the NYT.

Putting it in a text makes it feel real. Eugene's reply comes back fast.

Eugene: Wow! Really? That's amazing. You are the only person I know who has ever done that. What is it about?

"What *will* it be about?" would be more accurate. I can't seem to get the words out of my mind and onto the screen.

Lucy: It's about being the real-life inspiration behind Coetzee's Lucy. How it affected me. What he got wrong, etc.

My text stares back at me in all its prissiness. *What he got wrong, etc*? When did wrongness become a measurable concept in fiction? When did the extent to which a piece of fiction is true to life become a gauge of its worth?

Eugene: I think that's great. Good luck with the process. I'm looking forward to our date. Should be a fun night.

His use of the word "date" surprises me. Our arrangement for Saturday could easily be tidied away under the heading of two people hanging out together. Is he acknowledging it as a date because I am writing an op-ed for *The New York Times*? Is that the alchemy that has turned me from an acquaintance into a date?

Lucy: Me too. See you on Sat.

Disappointment flickers as he goes offline. Now I must apply my mind to my op-ed for *The New York Times*.

Op-ed for *The New York Times*. My op-ed for the *NYT*. I'm writing an op-ed for the *NYT*. Hello, have you met my girl-friend, Lucy? She's writing an op-ed for *The New York Times*. Opinion-editorial.

If you are writing an op-ed for *The New York Times* and no one commissioned you to do so, can you be said to be writing it? An op-ed for the *NYT* only becomes an op-ed for the *NYT* when it has been submitted and accepted. Until then, it is just words on a screen.

Except it isn't even that yet, because I am looking at the screen and there are no words on it. Now that I have to put them into sentences, my deeply held convictions are bleeding away. They are evaporating. I started off determined to consider both sides of the debate—mine and Coetzee's. But mine has disappeared, and Coetzee's is the only one I can see.

There is a slogan that gets printed on T-shirts and coffee mugs: "Be careful what you say to a writer. She'll save it up and put it in a book." Here's another one: "Don't annoy the writer. She'll put you in a book and kill you." I can barely open my Facebook feed without seeing these maxims. They frolic across the pages of my friends who consider themselves to be writers, which is all of them.

Did you notice the "she"? It is not there by accident. There's a reason why coffee-mug slogans use the feminine pro-noun. When women write things, it is cute and funny. When men write things, it is serious. For a woman to put you in her book would be flattering and amusing. For a man to do so would be life-changing. I throw words at the screen to this effect, to see if anything sticks. But Coetzee's perspective remains uppermost in my mind. It is part of the social contract that everything is fair game when it comes to fiction. Nothing is off-limits. Nothing is beyond the pale. If real life weren't allowed to be the inspiration for fiction, we wouldn't have the works of Shakespeare, Austen, Adichie, Naipaul, or Didion. It is not just important for authors to be able to write without fear or favour: it is vital. Hurt feelings cannot be permitted to intrude. The only post-publication discussion that has any validity at all is a critical one. A piecemeal breaking down of a text into its real-life inspirations is an ignoble enterprise, fit only for women and children.

I throw this at the screen too, and it sticks very well. I may never be able to unstick it. What won't stick is my counter-argument. What was that again? I can't remember. All I can hear in my mind when I try to grasp it is the sound of my own whining.

It's not fair
He wrote about me and I never said he could
He was watching me the whole time while pretending not
   to recognise me
He made me look stupid
He can't write about me without asking

I sound like a child. My entire academic career—all my training taught me not to think about literature in these terms. It taught me to reject this mindset. I can't bring myself to throw any of it at the screen. It is gibberish.

This has been a useful exercise. It has taught me to look more closely at this feeling of grievance I have been carrying around for nearly two years. What is at the base of it? Is it anything more than hurt feelings? John Coetzee hurt my feelings and I want him to apologise. Is that all there is to it? Yes . . . yes, it appears so.

I feel peaceful. How wrong I've been all this time. Writers don't owe anyone anything. They don't have to account for the words they put on a page or the order in which they put them. I have been trying to insert myself into the Coetzee Overnight Success narrative when the truth is, I don't belong there. I am not part of his story, and I have allowed him to be part of mine for too long.

This is what it feels like to be free.

I go out with Eugene on Saturday night. I wear skinny jeans with ballet flats and a sparkly top with spaghetti straps. It's the first time I've been out without my "I was raped" armour in two years. Men look at me and I look right back at them. It's wonderful to have my sexual confidence back.

The comedy show is hilarious. There is one guy who makes rape jokes throughout his set. It is edgy and ironic and self-reflexive. It is meant to show that rape jokes are never funny (except his, of course). I don't get triggered. The jokes wash over me. I laugh at some of them.

Eugene and I eat deep-fried tofu strips with sweet-and-sour sauce, and they are delicious. I look with pity at the table next to us. They are eating chicken nuggets and buffalo wings. They feast on the flesh of animals raised in misery and slain in anger. Who decides that the humble fowl is of less intrinsic worth than the human being? Or the ant, for that matter? And what about the humble protozoan? The simple eukaryote?

Is it not blatant species-ism to rank these creatures according to an arbitrary standard of complexity, thereby placing ourselves conveniently at the top? The Great Chain of Being went out with the Renaissance, except when it comes to deciding what is fit to be eaten. There is no philosophical justification for species-ism.

I decide to become a vegan, like Eugene. I whisper my decision into his ear between sets, and he smiles.

"Thank you!" He takes my hand in his. "Thank you for that. Our fellow creatures thank you. There is one less murderer in the world."

The skin-to-skin connection between us fizzes with electricity. Or is it chemistry? Perhaps it is both—electrochemistry.

The attraction is undeniable. I fantasise about what it would be like to have his hands all over me.

But first, there is an ethical dilemma I need to clear up.

During the interval, he pops round to the juice bar next door to get us freshly squeezed dairy-free smoothies.

"What's in this?" I ask, sipping the bright orange beverage.

"Carrots, oranges, beetroot and mango."

"I feel bad for the carrots and the beetroots."

"Tell me more."

"The whole plant had to die to supply us with food. It's not right. The carrot and the beetroot are the taproots. They anchor the plant in the soil, absorb water and nutrients from the ground, and store excess starch for the plant to live off in lean times. When we uproot them to feed ourselves, we're killing the whole parent plant. It is an act of violence."

"But plants are not sentient in the same way animals are." His dark eyes look up at me through sooty lashes.

"Well, actually, that's a common misconception," I explain. "Plants respond to stimuli and react to pain. They are capable of movement. There is evidence that they respond to music and voice. Really, the line drawn between plant life and animal life is arbitrary. It has no place in the mind of the person of conscience."

Understanding dawns in his eyes, proving that he is just as capable of rational thought as any woman. "But if we can't eat plants and we can't eat animals, what can we eat? There's nothing left."

I smile, pleased to be able to clear up his confusion. "Don't get hysterical. There's an answer. Listen and I'll explain. Have you ever heard of fruitarianism?"

"Fruitarianism?" He stammers over the unfamiliar syllables. "I don't think I have."

"You only eat that part of the plant that can be removed

without damaging it. Fruits, legumes, nuts, and certain brassicas can be included in that category."

"So . . . we could drink milk then . . . and eat eggs. And honey."

"No, that's not right. I'll explain the horrors of the dairy and egg-farming industries to you some other time. And as for honey—absolutely not. It is brazen robbery of the life-giving food stores of bees. Not to be thought of."

"You're saying I can eat anything I can pick that won't harm the parent plant?"

"Well, yes, there are those who are prepared to do violence to the plant by picking things from it. I prefer to wait for bounty to drop naturally from the plant. If you want to be an ethical eater, there's no other option."

"Thank you for explaining it to me, Lucy. You have opened my eyes. Would you like to come in for a cup of coffee perhaps, when you drop me home later?"

I laugh. His coquetry amuses me. "Perhaps. We'll see."

But I've already decided. I will indulge him by coming to his flat later and whiling away a few hours with passion. I won't stay the night. They always develop expectations if you do.

"I have to be up early tomorrow," I say, when he invites me in at the end of the evening. "I have a presentation in the morning. But I can come in for a little while." I'm laying the groundwork for my early exit.

He apologises blushingly for the state of his flat. I don't see much amiss. It's the usual boyish clutter—bright scarves draped everywhere, a Pilates ball by the sofa, a low-carb salad bowl abandoned half-eaten on the table.

I accept the offer of coffee, although I'd prefer brandy. While he fusses in the kitchen, I browse through his collection of CDs and DVDs. My expectations are low, so I'm not disappointed. *Pretty Woman, 10 Things I Hate About You, An Officer and a Gentleman, Sixteen Candles, Twilight.* The usual boyish fantasies of happily ever after.

Don't get me started on the music. He has every *Now That's What I Call Music* CD published since the turn of the century. Who even listens to CDs any more? Has this boy never heard of the digital age?

He brings a tray to the sitting room, looking flushed and nervous. Time to make him more nervous still. As he puts the tray down, I stand and back him up against the bookshelf.

"What are you doing?"

"Taking what I want." Then I swoop and capture his mouth in a masterful kiss. He struggles for a moment, like a bird trapped in my arms. Then suddenly all the fight goes out of him as he melts into my embrace. His capitulation comes a little more easily than I like. I prefer it when they put up more of a fight. But this will save time. I'll be out of here in an hour.

He pulls me toward the bedroom, but there's a perfectly good sofa right here. And no one expects you to cuddle or fall asleep on a sofa. I undo the buttons on his shirt with a practised one-handed move and back him up until his legs hit the sofa, forcing him to sit. He shudders and moans as my hard, calloused palms graze his nipples. His stomach is a little softer than I like—I prefer them tighter. Still, what he lacks in tone, he makes up for in enthusiasm.

He is panting now, practically begging for it. When we finally join, he utters a sob of gratitude. I make him come quickly and easily, and then take my time over my own pleasure. Afterwards, as he pulls a throw up to cover his chest, he casts me a look of blatant adoration.

I sigh. Why do they always insist on falling in love with me? Men don't seem capable of separating sex from emotion. You ring that bell for them, and next thing they're picking out china patterns. Perhaps it's their way of convincing themselves that they're not sluts to have slept with you. It's fine to have sex on the first date as long as you're in love with the woman, right?

It's all so predictable, I'm already bored. The way he looks at me with those liquid eyes. Not to mention how he clings to my arm.

I give him a devastating smile. "Early start in the morning, remember? I have to dash now, but I'll call you in a few days." I pull on my jeans and boots. "Stay cool, kiddo."

Then I'm out the door and heading for freedom, deleting his number from my phone as I go.

CHAPTER 12

I'm still sat at my desk trying to write my op-ed for *The New York Times*. That's what the English say, isn't it? I was sat at my desk . . . I was stood in the corner. In South Africa, we are more likely to say I was sitting at my desk . . . I was standing in the corner. Is it cultural appropriation for me to use the English form?

I laugh immoderately at the idea.

Cultural appropriation only becomes relevant where there is a current or historical imbalance of power between the two cultures—where the culture that is doing the borrowing is mainstream and the culture that is being plundered is marginalised. As a white South African, I can borrow the cultural spoils of Britain as much as I like and suffer no penalty other than to be considered pretentious.

A flash of light ignites my brain, and the room is filled with the chorus of a thousand angels.

Would that not be a fruitful line for me to tug in my op-ed for the *NYT*? Cultural appropriation?

John Coetzee has appropriated my story, one that was mine to tell. He seized it with his greedy, patriarchal fingers and snatched it from me. He has profited from it, both in monetary terms and in the career capital that has accrued to him.

In terms of race and class we are on an equal footing, but in every other respect he is my senior. He is older than me. He was a professor in the English Department while I was a junior lecturer. He is a man and I am a woman. There are not many things you can claim for yourself once you have been raped, but surely the right to tell your own story is one of them?

Yes. I can work with this.

I must whip up the outrage sufficiently so that anyone who points out that we could both tell the story is drowned out. Or dismissed as a cis-het, heteronormative, privileged, patriarchal misogynist.

The trouble with writing an op-ed for *The New York Times* is that you can't be emotional. This isn't *Jezebel* or *Bitch Media*. The *NYT* expects facts and reasoned argument, those trappings of normative oppression. The *NYT* is the very home of respectability politics. If I don't play by the rules, I won't be let in the door.

Being let in the door is important to me. John Coetzee can ignore me in every other forum, but if my story makes it to the *NYT*, he will be forced to pay attention.

* * *

L. BASCOMBE: How was your date with the vegan?

ME: I already told you.

L. BASCOMBE: No, you told me the fantasy version. I'd like to hear what really happened.

ME: Aren't you interested in why I felt the need to create such an elaborate fantasy scenario? Isn't that more of a window into my psyche than a real-world date?

L. BASCOMBE: I think it's clear to both of us. The only way you can contemplate moving forward in a sexual relationship is if you frame it in a familiar narrative—perhaps one you grew up with as a child. I'm guessing that you read a lot of romance novels as a teenager. After what you have been through, you find the traditional seduction scenario hard to stomach, so you turn it on its head with you as the experienced seducer and the vegan as the ingénue whose innocence is being pillaged.

ME: I suppose you're right.

L. BASCOMBE: I'm more interested in what really happened. If it had been a happy experience you would have been content to dwell on it, rather than to erase it with fantasy.

ME: It was underwhelming. I think that's the right word. And I'm afraid he found it so, too. I fear he won't want to see me again because it was such a lacklustre evening.

L. BASCOMBE: So, it was boring? You didn't click? You didn't have much to say to each other?

ME: All of the above.

L. BASCOMBE: Then why would you want to see him again? So you can spend another boring evening together? Why go back for more?

ME: It was my fault that we had so little to say to each other. I need to try harder. I need to be better.

L. BASCOMBE: Why wasn't it his fault?

ME: Why do I have to explain this to you? He's a vegan. He is the best-looking person I have ever seen off a movie screen. He has a great Instagram account. It's grainy and raw and real. He knows people who work in television. Obviously it's my fault. How could it be otherwise?

L. BASCOMBE: Perhaps he is just dull.

ME: Then why does he have so many followers? Why does he hang out with cool, beautiful people? I have a small life. He has a large life. Finis.

L. BASCOMBE: In your quest for another dull evening, have you contacted him again?

ME: No. I don't want to seem clingy.

* * *

I finished my op-ed for *The New York Times* and sent it off.

Moira read it and thought it was very good. I expect to hear from them soon.

While I wait, I fork peaches out of the tin into my mouth and do line edits for publishers. After an unprecedented spell of going out, I slip back into staying home. It is easily done. There is not a ripple on the surface of the pond to indicate that I ever left it.

But I get a call from the insurance company. This means I have to go out again.

"This is Jono from Very High Premiums Insurance. Am I speaking to Lucy Lurie?"

"You are."

"I am processing the householder's insurance claim for Mr. David Lurie. I see you signed the form detailing items lost in the fire. I wonder if I could speak to you about that?"

"Go ahead."

"I'd prefer to do this in person. I can come to your house if that would be convenient. Or any other location."

"Let's meet for coffee."

We arrange a time and a place. My sins have found me out. I am going to be questioned about nineteenth-century stinkwood dressers. I will be revealed as a liar.

I phone my father to tell him about this development. He won't be happy. Anything that might delay or diminish the payout causes him distress.

He is quiet as he absorbs the disappointment. "I was expecting this."

I don't think he was, but he likes to maintain the illusion of control.

"Yes, it was only a matter of time. They are simply being conscientious. There is a lot of money at stake, and they want to be sure of dotting their i's and crossing their t's."

"What must I do? What must I say?"

"Stick to the truth. The inventory you compiled was accurate.

You can personally vouch for each piece of furniture. Don't change your story. Don't elaborate."

But that's not the truth, Daddy.

"I'll try."

"Don't get flustered, girl. You lose your nerve too easily."

"I won't. I'll stay strong."

* * *

Jono from Very High Premiums Insurance wears a grey suit with grey socks and grey shoes. His face is shiny with youth. His hair has been brushed and gelled to cling to the shape of the skull. He shakes my hand and makes eye contact like they taught him in business school.

"Miss Lurie. Good to meet you. Jono from Very High Premiums. Would you like tea or coffee?"

I ask for tea and sit on the edge of my chair. It is a classic marker of guilt, but I can't help it. I feel guilty because I am guilty.

"Just a few issues to run through." He consults a clipboard and cross-references it with something on his laptop screen. "Your father said that his collection of antique furniture was amassed over many years. Can you tell me about that?"

"Of course. Some of it was given to my mother and father as a wedding present by my mother's family. They were farmers in the Worcester district for generations, and had an impressive collection of furniture. My parents were also in the habit of frequenting auction sales and flea markets on weekends. I believe much of their furniture was sourced in that way."

My mother loved trawling second-hand shops and flea markets. My father hated it. When she died, he got rid of most of what she had collected. I remind myself that I don't remember exactly what he sold and what he kept. I was twenty at the time. I was at university. I didn't pay attention.

He keeps his gaze fixed on the clipboard. "On the night of the incident, can you remember whose idea it was to start the fire?"

The question snatches the breath from my lungs. I am a landed fish, begging to be thrown back into the water. Jono keeps his eyes on the clipboard. The Dale Carnegie school of eye contact has been abandoned.

Is this what he wanted? To question me about that night?

"Do you remember, Miss Lurie? Do you remember who decided to start the fire?"

"We didn't know that a fire had been started until it was almost upon us. My father came to tell me to get up—to get out because the house was on fire. Smoke was already billowing into the sitting room. I wanted to grab a few things, but he told me to leave everything and get out. I didn't hear them—the intruders—discussing it. I didn't know they were thinking of such a thing."

"Right." His eyes flick up to meet mine for a second, and then he looks down again, tapping his mouse. "Whose idea was it to rape you? You must remember that?"

There is a rushing sound in my head, as though the blood that usually washes around in there has receded. It is low tide in my brain.

"I don't know who any of my attackers were. I can't say to you that this one decided this, and that other one demurred. There were six of them, and they were speaking isiXhosa. That's all I know."

"Would you recognise them if you saw them again?"

"Yes, but there's no chance of ever seeing them again. It's been two years. No arrests have been made. The case has gone cold. I am not sure it was ever warm."

"Can you remember whether they discussed raping you? Did one of them suggest it and the rest fall in line, or how did it work?"

"It seemed to be their plan from the start. Their only concern was whether there was enough time. They argued about that. They lined up and waited their turn. Then they left. They must have started the fire on their way out."

"And they took cash?"

"A small amount, yes. They took what was in my bag and in my father's wallet." I have already told this to the police. More than once.

"What do you think their purpose was in coming into the house that night?"

"To rape me." It's the first thing that comes to mind. "To rob us. And to start the fire."

Jono from Very High Premiums drains his coffee cup and stands up. "Thank you, Miss Lurie. That was helpful. Very helpful indeed."

Only after he has gone, does it strike that those were very strange questions for an insurance investigator to ask.

This has happened before. There are people who want to talk to me about what I went through. They want me to describe it to them, to answer their questions. They will keep asking, circling ever closer to the act itself, until I call a halt. I have to set limits. I have to decide so far and no further. Otherwise they will keep asking.

Back home, my father is on the phone almost before I walk in the door. I am pleased to be in a position to reassure him.

"What did he want? What did he ask you?"

"You can relax. He seemed uninterested in the furniture. He asked me a few questions about how and where you had collected it over the years, and that was it."

I hear my father releasing a puff of breath. "Good. That's good."

"He seemed happy with my answers."

"Good work, my girl."

His praise makes me glow.

"Did he ask you anything else? Anything that wasn't about the furniture?"

I hesitate. If my father knows that the insurance investigator was taking a prurient interest in what happened to me, his approval will evaporate.

"No," I say. "That was all. It was a short meeting."

* * *

The New York Times has turned me down.

So now my op-ed for the *NYT* is just an op-ed. Or rather, it is something I once wrote that will never see the outside of my computer.

"Send it to *HuffPost*," suggests Moira. "They will publish literally anything."

"That's the problem. John Coetzee will be able to ignore a website that publishes literally anything. He wouldn't have been able to ignore *The New York Times*."

"Okay, but you could publish it in more than one place. Let's say, *HuffPost*, *Salon* and *Jezebel*. The three of them together would be the equivalent of one op-ed in the *NYT*, wouldn't they?"

I'm not sure they would. "Three left-wing websites with a reputation for wild-eyed feminism? Won't that work like homeopathy? The more of them I published my story in, the weaker my argument would become."

"I see what you mean. John Coetzee exists on a plane of importance that can afford to ignore websites. They are moths battering themselves against the invincibility of his flame. It's the same with Jonathan Franzen."

I told you Moira was a star-fucker. The big-man trope of modern publishing has hooked her and reeled her in. Her cheeks flush and her eyes glow as she imagines battering herself to flinders against the flame of John Coetzee's magnificence.

"You know, you could go even more low-brow than *Jezebel* and *Bitch Media*," she says.

"What do you mean?"

"I'm talking about the kind of publishing that has no gate-keepers. The kind that will never turn you down, edit you, question your decisions, or invite you to reflect before pressing send."

"You mean . . . vanity publishing?"

Moira laughs. "You are such a product of the academic establishment, Lucy. It's not called that any more. No, I'm talking about putting your story out there as a blog and launching a social media campaign to publicise it."

"So, John Coetzee, who would pay no attention to *HuffPost*, is supposed to be alarmed by my bloggings and tweetings?"

"He would be if they gained traction. No one is immune to a Twitter storm. Not presidents, not royalty, not celebrities, not academics. It's the rolling stone that gathers all moss. Twitter storms have ruined lives. How do you think #MeToo got its momentum?"

"I'm not interested in starting a lynch mob. I don't want to ruin anyone's life, not even John Coetzee's."

"Yes, but listen." Moira's voice is honey. She is Mephistopheles to my Faust. "You won't be ruining anyone's life. That's an extreme example. You are trying to raise aware-ness of the masculinist tendency to co-opt women's narratives. He won the Man Booker Prize off the back of your pain, Lucy."

He did indeed. He won the Man Booker. Because of *my* pain. It was my story to tell, and he co-opted it. I need to lean in and reclaim my narrative.

"How?" I say. "How do I do it?"

Mephistopheles smiles and touches my shoulder. I smell brimstone.

"Should I publish my op-ed as a blog, and then tweet the link?"

This suggestion finds no favour. Mephistopheles' pointed teeth disappear. "That is not an avalanche. That is a stone dropped into a pond. It will disappear without trace. You can do better."

"Tell me, daemon. I place myself in your hands."

"Break the op-ed into several smaller pieces. Make them more emotive. Think Caitlin Moran, not Gayatri Spivak. As you publish each one, share the link across all your social media platforms, with emphasis on Twitter."

"I have a Twitter account, but it's a dusty and defunct thing with maybe thirty followers. You can't start an avalanche on flat ground."

"That doesn't matter. You are going to tag specific people and organisations in your tweets. So your first tweet might read, 'I was gang-raped while my father was forced to watch. RT to spread awareness @WomenMedia.' They are a powerful organisation. If they do retweet it, it will reach twenty-five thousand people."

My stomach roils at the prospect of turning my experience into a True Confessions headline.

Moira upbraids me for my squeamishness. "How do you expect to put pressure on Coetzee if you're not willing to get your story out there? It won't all be True Confessions headlines. You will change your register depending on your audience. So, for @FeministWarrior99, for example, you might tweet, 'Patriarchy punished me twice for my rape. Please RT.' And so forth."

Bleakness rolls over me, blanketing my senses, and numbing my limbs. I don't know if I can do this. The thought enervates me. But the alternative is equally unattractive. To continue huddling in my little house, scooping syrupy peaches from the tin, washing erratically, eking out a living from my proofreading. Unable to wrench my life onto a different track because the one it is on is a groove so deep and dark that I can't see a way out.

I need, as they say, to move on.

* * *

I start that same night by turning the first part of my assault into a six-hundred-word blog post that takes the story up to the point where my assailants seized me and made it clear that rape was on their mind. I write it from the premise that a housebreaking is different for a woman than it is for a man. The threat of sexual assault is always present.

I tweet the link, I Facebook it, I share it on Instagram and Snapchat. I preface it with a thoughtful paragraph about how the only way to make sense of what happened to me is to raise awareness of how rape survivors (yes, for this cause, I can bring myself to use the term) need to reclaim their own stories. It is shared across all social media platforms, perhaps fifteen times.

The next day, I write the next instalment—taking the story as far as the moment my eyes locked with my father's over the heaving shoulder of my assailant. This time, as well as sharing the link generally, I target it at specific media organisations and people of influence in the women's rights arena—influencers, I believe they are called. Radio hosts, TV personalities, Twitter stars. It is shared about twenty times by ordinary mortals, and once by a radio-show host with a Twitter following of fifty thousand people.

On the third day, I write about how my attackers finally left, and how my father tried to get me into a bath. Then we realised that the house was on fire and barely escaped with our lives. This time I target the story at the True Confessions crowd—*YOU* magazine, *Huisgenoot*, *Drum*, and websites like AllAboutWomen.com. I call my piece "They raped me and burned my house down." Today the shares and retweets reach over fifty. I get a direct message from a magazine asking if they can run my story in their next issue. There is a certain amount of hand-wringing online about how my father did the wrong thing by trying to get me into a bath, but also about how understandable it was that he wanted to clean and comfort me.

On the fourth day, I write about the secondary victimisation I experienced at the hands of the authorities—the tests and examinations, the questions. There is nothing new in this. It is in the very nature of rape that the evidence collection process will be intrusive and unpleasant. I make it new by writing with great physical immediacy.

I know it's good even as I write it. You get that feeling sometimes. The words pour out of you in a gush of goodness. It feels adroit.

This time, I target the post at mildly feminist bloggers and websites. A blogger with a following of seventy-five thousand people tweets my link with an endorsement saying that it's "an important read." This causes my individual page views to sky-rocket.

I leave it for a few days and watch as the page views for my earlier posts start to climb and climb. The feminist blogger asks if she can feature me on her page. She sends me some questions by email, and I send the answers back the same day. She expresses surprise at my diligence. She doesn't know I'm on a crusade, and that she is one of the horses I am riding into battle.

The next part is harder to write. I trip over those caveats that troubled me earlier—my awareness that fiction is fiction, and that everything is fair game to the writer. I stick to identity politics. As a man, Coetzee had no right to appropriate my story for his own ends. Fortunately, the political purpose that my story served in his novel is genuinely dubious. I have valid grounds for complaint.

It is bad enough that my rape was appropriated by a male writer, but he used it to construct an unsound messiah-redemption narrative for South Africa too.

I break the last part of my story into two parts—a description of how Coetzee misappropriated my story, and then how it garnered him fame, fortune and literary prizes. He waxed fat and successful. I shrank until my life became a tin of tuna and a blanket over my knees. It would wring the hardest of hearts. Clearly, his success was directly responsible for my failure. Cause and effect.

I decide to go international with this part of my story. The South African media is not big enough to contain the breadth and depth of my grievance. I tweet the literary magazines and the book-review sections of newspapers like *The Guardian*, the *Independent*, *The Irish Times*, and the *Los Angeles Times*. I tweet left-wing and feminist websites like *Salon*, *Bitch Media*, *Jezebel*, and the *Daily Beast*.

It's at this point that I hit a wall. No retweets, no comments, no response whatsoever. The local media lapped up my story. The international media doesn't care.

I manage to locate John Coetzee's literary agent on Twitter. She is a charming, fey creature in the Manic Pixie Dream Girl mould. She tweets full-length mirror selfies of her eccentric charity-shop outfits each morning. She recently acquired a photogenic kitten, named it George Michael, and created a troubled-rock-star persona for it.

I tweet her my blogs in chronological order with enquiring comments like, "Whose story is it to tell?" and "Monetising women's pain?"

This gets under her skin because she retweets them with her own comments, like "Troubling . . ." and "Thought-provoking . . ."

It catches fire. The agent's tweets—with my blogs attached—are retweeted thousands of times. In the space of twelve hours, five news websites run op-ed pieces questioning the propriety of what Coetzee did. Many attempts are made to reach him for comment, but he remains silent. His agent, who sowed the wind with her tweets, now reaps the whirlwind of being fired from representing him.

The next morning, an enterprising journalist tracks him down at his favourite coffee shop in Adelaide. This provokes him into an unwise outburst. "I made that bitch famous," he says, Kanye-style. But what is acceptable in rap culture sounds tone-deaf coming from the mouth of white South African privilege.

Public sentiment turns against Coetzee. He becomes the poster boy for misogyny. His brand is damaged, and no one wants to be associated with it. At first, it is his more minor awards that get taken away from him—middleweight literary prizes that have little resonance in the court of public opinion. Then copycat fever catches hold, and no one wants to be the last to take their award away.

When the Man Booker committee caves and announces that they are rescinding their prize, *The New York Times* runs a story on it. I get a request from the managing editor to write an op-ed about the whole thing. An op-ed for *The New York Times*.

Coetzee was nominally in hiding before. Now he goes into hiding for real. It used to be an open secret that he lived in Adelaide. His agent always knew how to get hold of him. He would pop up at selected literary festivals and other glittering events celebrating the elite of the Anglo-American literary world. He could always be persuaded to give a talk if the event were sufficiently five-star.

Now his agent doesn't know where he is because he doesn't have an agent any more. There are sightings of him in the Cape Town area. Unconfirmed reports say he is living rough in the Bo-Kaap.

As John Coetzee's star wanes, so mine waxes. I recover from my agoraphobia and start dressing normally. I get my job back at the university, and within a few years I have tenure. On the same day that I receive my letter of tenure, I finally succumb to Eugene's repeated entreaties to marry him. We have two children—a girl and a boy.

When I turn thirty-eight, I achieve the necessary mental balance to write my own novel about my experience. It is the ultimate act of taking back one's power, of reclaiming one's narrative. The Man Booker committee votes unanimously to give me the prize that year, and when they do, they explain that it is not just any award they are giving me; it is Coetzee's award.

* * *

Would it make me happy to see Coetzee living homeless in the Bo-Kaap? Would I want his award to be taken away from him and given to me?

The answer is yes to both questions.

But that isn't a part of myself I want to encourage. If, as the inspirational memes would have it, we all have two dogs living inside us—the noble wolf and the snapping cur—we can choose which one to feed. I choose to feed the wolf and starve the cur.

I won't embark on Moira's social media campaign. Not because I think it has no prospects of success, but because I think it has too many.

It is tempting to bring one's enemies low like this. Instead of internalising your anger and letting it consume you, you leak it onto social media—a corrosive force that consumes all in its wake.

I am not going to do that. Not because I am a good person, but because the disgust-hangover would be too awful, and I am already sufficiently disgusted with myself every day.

CHAPTER 13

I have an appointment with Lydia Bascombe. I can trust her to make sense of the midden that is my mind.

L. BASCOMBE: There can be no reconciliation without reparations. History has shown that. Here in South Africa, we have seen what happens when you sweep history under the carpet of rainbow-ism. Those issues you thought you had pushed out of sight will fester until you can't ignore them any longer.

ME: But what am I sweeping under the carpet? What?

L. BASCOMBE: The harm that John Coetzee did to you. You can't forgive him until you have exacted payment for your suffering. It is not possible.

ME: He doesn't even know that he harmed me. He is oblivious.

L. BASCOMBE: That doesn't matter. Take the case of the Rwandan genocide. In the years following the genocide, the Hutus as a people flourished and grew prosperous. They got over the genocide. They put it behind them. The Tutsis, on the other hand, suffer from depression, unemployment, high suicide rates, and a general feeling of hopelessness. As a people, they are not doing well. It says so in *The Guardian*, so it must be true.

ME: I don't know what any of this means.

L. BASCOMBE: The Hutus were responsible for the genocide. Well, the Hutu-majority government was. And while there are museums and other official attempts to recognise the genocide, the Hutus never had to pay a significant price for what they did.

ME: A bit like white South Africans, then?

L. BASCOMBE: If you like. When a historical injustice passes without serious consequences for the perpetrators, the victims are unable to heal. They remain stuck in a situation where the weight of their trauma prevents them from moving on. Perpetrators of the worst atrocities in history have the ability to move on very quickly from what they did. They might feel some superficial remorse, but it doesn't stop them from succeeding.

ME: Like the Germans after World War II? You have German ancestry, don't you?

L. BASCOMBE: Victims are retraumatised by having to witness their former oppressors flourishing like the green bay tree. This acts as a barrier to their ability to succeed. That is what is happening with you and John Coetzee. That's why you are the way you are.

ME: There is only one flaw in that theory. John Coetzee is not my oppressor. He isn't the person who raped me. He just wrote a book about it.

L. BASCOMBE: He was a secondary perpetrator. His book and its success had the effect of inflicting secondary trauma on you. You can't deny that.

ME: No.

L. BASCOMBE: You should have launched that social media campaign. You could still do so. It would be healing for you to see him brought low. Only then would you be able to pull yourself out of your tuna-and-tinned-peaches existence.

ME: I didn't know that therapists advocated revenge as a tool of healing.

L. BASCOMBE: Perhaps they don't, but you have never been

able to distinguish between what I really say and what I say in your imagination, have you?

* * *

I leave her office in a state of bewilderment.

Fantasy and reality are conflating in my mind. I can't remember what Lydia Bascombe said. I know we talked about the idea of a social media campaign, but there was another conversation going on inside my head, and now I can't distinguish it from the real one. Have I confided in her about the precise extent of my delusions? Would she have me committed if I did?

I get home and burrow under my crocheted blanket. It shows a tendency to unravel in places, but not in as many places as my mind is unravelling.

A knock at the door lifts me groaning from my armchair. Phones and doorbells. Doorbells and phones. I can't decide which I hate more.

I open the door to find a small child standing outside. It is a boy in quaint clothing—knickerbockers and a button-down shirt. They are not clothes from another era, but the kind of branded throwback items that hipster parents pay a fortune for. When Eugene has children, he will dress them like this.

"Can I help you?" He must have thrown a ball over the wall into the hardscrabble patch of weeds on the side of my rented house.

"I need to talk to you. May I come in?"

So, not a ball then. This is a confident lad, unafraid of putting himself forward.

I stand back and make a sweeping motion with my hand. "Please do."

I show him into the sitting room and inform him that I have only water to drink. Perhaps he would like a glass? He stares at the splashes of tea on my table and the abandoned, unwashed mugs, and asks for coffee. I explain that I only have instant, and he says that will be fine this once.

I make him a mug of coffee, and he settles into a chair opposite me.

"I thought you lived on a farm in Worcester," I say.

"No, that's not me. You're thinking of someone else."

"What do you want to tell me?"

"I need to explain that my place is here in the urban world. Here is where the transformation needs to begin, in the economic engine of the country. The countryside hasn't been a significant player in this country's narrative for two hundred years."

"What is your role? Are you the sinless Christ-child?"

"That is too passive a descriptor. I am not the lamb, but the warrior. I am a reformer."

"I don't understand why I had a role in this. Why was my blood needed to create you? Why could the reforming warrior not have been a black child? Why did you have to be a mixed-race boy?"

"Because John Coetzee couldn't resist inserting whiteness into a prominent role in this country's future. He couldn't accept that white people have become irrelevant—that their story has been told. He had to make them central to the narrative, even abased and humiliated by rape."

"Is the humiliation mine or my father's?"

"It is your father's humiliation because you don't experience it as such. You accept what happens to you, and it makes you stronger. You take your place in South Africa's future as the consort of Petrus. It is your father who is left bewildered and out of time, aware that the world has moved on without him."

"But I don't want to accept what happened to me. I am not the peaceful, consenting fiction-Lucy. I am a rage-filled harpy."

He stands and takes his mug to the sink. "You need to work on that."

* * *

The child leaves on the heels of a text from Eugene.

Eugene: How goes it with the white whale?

An interesting opening gambit. It focuses on me and my priorities, while also demonstrating a shared knowledge between us—a kind of verbal shorthand.

Lucy: No progress so far. NYT op-ed rejected. Thought about launching social media campaign to smoke him out but decided against it.

Eugene: Those can be brutal for all concerned. Had a meeting in your neighbourhood this morning and noticed the cops outside your house. All okay?

This is the last thing I expect him to say. The very last. I was out at Lydia Bascombe's office this morning for my appointment, but that doesn't mean the police were here. They must have been at the house next door. Eugene must be mistaken.

Lucy: Must have been one of the neighbours. No cops here this morning.

Eugene: But there were. I saw them. They knocked on your door for ages.

Adrenalin fizzes through my veins, making my fingers shake so that I can hardly type.

Lucy: This must be a mistake.

Eugene: Did you have a break-in recently? Or maybe your car was tampered with?

Lucy: No. Nothing like that.

Eugene: I've upset you. Sorry! Perhaps there's been a development in your case?

That would be the logical explanation, but my brain and body don't think so. My reptilian brain has woken up and taken over. I feel as though the police have found me out. But what could they have found out? I haven't done anything.

Lucy: After two years? Unlikely. My case is gathering dust at the bottom of a filing cabinet.

Eugene: It must have been for something else. But don't worry about it. If they really want to speak to you they'll come back, or phone. How have you been since I saw you?

We last saw each other at the comedy club—the under-whelming date that L. Bascombe tried to convince me wasn't my fault. But it was. When a social butterfly and a social tortoise don't get along, it is always the tortoise's fault. I doubt the butterfly would have contacted me again if he hadn't been curious about the police. Maybe I have something to thank them for.

Lucy: Okay.

I look at this response before I send it. Even the tortoise in me knows it is inadequate. Some elaboration is required. But what? I already told him about my op-ed for *The New York Times* and the social media campaign that never happened. What else is there?

Did I ever know how to do this? Was I good at social banter before the rape knocked it out of me?

Lucy: Okay, thanks. Working mostly. How have you been?

This is better than "okay," but not by much.

Eugene: Busy. Need some down time. Been thinking of walking the Olifantsbos coastal path. Would you like to come?

Lucy: I would, thanks. Are you getting a group together?

I send this before I have time to think about it. It is an unsubtle way of asking whether this is a date. I should have waited.

Eugene: I can if you like. We could invite your friend Moira, and maybe my cousin Raz.

So it was going to be a date. And I just turned it into a non-date with my question. I think about trying to retract (*It doesn't HAVE to be a group. It can just be the two of us if you like*), and my toes curl. Better to leave it. If it goes well, we can have a one-on-one date some other time. And it's not as though our one-on-one dates have gone well up to now. Perhaps the presence of other people will change our chemistry for the better.

Lucy: Sounds great. I'll confirm with Moira and you can ask your cousin. Olifantsbos is the one with the shipwrecks, right? I've always wanted to walk there.

Now I'm enthusiastic about this weekend. Moira and Raz will save us from awkwardness. We will find common ground and fruitful topics for discussion. And I will get to look at shipwrecks. It will be good.

* * *

But first, another home invasion.

The doorbell rings. I worry that it may be the trendy imp again—my fictional mixed-race child come to save South Africa from its troubled past. I don't want to talk to him.

It's the police.

I panic and try to close the door in their faces, but one of them steps forward and plants his foot in the gap so the door bounces off his shoe.

"I'm sorry. I don't know why I did that. I have nothing to hide."

It is a man and a woman. They are wearing the quasi-militaristic, belted uniform of the local police force. Khaki trousers tucked into combat boots. Blue shirts tucked into the khaki trousers and wrapped around with gun holsters. I last had contact with the police two years ago when they took my statement and collected my rape kit and clothing at the hospital. The associations aren't good, but they aren't terrible either. They did their jobs then, and they did them with reasonable competence.

"Are you . . . uh . . ." the man glances down and consults a notepad. "Lucy Lurie? Are you the daughter of David Lurie?"

"Yes, I am. Please come in." I am anxious to show them that I didn't mean it when I tried to shut them out. I wave them into my sitting room and offer them a choice of beverages. They accept tea with powdered milk and sugar.

When we are all sitting around with teacups balancing on our knees, they get down to business.

"Your father's insurance company is processing a claim for damage sustained during a fire at his property near Worcester. Are you aware of this?"

"Yes. Oh, yes." This is just about the insurance claim. What a relief. "It has taken them an unconscionable time to process the claim. Unconscionable." I don't think I have ever said the word "unconscionable" out loud before, and now I have said it twice in a few seconds.

"The original police report was incomplete. That's why we are here—to fill in the blanks."

"Okay." I lick dry lips. "Yes, that's fine. I should text my father to join us. He can answer more questions than I can. He remembers more of the details."

The woman removes the mobile phone from my grasp. She places it on the coffee table, where I would have to get up to reach it.

"That's not necessary. We will interview him in due course. First, we are speaking to you, and then we will speak to him."

"Right. Absolutely. That's fine. I'll let him know you're coming so he can clear his schedule." My father doesn't like being caught by surprise. I want him to have time to prepare for this interview. The police officers say nothing. I take this as tacit consent. As soon as they leave, I will let my father know that they might be on their way.

"The night you were attacked on the farm, did you recognise any of the men who came into the house?"

Well, there was Petrus.

I nearly say it, but manage to stop the words in my throat before they emerge.

"Who is Petrus?"

I did say it. Out loud. The veil between reality and fiction is in tatters.

"Petrus is no one. He is a character in a book. Even in the book he didn't do it. I don't know why I said that."

The police officers are on high alert now. They lean forward in their chairs—teacups abandoned on the coffee table—notebooks at the ready and pens poised.

"You say that one of the men was called Petrus," says the woman. "Was he a farm worker you recognised? A piece-worker, perhaps, or a seasonal labourer?"

"No, no. I made a mistake. Petrus isn't real."

"You don't have to protect anyone," says the man. "After what he did, he doesn't deserve your protection."

"Can I fetch something?" I don't know why I feel the need to ask permission to stand up in my own home, but I do.

They nod. I walk to the bookshelf and pull out John Coetzee's book. Then I sit down and show it to them.

"This man wrote a book about what happened to me. He called one of the men Petrus, so that is a name I always associated with them. But it's not real."

The policeman makes a note of Coetzee's name. "Did this writer have special knowledge of the attack? Where does he live? Perhaps he can tell us where Petrus is now."

As tempting as it is to sic the police onto John Coetzee, I have to concede that there isn't much point. If he lives in Adelaide, they won't be able to make his life difficult.

"I don't know where he lives," I say. This is true. I have my suspicions, but I don't know for certain. "Forget about the book. It isn't important. I shouldn't have mentioned it. I didn't know any of the men who attacked me."

"Did your father recognise them?"

"I don't think so. He didn't say that he did."

They make a note on their clipboards.

"How often did you visit your father on the farm? You weren't living there at the time?"

"No, I was just visiting. I lived in a shared house in Cape Town at the time. I was a graduate student at Constantia University. I'm not sure how often I visited. A few times a year, maybe."

"Why were you visiting on that occasion? It wasn't Christmas or Easter. Or someone's birthday."

I'm not sure how she knows that, but she is correct. There was no special occasion. "My father invited me for the weekend. He said it had been too long since he'd seen me. I hadn't been home in a while."

"And what did you do before the attackers broke in?"

This strikes me as a strange question. Does he want to know what canapés were served before dinner (none) and how much sherry I was permitted (half a glass)?

"We had dinner together. I wanted to go out to a restaurant in town, but my father said he would cook, and he did. We had just finished our coffee when they broke in."

More notes are made.

The policewoman looks up. "What did your father do while you were being raped?"

He watched.

"There wasn't much he could do. The men took him to show them where the safe was. Then we were all in the same room. He was forced to witness what happened. They had knives."

"And why do you think they broke into your father's farmhouse? What was their purpose?"

To rape me.

"I suppose they were looking for something to steal."

"But they didn't steal anything, did they? They raped you and set fire to the house, and then they left."

"I believe that's true. Yes, I was told at the time that nothing was taken apart from a little cash."

"So do you think they accomplished what they set out to do?"

"If they got away with nothing, then I guess not. Perhaps they were interrupted."

"By what?"

I shake my head. In my memory, my father chased them away, but I have never been sure about this.

The policeman stands up. "That's all we need for now, Ms. Lurie. You have been very helpful. Constable Mwire will stay with you while I go and speak to your father."

He lets himself out of the house. Once again, I feel as though events have taken a strange turn. Then I remember that I wanted to alert my father, so I reach for my phone.

Constable Mwire nudges it out of the way.

"I'd like to use my phone, please."

"Please wait for a few minutes. Let my colleague get there first."

I sit in the armchair with my hands folded in my lap, feeling as if I have fallen into a Kafka novel. I have no idea what my rights are. My knowledge of the law is culled from television shows and social media. It doesn't seem right that a police officer can occupy my home in this way and refuse me access to my phone. Am I a suspect? What am I suspected of?

"You are under suspicion of having not taken adequate measures to prevent your rape. You didn't say 'no' clearly enough or firmly enough for the men to understand you. You didn't scream. You didn't fight. We are investigating you for your acquiescence in this felonious act."

She doesn't say this.

I ask her nothing and she says nothing. We sit in silence. I can hear her breathing. The shadows move along the floor as time passes. Her phone buzzes, and she picks it up to read a text. Then she stands.

"My colleague is with your father now. I will join him. Thank you for your co-operation."

Once she has gone, I ring my father. He doesn't answer.

CHAPTER 14

T he Olifantsbos hike is one of those life events that almost convinces me that I could be different from the way I am.

We have agreed to meet at eight in the morning, so that we don't walk in the midday sun. This means I have to set my alarm for half-past-six. I have almost forgotten how the alarm on my phone works, so I test it several times. Even then, I don't quite trust it. I don't sleep well the night before. I keep waking up and looking at the time, convinced I have overslept.

At half-past-six, I am relieved to leave my bed. I take a shower because it seems like the right thing to do. My three companions will have showered, and so I will too. While I am in the shower, I wash my hair. I have to wash it three times before it feels clean.

I towel myself dry, aware that I have emerged from the water a different creature.

This person who is awake and showered before seven is an unfamiliar version of me. I feel washed clean of sin and born again. The puritanical virtues reside in my sinless self—early rising, hygiene, brisk exercise in the morning air, sexless camaraderie with others.

This is how you get over a rape. You clean yourself from the inside out. You are a sponge held under a running tap. Each time you are squeezed out and filled with fresh water, you become cleaner and cleaner until no speck of contamination remains.

I need to put something pure into my body. Tinned peaches for breakfast may be technically a fruit, but they are not pure. They are processed, preserved, coated in sugar, and therefore not up to the task of washing me clean of sin. I rush out the door and down the street to a shop, where I buy organic apples. If they don't do the trick, nothing will.

I put my contact lenses in for the first time in a year.

I am waiting at the entrance to the reserve at five minutes to eight. No one else is here. I am the first. This is virtue of a magnitude I have been incapable of for two years.

The others arrive at almost ten minutes past eight, full of apologies. I accept their contrition with the patient good humour of one who has been cleansed by organic apples. Eugene and his cousin Raz arrive together, and Moira a moment later. Raz looks like a version of his cousin who has faded in the wash. Where Eugene's hair is glossily black and Byronic, Raz's is flecked with grey, receding, and cropped close to the skull. Eugene holds himself upright like a young David. Raz is a little stooped and his paunch is losing the fight against gravity.

Nevertheless, Moira seems quite taken with him.

She holds onto his fingers after shaking hands. "Well, aren't you the handsome one? Why didn't Lucy tell me that her new boy had a good-looking cousin?"

She sounds like someone from a movie.

We set off along the marked path with Moira and Raz leading the way, and Eugene and me following. My self-satisfaction took a knock when I saw what the others were wearing. I thought I had dressed appropriately for the occasion, but I was wrong. Maybe five years ago, when I last did something like this, it would have been appropriate. I am wearing a pair of jeans, a baggy, long-sleeved T-shirt, and trainers. A hoodie of sorts is knotted around my waist by its sleeves.

The others are wearing professional hiking gear in engineered fabrics that cling to the body and undertake to "wick" sweat away from the skin. They don't wear trainers, but hiking boots with textured, trail-gripping soles. Their sunglasses wrap around their heads, so they can't fall off, and their hats are made of shiny, sun-reflecting neoprene. Armstrong went to the moon with less technology than these people have employed for a morning walk.

This morning I was proud of myself for having reduced my suit of armour to a pair of jeans and a loose T-shirt. I felt like a Victorian maiden flashing her ankles. Now I know that I still look wrong.

I prod my psyche in an attempt to figure out how I feel about this. Do I wear my rape as a badge of honour? Do I choose to single myself out as the girl who was raped? Or are my multiple layers of clothing a genuine expression of the vulnerability I feel? I can't answer this, not even in the privacy of my own head, because I don't know any more.

As we walk, Moira chats animatedly to Raz. She laughs at the things he says, flinging her head back and exposing her throat. She touches his arm constantly, establishing a zone of intimacy between them. He is reserved at first, but she wears him down. Soon he is chatting and laughing too, and giving her little dabs and shoves.

"They're hitting it off," I say to Eugene, swallowing resentment like sour milk.

"Your friend has a gift. Raz tends to be shy, but she's taken him out of himself. He's having fun."

"That's good."

Are we? I wonder. *Having fun?*

Is this what fun feels like? The sun is hot on my cheek, making me wish I'd brought sunscreen, but my body is still cold. I have to resist the urge to walk with my arms folded around my chest for warmth. I make myself swing my arms like the others are doing.

The scenery is pretty. At least, it would be pretty if it were framed and cropped in a photograph, with a dramatic filter applied to play up the contrasts between blue and green. As it is, it seems messy—as though the set designer hasn't got to work yet. There is low-growing, grey-green scrub everywhere, and it is not picturesque. We have passed several places where litter is caught in the scrub.

The rocks are untidy and asymmetrical. There are drifts of shingle that we avoid. We are walking partly on a trail and partly on the beach.

Conversation does not flow between Eugene and me. His beauty makes me tongue-tied. I want to impress him, but fear of failure keeps me silent. It's much easier when he is just a photograph on my screen and the messages fly between us.

Then we come to the first wreck, and everything becomes easier. The sight of the twisted iron skeleton strikes even Moira dumb. It has ribs that reach up out of the sand, like the carcass of a buck. The predator that has been chewing on it is the sea.

We have been alone on the trail until now, but no longer. There is a man inspecting the wreck. He stands ankle-deep in the water. We were warned at the visitors' centre not to clamber over the wreck or even venture too close. There is submerged wreckage everywhere, and it is heavily corroded. By getting too close you are risking injury, tetanus, and other undesirable consequences.

If I am dressed inappropriately, this man is entirely out of place. He wears long khaki trousers with a deep crease ironed into the front. His jacket is navy blue and fitted tightly at the waist. It reaches almost to mid-thigh, with brass buttons down the front. The lapels are wide and decorated with various pins. This makes him sound rather neat and point-device, but he is anything but.

The cuffs of his trousers are sodden and frayed. He must have been wearing boots, but now he is barefoot. One of the buttons on his jacket is missing and another is hanging by a thread. His hair is over-long and hangs into his eyes. It is his eyes that are especially arresting, because they are aflame with the light of madness.

I have been longing to inspect the wreck, but now I want to hurry past and get away from this man.

It is too late. He has seen us. He strides up the beach towards us. I stand still in dismay, but the others keep walking towards the water's edge.

"It was murder, you know," he says in a loud American voice. "Sabotage. The compass was out by 37°. We were in heavy fog and there were U-boats all around. We hugged the coast as closely as we dared."

"Why?" I ask. "Why sail so close to land when you couldn't see two feet in front of your face? Was that not reckless?"

"It was our practice in bad weather, especially in war time, when the German submarines patrolled these waters constantly, looking to pick off Liberty ships like ours."

"You must have known you were terribly close to the rocks."

"I tell you I didn't!" he thunders. "I thought we were near Robben Island. The compass was out by 37°. But what else would you expect from a ship that was built by women?"

"The *Thomas T. Tucker* was built by women?"

"Most of the Liberty ships were. She was laid down by the Houston Shipbuilding Corporation in June of 1942. The men had all gone to war, so women were building the ships. And you see the result. She was on her maiden voyage from New Orleans to Suez when she ran aground here."

"You were the captain. You were disoriented and too close to shore. You ran her onto the rocks."

He turns away from me. "It was a terrible day. Just terrible. Dark as night in the fog. And a sound to freeze your blood. The sound of your ship running onto the rocks. The stern splitting asunder, and a terrible groaning like souls in hell. I can't sleep for hearing it in my head. She started taking on water almost immediately. I called for the lifeboats, but there were rocks everywhere, so they were next to useless. We swam and clambered to safety. Our uniforms were in tatters, our legs and feet running with blood."

Eugene comes to stand next to me. "What are you looking at?"

"Captain Ellis. He was in charge of this vessel when it foundered."

He thinks I am joking. "Never shake thy gory locks at me?"

"Something like that."

"That's cool. Help me choose a filter for this pic. The Crema is nice and moody, but the Slumber gives it more of a sepia look. Which do you prefer?"

I pick the Crema, but he decides to go with the Slumber. When everyone has finished taking photos, we agree to walk on. I don't bother with pictures because I was there. I saw it. I heard the screams and saw the terrible listing of the ship as it came to rest on the rocks.

We find the boiler of the *Thomas T. Tucker* further up the beach. And beyond that, we come across the wreck of the Dutch coaster, the *Nolloth*. There is no one around. It ran aground in 1965, so perhaps everyone is still alive.

Moira and Raz have been restored to full vivacity now that they are away from the dampening chill cast by Captain Ellis. The banter flows like wine between them until they are drunk on it.

"This is the best day of my life," declares Raz.

"Because it's the day you met me?" asks Moira.

"Because the sky is blue, and the oystercatchers are strutting around, and the gulls are wheeling above. It has nothing to do with you."

"You took one look at me and realised what had been missing from your life all these years."

"I took one look at you and realised the importance of shaving every day."

"Are you implying I have a moustache? I don't have a moustache, do I?" Moira appeals to the rest of us, but her eyes are firmly on Raz.

"Well . . . it's not a very big one."

"It must be my Mediterranean blood. I'm half-Greek, you see."

"Which half?"

"The top half, apparently."

They are hilarious, these two. The Hepburn and Tracy of Cape Point. And still silence hangs between Eugene and me. The repartee fails to sparkle. The wit does not flow. Our lack of rapport is highlighted by the ease that exists between our companions.

I don't like to be beaten, especially by Moira, so I initiate a conversation.

"Do you like hiking?" I ask, at the exact same moment he says, "What did the police want with you the other day?"

There is no question as to whose conversation starter is the more compelling. Mine hops out of my mouth and lands on the sand between us, where it sinks away like sea foam. His hangs in the air—a big bully of a topic, demanding an answer.

The possibility of saying that I don't want to talk about it doesn't even occur to me. He has asked, and I must answer. The silence between us must be banished.

"They came to talk about the day my father and I were attacked in the farmhouse. They said the insurance people had raised certain questions."

"How strange, after all this time. Do you think they have new leads?"

"It didn't seem like it. They kept asking me if I knew them— the men who attacked me. If my father knew them. If we'd ever seen them before. But we hadn't. They were strangers."

"In Coetzee's book they weren't strangers, were they?"

I am surprised to find that his mind runs on similar lines to mine. From my story to Coetzee's story, and back again. Perhaps it is only because we have spoken about it. He knows it is a preoccupation of mine.

"That's right. In Coetzee's book, Lucy and her father both knew the men. They were labourers who worked on the farm, plus a wildcard character who was known to be volatile. It was an intimate crime—between people who had known each other a long time. In my case, it was a crime between strangers."

"Do you think they believed you?"

Again, the workings of his mind astonish me. He has put his finger on precisely what has been troubling me.

"No. I don't know why, but they didn't believe me. They wanted to question my father and me separately from each other. They wouldn't allow me to warn him that they were coming. It was as though they didn't want us to collaborate— to have time to get our stories straight."

"That is certainly strange. You were the victims of this crime. Do you have any theories?"

I want to end this conversation on the grounds that it is making me unhappy, but to do so would take more resolution than I am capable of.

"I think they don't believe me. They suspect that my father and I invented the rape story between us and set fire to the house ourselves to get the insurance money."

Eugene looks taken aback. "But you were examined, weren't you? They have evidence proving what happened to you."

He sounds so certain, so quod erat demonstrandum. He has no idea of the extent to which a rape victim feels disbelieved. But he is right. They do have physical evidence. Unless they have lost it.

"Yes, there is evidence. I don't know why they're behaving like this now."

Actually, I do have an inkling, but I won't share it with Eugene. I barely have the resolution to take it out and examine it in the privacy of my own head.

I think (I fear) that my father's inflation of the value of the household contents has triggered alarm bells for the insurance company. Now they are re-examining the whole claim. They suspect it to be fraudulent and have decided to involve the police. Any moment now, my father will be notified that the insurance company have decided to repudiate the claim.

It is his own fault for being greedy. If he had estimated the household contents at their correct value, he would have been paid out by now, and we would both have been spared this scrutiny.

But what a venal sin. What a small, forgivable, human thing to do. Who among us wouldn't try to see how much we could take the insurance company for? (Not me, but that's because I have an exaggerated respect for the law.)

I choose not to share this with Eugene because I don't want to expose my father's failings to his pure vegan gaze.

We walk back the long way, turning our expedition into a five-kilometre hike rather than a three-kilometre one by adding Sirkelsvlei to the route. And then suddenly we are back at the parking lot. Moira and Raz are edging towards their cars, whispering and giggling. Eugene suggests that we go somewhere for coffee to round off our morning, but they make unconvincing excuses.

Moira texts something into her phone. Raz's phone beeps. He checks the message and they smile at each other. It couldn't be any clearer that an assignation has been made. There is a flurry of cheek-kisses and handshakes, and they peel out of the parking lot, unable to wait another moment before getting their hands on each other.

I wait for Eugene to suggest that we still go for coffee—just the two of us. But he doesn't.

"Oh, well. Another time then," he says.

* * *

I get home in time for lunch. I separate two slices of white bread from a loaf in the freezer. I cut slices of cheese and place them on the bread. Then I heat this in the microwave. I am just settling down with this meal when the doorbell rings.

It is a female child this time.

"I was about to eat my lunch," I protest.

"I'm sorry. I'll come back another time."

She looks so downcast I can't bear to send her away. "No, it's okay. You can come inside."

She approaches diffidently, unsure of her welcome.

"You are very different from your brother," I remark.

"No, no, sorry. He is not my brother. I am he, female. And he is me, male."

"Would you like a glass of water? Or some cheese melted onto bread?"

"No, thank you. Sorry, I didn't want to put you to any trouble."

"You apologise a lot. Why do you say sorry all the time?"

"If I occupy space too emphatically, I will be accused of aggression. I have to be accommodating. It is a question of survival."

"Does it work?"

"No. My existence makes men angry. It's okay in private spaces, but in public I have to be careful."

I chew a morsel of bread and cheese and watch her perched on the edge of the sofa. She is careful not to take up more space than necessary. "Are you also the Christ-child?"

"I am too female for that. The Christ-child can be born of

me, but I can never be him. The most I can do is bear the new generation. I am a conduit, no more."

"Do you think John Coetzee considered the possibility that you might be a girl?"

"No. He refers to the child as 'he'—as a child of this soil. The father in the book asks the daughter whether she loves 'him' yet. Referring to the baby, you understand. The possibility that the child may be female is not considered."

"The redeemer-narrative doesn't work if you are a girl. Females are not redeemers. The only way it can continue to make sense is if—as you say—you are the conduit that gives rise to a line of redeemers."

"Am I a vessel then, and nothing more?"

"You are a vessel," I agree.

"Then I choose not to be born," she says, as she disappears.

I chew the last mouthful of my sandwich in silence. I can't blame her for choosing non-existence. Her male self has better prospects than she does. It makes sense for her to pass the mantle on to him.

I contemplate the afternoon ahead, wondering what happened to the energy I had this morning. What happened to the person who was up and showered by six-thirty, who went for brisk hikes in nature reserves on Saturday mornings? She has dissolved like the mirage she was.

My head slips back and my jaw droops like a tired lily. Soon I am noisily, droolingly asleep.

My phone explodes into life, causing my heart to pound in a way that can't possibly be good for it. I don't recognise the number. It is a local landline. I am too dazed to ignore it.

"Hello?"

"It's me."

It is my father. Something is wrong—I can hear it in his voice.

"I'm at the police station. They brought me here. You need to come."

My brain labours to process this. Why would they have taken him to the police station, and why do I need to come? Perhaps they want to question us together. But today is Saturday. I must be missing something. My mind hasn't woken up yet.

"You're not . . . you're not under arrest, are you?" I feel stupid even asking the question.

"Yes, that is what has happened. I am under arrest. They are keeping me in the police cells, but they let me make a phone call."

"But that is ridiculous. They've gone too far this time. I'll come right away, and I'll bring your lawyer. What is his name again?"

"It was Corno Claasen, but I think he has left the firm. He was going to retire. The firm is called Claasen, Nkabinde and Marriot. You need to phone them and get them to send someone to the Mowbray police station immediately."

Adrenalin floods my body, banishing the last wisps of sleep. I am ready to do this. I am ready to gallop to my father's rescue. No son could be more capable or more determined. My fear of driving is nothing next to my need to be of service to my father.

Twenty minutes later, I am in my car rushing to Mowbray. I phoned the attorneys and they told me someone would meet me there. They said they took very few criminal cases, but I reminded them that my father was a long-standing client and that this was a matter of alleged insurance fraud, and therefore more civil than criminal anyway.

The traffic is light for a Saturday afternoon and I make good time. I come down off the highway to Main Road in Woodstock, where the traffic lights are in my favour until I get to the big intersection at Roodebloem Road. As I bring the car to a stop, I am boxed in. There are cars in front of me, behind me, and on either side of me. The usual collection of hawkers and beggars moves between the cars, selling phone chargers, and asking for money.

My door isn't locked. As a hawker approaches, I slide my hand sideways and lock the door with a clicking sound that reverberates up and down the street. The man motions for me to roll down my window, which I do.

"You locked your door as I approached," he says. "Would you have done that for a white man?"

"Of course. One is always vulnerable at intersections. It had nothing to do with the fact that you are black."

He stares at me in silence. The interrogation in his gaze unmans me. Unwomans me.

"You're right," I say. "It had everything to do with the fact that you are black. I profile black people all the time, especially black men. I associate them with criminality."

"And how do you suppose that makes me feel?"

"Hurt. Abused. Angry. Overwhelmed by frustration and a sense of injustice."

"Precisely."

"I'm sorry. But I do have an excuse."

"And what might that be? You were mugged by a black man? Your house was broken into? Your mother had a bad experience with a black man?"

"I was raped by a group of black men nearly two years ago. They broke into the farmhouse I was visiting with my father and raped me. They set fire to the house and we barely escaped with our lives."

The accusation in his eyes doesn't fade. "You do realise that your individual suffering does not weigh in the balance against the systemic and historical suffering of my people over many generations—three hundred and fifty years, to be precise?"

"I do realise that. But I can't control my visceral reaction when a black man approaches me. Something inside me flinches. My therapist calls it a form of PTSD. It is the thing I resent most about having been raped—the fact that it has turned me into an emotional racist. I know I was already the beneficiary of a racist society that privileges my skin colour above all others. But now I have become a visceral racist as well, and I resent that."

"This isn't about you," he says. "It's about me. You are attempting to hijack this narrative—to recast it with yourself in the starring role."

"I'm sorry," I say again.

"Would you like to buy a stick-on holder for your licence disc?"

"No, I would not."

"Then your sorry-ness extends to words only. You are not sorry enough to pay a few rand that would make very little difference to you, but a great deal to me."

The traffic light changes to green, and I drive on.

At the Mowbray police station, there is no sign of my father's car. I wonder if he really is here. Perhaps I only imagined that he phoned me. I've been doing that a lot lately. Then I remember that he was arrested. They probably went to his flat and made him get into their vehicle. They would have driven him here.

My father's car might not be here, but a gleaming BMW seems to be waiting for me. When I get out of my car, a middle-aged woman climbs out of it. She introduces herself as Abigail Nkabinde from the attorneys' firm.

"I'm here to ensure that your father's rights are protected. We will try to secure the best possible outcome for him."

I thank her, and try to ignore the misgivings plucking at me.

If I am a reluctant, post-traumatic racist, my father is an enthusiastic, dyed-in-the-wool one. He believes that the elevation of any black person to a position of responsibility is "political correctness run mad." To say that he will not be happy to have a black woman representing him would be a dim understatement of the case. But it is a Saturday afternoon, and lawyers are thin on the ground around here.

"This should be easy to sort out," I tell Ms. Nkabinde. "They suspect my father of insurance fraud. I'm not saying they are right, but there is no reason to detain him over the weekend. Perhaps he will have to forfeit his insurance payout, or even pay a fine or something, but there is no reason for this excessive zeal on the part of the police."

The lawyer gives me a look. "Why don't you take me to my client?"

I squirm. Watching my father interact with black people like a feudal lord bossing the serfs around makes me uncomfortable. Not uncomfortable enough to confront him about it. Not since I was a teenager and steeped in self-righteousness. But that's what we're supposed to do, isn't it? As politically aware white South Africans we are supposed to take every opportunity to educate our less conscientised brethren. We are supposed to take a stand at braais and around dinner tables. We're meant to pound our fists and say, "Enough. Your attitudes are unacceptable. You can't treat people like this. We won't allow it."

How many of us do that, I wonder? I imagine myself saying to my father, "Don't speak to Abigail Nkabinde like she's a lesser human being. She is your lawyer. She knows more about the law than you do. She is here to help you and she deserves the same respect you would give to a white man in her position."

It would lead to an irrevocable breakdown in our relationship. I would become estranged from my only living relative. A wave of self-pity washes over me as I think of the sacrifice I'd be making in the name of political duty.

"Why don't I go and speak to my father while you negotiate with the police?" I suggest.

"I need to speak to my client."

She will pay for her implacability by being patronised.

We announce ourselves at a desk called Customer Services. A police officer disappears for a minute. Then he comes back and escorts us to an interview room where my father is sitting. I half expect to find him in an orange jumpsuit, but he is wearing normal clothes. A crocodile peeks out at me next to the breast pocket of his mauve shirt.

I step forward to run interference between him and the lawyer.

"Hello, Dad. How are you? I'm so sorry this has happened. But we'll get it sorted out, I promise. I phoned the lawyers like you asked and it turns out that Corno Claasen has retired, just as you thought. They've sent their very best criminal attorney, Dad. This is Abigail Nkabinde, Dad—she's one of the *partners*."

I have to breathe in deeply before I pass out.

The lawyer steps forward with her hand extended. "Mr. Lurie, it's good to meet you."

I wait for my father to turn towards me, eyebrows raised in incredulity, demanding to know the meaning of this. Instead he grasps her hand and shakes it warmly.

"Hello, ma'am. Hello. Thank you for coming. This is good. This is very good." He turns to me, rubbing his hands together. "You've done well, girl. Now we'll get somewhere at last."

I bask in the unaccustomed praise. "We'll get you out of here soon, Dad. It's ridiculous for them to have arrested you at all. This is a misunderstanding. Just tell Ms. Nkabinde exactly what they're accusing you of, because I would have thought that insurance fraud was more of a civil matter than a criminal one."

A glance passes between my father and the lawyer. She steps forward, interposing her body between us. "Ms. Lurie, I'd like to speak privately with my client. Could you wait outside?"

"That's not necessary. I know all about it. I was part of it, in a way. They'll probably call on me to testify."

She touches my elbow and guides me out of the room. "This won't take long, Ms. Lurie."

The door is shut in my face. I try not to take it personally. Attorney-client privilege is king. This isn't about me. I need to let the process run its course.

I take a seat on a bench in the passageway. I smell dust and lemon polish. It is the smell of boarding schools and public institutions. It is a smell that strips away one's illusions of self-determination. You become a cog in the machine, but not a useful cog. Not a cog that knows its place. You become a cog that rattles around uselessly while the other cogs move together with oiled precision. They are going about their business—policemen and women in uniform striding up and down the corridor, clutching paper. Their weapons jut from their hips, thickening their silhouettes and giving them a wide-based gait.

I retreat into the world of my phone, scrolling through social media posts and news sites. It is a soothing world. Everything that appears in my feed is designed to reinforce my world view. I permit no cognitive dissonance to intrude. It is a world I can lose myself in for hours.

I am in the middle of reading about "10 things that Muslim women wish white feminists would stop doing" when I become aware of a weight descending onto the bench next to me. It is a policewoman. She is fanning herself with a manila folder.

She glances at me and smiles.

"Whoo!" she says. "Hot today."

I nod in agreement, although it isn't particularly hot. The way she is sweating, I suspect she is having a hot flash. She is of menopausal age and seems grateful for the opportunity to sit down.

"Is it always this busy?" I ask. I am anxious to get back to my scrolling, but she expects conversation.

"Not always. Not on a Saturday afternoon. But today we have made a significant arrest, and that generates a lot of paperwork. It is just a matter of time before the media hears about it and then we have to be prepared. There will be a media briefing this evening."

I am so disconnected from quotidian reality that I have no idea what she is talking about. I know more about Buzzfeed listicles than I do about what is happening right now in Cape Town.

What high-profile case is she talking about? I am ashamed of my cluelessness.

"Oh, yes . . ." I say vaguely. "That was the case about the . . ."

"That girl who was gang-raped on a farm a couple of years ago. Do you remember that story? It was all over the news. We still haven't caught the guys who did it, but this is the closest we've ever come. Because who do you think organised the whole thing? Her father. It turns out he hired the men to break in and rape his own daughter. Can you believe that? Some people are wicked, hey? It looks like he did it for the insurance, because he got them to burn down his house afterwards. Anyway, we've got him now. He is being questioned with his lawyer."

I open my mouth and the words come out as steady as a ship on calm seas. "How do you know it was him?"

"We got a tip-off. Probably from one of the guys he hired, who is now looking to make a deal. The station commander is very happy. This is going to be a big feather in his cap."

She heaves her weight forward and stands.

"I'd better get on. You should go and wait over there by customer services. Some space has opened up. They'll attend to you soon."

I thank her and take her advice. I go to customer services to wait with the other citizens of this municipality who are queueing to report stolen cars, traffic accidents, pickpocketings and burglaries.

On some level I think I always knew. There was something in my subconscious warning me about what had really happened—a certain level of awareness that tipped me off. Something that seemed to tell me he was involved from the very beginning.

No. I can't keep it up. Not even inside my own head.

I didn't know. I had no idea. My mind is blank. There is a stillness inside me, like breath drawn in before a scream. The emotion that struggles to the surface is incredulity. I don't think this can be true. This isn't something that fathers do.

As I look around the waiting area with eyes that have been struck blind, one image resolves itself. The lawyer, Abigail Nkabinde, is getting two cans from a vending machine—one for her and one for my father. I get to my feet noisily, and she glances in my direction. Our eyes meet for a second before her gaze flicks away from me as if I am hot.

Pity and disgust. Disgust and pity.

She keeps her head down and bustles back to the interview room to resume her support of my father in the face of police interrogation.

There is nothing for me to do here. I will go home. Would a concerned friend warn me not to drive in this condition? Possibly. But there is no one here, and I don't like myself enough to insist on taking a taxi.

It is dark now. The sun went away while we were in the police station. I must get back for supper. I know I am driving erratically, but I can't seem to correct this. If a policeman pulls me over, perhaps he will take me back to Mowbray police station. I could join my father in jail.

The red light at Roodebloem Road catches me, as it always does.

The population of itinerants has changed over to the night shift. The panhandlers are gone. Now it is just beggars. It is a chilly night, but one man is dressed in rags only, with bare feet and limbs. He clutches at his thin arms and shivers. As cars arrive, he abases himself on the road in front of them. When they drive away, he stands up again.

It is theatre, yes. But there is truth behind the performance. He is poor and desperate, and we are well-heeled and comfortable. As I wait for the light to change, he stands up and starts moving up and down the line of cars, asking for money. He approaches my car and I wait for the fear to kick in.

It doesn't.

He comes right up to my window. My usual reflex is to lock the door, but this time I don't. Instead, I feel in my bag for some money and hand it to him through the window. He thanks me and moves on to the next car.

CHAPTER 15

Your father?"

"Yes."

"I don't believe it. I just don't believe it."

I have made Moira's day. I can feel the glee coming off her in waves. And the fact that I told her about it before it was announced in the media is the icing on the cake

I don't resent her attitude. It is very human. We are far enough removed from the incident for the horror of it to have lost its freshness. I've been living with it for a long time, and Moira has been living with it through me.

"Are you sure it's true, though? That policewoman might have got the wrong end of the stick. In fact, she probably did. Let's face it, it doesn't sound likely."

Moira hopes it is true. The disappointment in her voice is palpable. I am able to reassure her.

"I didn't believe it at first either, but when I saw how the lawyer reacted to me, I realised it was true. And my father hasn't contacted me since that first phone call. Normally he would be ringing me night and day to bring things to him and do things for him, but I haven't heard a word."

"Why, though? Why would he do that? I don't understand."

"I'm not sure. The insurance fraud makes sense. He has always hated the house in Worcester and everything in it. I can see him taking a match to the whole lot. He has the life he wants now. The bachelor flat. The lock-up-and-go lifestyle. No family obligations."

"What gave him away after all this time?"

I can answer this because I was part of it. "He got greedy. The insurance company have been dragging their heels over the payment. I think they often do when there's a fire involved. There is always a question mark hanging over a fire. Did the owner set it himself? But they were on the point of paying out when my father made his mistake. He wildly over-valued the contents of the house. Every painting was an old Master. Every ornament was a fragment of the True Cross. It made them suspicious, so they started looking more closely at the claim."

"That makes sense."

Moira's frustration is obvious. She doesn't want to talk about insurance fraud. I take pity on her.

"He didn't want them to steal anything like money or electronics, right? He took those with him when we escaped."

"Okay."

"But there had to be a motive for breaking in besides just setting fire to the house. So, the motive was rape."

"Right."

Moira looks at me. Her mouth is open as if she wants to say something, but no words come. I don't mind. I would rather have her here, struggling with inarticulacy, than be left alone with my thoughts.

"What are you going to do?"

"I am going to live. I am going to work and eat and sleep. I might see Eugene if he contacts me again." A memory starts to glow in my brain. "I meant to ask—have you seen his cousin again? Raz?"

Moira smiles. "No. But it was good while it lasted."

"How long did it last?"

"An afternoon."

"Okay."

"I see that look on your face. You're casting me in the role of slutty best friend. I'm the loud and amusing one who keeps you entertained with her sexual exploits. But from my point of view, I'm the star of the movie, and you're the weird best friend struggling to come to terms with her difficult past."

"I don't think of you as a sideshow. You're not my light relief."

But of course she is right. Other people are the bit players in the absorbing big-screen drama that is my life. The role of villain was played by the men who raped me, but now their part has been usurped by my father.

If my father is the major villain and my rapists are the hired goons, what does that make John Coetzee? It isn't easy to assign him a role in this revised narrative. I see him as a kind of Faust-Machiavelli-Uriah Heep hybrid. He is the great manipulator who profited from my tragedy.

It annoys me that his narrative has remained stable while mine has changed. Fiction-Lucy is still the Madonna, chosen to bear the redeemer-child who will lead South Africa into the promised land. I was one kind of victim, and now I am another. I was an unfortunate casualty of that South African phenomenon known as the farm invasion. Now I am an even more unfortunate casualty of my father's viciousness. No longer farm violence, but that far more common beast, family violence.

* * *

ME: Am I your most interesting client? I am, aren't I?

L. BASCOMBE: I couldn't possibly comment. Why does it matter to you?

ME: Am I not allowed to be interesting? The media finds me so. Since they got hold of this story, they have been fascinated by what I went through.

L. BASCOMBE: That should suffice. You have my professional interest.

ME: What does your professional interest say about this latest development?

L. BASCOMBE: It is . . . significant. It must have changed your perspective in various ways. But I think the most important thing is that you shouldn't feel guilty.

ME: Guilty? What do I have to feel guilty about?

L. BASCOMBE: I mean you shouldn't waste time thinking about your childhood and wondering what you might have done to anger your father so deeply that he would want to do this to you.

ME: It hadn't crossed my mind.

L. BASCOMBE: Well, good.

ME: Until now. You're saying I did something to deserve this?

L. BASCOMBE: No, no. I'm saying you mustn't think that.

ME: I suppose I might have been an annoying child from time to time.

L. BASCOMBE: Now you are being deliberately contrary. I would never blame the victim in a case like this.

ME: You have planted a seed in my mind. I will consider it.

L. BASCOMBE: You are trying to make me feel unprofessional.

ME: I thought this session was about me.

L. BASCOMBE: It is. Of course it is. Have you had any contact with your father since he was arrested?

ME: No. They are calling him a monster, you know. The media. They are calling him the Monster of Worcester.

L. BASCOMBE: And how does that make you feel?

ME: It makes me wonder what a monster is—what a monster looks like. Does it wear Lacoste golf shirts and offer me a glass of sweet sherry when I am invited for lunch? Does it worry constantly about whether I am doing okay financially and hide its relief when I say that I am? Did it sometimes bring an ice lolly for me from trips into town when I was a child?

L. BASCOMBE: Medical science struggles to understand psychopathology. Has your father had a difficult life? Unresolved traumas?

ME: Not to my knowledge.

L. BASCOMBE: There must have been something. It's not necessarily a major event like death or abuse, but something that might seem quite trivial to the outsider.

ME: His parents were happily married. They died when he was an adult. He lived a comfortable, middle-class life. He never went to boarding school. He married a woman who came from a moneyed background. He has been solvent and enjoyed good health his whole life. He lost his wife eight years ago, but seemed more relieved than grief-stricken. That's not my definition of a hard life.

L. BASCOMBE: You can find no mitigation for what he has done? His crime is unforgivable as far as you are concerned?

ME: I didn't know it was my job to forgive him. I didn't realise the onus was on me to decide that.

L. BASCOMBE: It is going to be very hard for him to move forward without knowing that he has your forgiveness. It will hold him back.

ME: Why do we care whether he moves forward or not? He'll be spending the rest of his life in prison.

L. BASCOMBE: We'll see.

* * *

White South Africans react with relief when an act of apparently random violence turns out to be personal. I know this to be true because I have reacted that way myself.

Random violence makes us nervous because it could happen to any of us. If people all around you are being hit by comets, you start worrying that you could be hit by a comet too. And you know there is nothing you can do to protect yourself because comets strike without warning. There is no hiding or evading to be done. You could be in a high, high building or a deep, deep hole, and still be hit by a comet.

But if you find out that the comets aren't random acts of God at all but are sent by someone with a specific grudge against the victim, you start to feel safer. You tell yourself that no one in your life hates you that much, so you're all right.

When Shrien and Anni Dewani were attacked in Gugulethu on their honeymoon, I felt the same dismay as other middle-class South Africans—the shame that tourists were not safe in our country. And when the accusations started to fly that Shrien Dewani had orchestrated the hit on his wife, I felt relief: South Africa wasn't at fault after all.

Then there was the case of Ina Bonette who was kidnapped, tortured and raped, and whose son was murdered in front of her. It turned out that her estranged husband had orchestrated and participated in the whole thing. The media dubbed him the Monster of Modimolle.

He didn't look like a monster any more than my father does. He looked like a middle-aged white man of the sort one sees in South African small towns.

Evil really is banal.

I know there were people who read about what happened to me, and felt a shiver of dread. A home invasion makes you feel as if you are not safe anywhere. And being raped inside your own home is a nightmare for any woman. What happened to me must have made the threat feel closer. It must have made them feel less safe in their beds at night.

Now when these women read in the media that the whole thing was orchestrated by my father, they will feel relief. They will review the men in their own lives and conclude that they are safe because not one of them poses such a threat.

What they don't realise is that I once felt like that too. I also believed my personal circumstances made me safe from danger—that there was no man in my life who hated me enough to hurt me.

* * *

My father phones the next morning. It is seven o'clock and I am still asleep. A glance at my phone tells me it is a local landline number, one I don't recognise.

"Hello?"

"I need you to do some things for me. This is all a misunderstanding, but that lawyer hasn't managed to get me out yet. There will be a bail hearing on Tuesday and then I'll be out of here, but until then there are things I need. Have you got a pen and paper, girl?"

"I . . . yes."

"You must go to my flat and bring me some money and some cigarettes."

"Cigarettes? I thought you stopped smoking."

"They aren't for me. Cigarettes are currency in here. I need them to get privileges from the guards. You will find them in the drawer next to my bed. I also want some books, so that I don't get bored. Just bring me three from the shelf. It doesn't matter what."

There's a pause while I write this down.

"Are you still there, girl? Are you listening?"

"Yes."

"You must come here at three o'clock this afternoon. I am still at Mowbray in the police cells. They will let you see me at three. Don't forget, hey?"

"I won't."

"You have that key I gave you? The one for my flat."

"Yes, I have it."

"Good. You are the only one, see? You are the only one who has the key."

It is all a misunderstanding and I am the only one who has the key, so I go to my father's flat at midday and let myself in. This is the first time I have been there without him. I've had a key since he moved in, but have never used it before.

This is the scene of our occasional Sunday lunches. Approaching the front door makes me taste sweet sherry at the back of my throat. The flat has been empty since Saturday. The air is settled and heavy. As I push the door open, the displacement makes dust motes dance upwards, before falling back to earth exhausted.

I can smell my father in the air. It is the smell of his exhalations and eructations. It is the smell of his sweat trapped in clothes that are not washed frequently enough, and of urine left to accumulate on toilet seats. His housekeeper hasn't been around in a while. His level of self-care is adequate, but not exemplary.

It is still better than mine.

There is a bread roll on a plate in the kitchen, with several bites taken out of it. I imagine it is what he was eating when he was arrested on Saturday. How annoyed he must have been to have his lunch interrupted.

I have never been in his bedroom. A duvet has been pulled over the bed, but it is not properly made. I pull the duvet down, exposing the intimacy of sloughed skin cells, pubic hair and random stains. I ask myself what I am doing, but no answer comes. I tug the duvet back into place and open the drawer of his bedside pedestal.

There is an open pack of cigarettes in there, just as he said. I put it in my bag and take three books from the bookshelf. They are *The Crimean War: A History*, *The Rommel Papers* and *The Science of War*.

What else did he ask for? Oh yes, money.

I look for money, but this is one secret the flat does not yield. There are coins on a shelf in the bedroom, but they don't add up to anything significant. I can't find real money—an amount that would make his life easier in jail. I search half-heartedly for a safe, but I'm not sure what I would do with one if I found it. I don't know the code. We don't have that kind of relationship. I have a key to my father's flat only on the under-standing that I never use it. If he gave me a code for his safe, he would have to change it afterwards.

What could he have meant by money? I can't ask him, because I don't think you can phone the police station and ask to speak to a prisoner.

Then I realise he meant that I should bring him money—my own money.

There is a part of me that protests against my compliance with these requests. Why should I help him? He is accused of doing something truly dreadful. Do I owe him filial obedience?

Objectively, I know I don't, but it seems petty to refuse to do this small thing for him. So I will take his cigarettes and his books. But will I also give him money? *My* money?

I will decide later.

I throw the bread roll in the bin and wipe crumbs off the kitchen counter. I put the plate in the dishwasher. I consider giving the toilet a quick swirl with detergent, but that is a bridge too far. The impulse in me to regard the housework as my duty is astonishingly strong. I am in the house of a male rel-ative, and as such am powerfully inclined to regard it as my province to clean and care for it.

Not to do so seems sluttish and neglectful. I bustle into the bathroom, filled with housewifely fervour. There is a bottle of detergent in the cupboard and a toilet brush next to the toilet. I squeeze a line of detergent under the rim and around the toi-let bowl. Then I stand with my forehead resting against the wall and the smell of ammonia in my nostrils.

I turn my head as someone walks into the bathroom.

It is the girl child. This is the happy, carefree child I met at the house in Worcester, not the troubled, questioning one who visited me at my home.

"Why do you hesitate?" she asks. "Why do you not clean the traces of your father from the lavatory bowl?"

"He did a bad thing to me. A terrible thing."

"That doesn't absolve you of your duty. I would do it if I were in your position."

"Here, then. Take it." I hold the toilet brush out to her.

She shakes her head, her braids dancing around her face. "No. Because I am not in your position. I can only be in my own position."

"You have been brought up on the farm under the aegis of Petrus, have you not? Did he teach you to consider the domestic sphere as your particular responsibility?"

"Of course. The boys have their duties in the fields, and the girls have their duties in the fields and in the house. While the boys play their games in the evenings, we prepare the food, serve it, and clean up afterwards."

"So it is not Uhuru, this life that John Coetzee conceived of."

"It is a life of great racial harmony and belonging. Everyone has their place. Everyone has their role. Everyone is at home in this country."

"But it is still a place of gender inequality."

"My creator didn't see that as a problem that needed addressing."

"Do you mean God?"

"I mean John Coetzee."

I stand and stare at the toilet bowl, detergent in one hand, toilet brush in the other. When I look around again, the child is gone—and with her, my enthusiasm for cleaning. I bundle up the books and leave, locking the door behind me.

* * *

I stop at an ATM machine to draw money on my way to the police station.

The first person I see when I get to the station is the lawyer, Abigail Nkabinde. She stands as I arrive and walks towards me, blocking my progress with her body.

"Hello, Ms. Nkabinde. Are you here to see my father too?"

"He told me you were coming to see him, so I came here at once. I will accompany you on this visit."

"That's not necessary. He asked me to come. He asked me to bring him some things. I'll give them to him and then leave."

"Nevertheless."

There is a subtext here that I don't understand. I wasn't looking forward to seeing my father alone, but I am looking forward to seeing him in the company of this woman even less. She has the air of a guard dog, but whom is she guarding? Do I need protection from my father, or does he need protection from me?

She seems to feel that elucidation is required because she says, "Unless I am with you to smooth the way, it is unlikely that you will be permitted to give your father anything at all. I am here to help."

I don't believe this. I don't think she left her office close to rush hour on a Monday afternoon simply to smooth the way. I pretend to believe it.

"Give me the cigarettes and the money you brought for your father."

I hand over the box of cigarettes and she waits while I fiddle in my wallet for the money I drew on the way here. I hand that over, too. She takes a handful of cigarettes out of the pack and peels off five hundred rand from the slim sheaf of money. She gives the rest back to me.

"I don't understand."

"This is for the guard. If I don't give him his cut, he won't allow us to give anything to your father. It is against the rules, but he will look the other way if we make it worth his while."

Ms. Nkabinde looks at the meagre amount of money left in my hands.

"Is that all you brought? It's not much, is it?"

"It was all I had in my account. I should get paid for an editing job soon, but until then I can't manage any more."

"There was no money at your father's apartment?"

"Not that I could find. Only coins."

"You drew your own money to give to him?"

"Yes."

She opens her mouth to say something and shuts it again. There is a world of pity in her eyes. For a moment, I see myself as she must see me—the very model of a modern Stockholm syndrome. Then it is gone, and she is all business again.

"I'll see if they are ready for us."

She goes to the customer services counter and has an emphatic conversation with the constable on duty. When she turns back to me, she is smiling.

"Let's go," she says.

She leads me to the same interview room I was excluded from on Saturday. This time I am allowed in. My father is waiting there. He is still wearing his normal clothes. There are shackles on his ankles, but his wrists are unencumbered. There is a guard in the room. Ms. Nkabinde consults briefly with him, and hands over the money and cigarettes. He takes a step back, and leans against the wall, watching us closely.

I approach my father, intending to take a seat at the table opposite him. The lawyer blocks me again. She interposes her body between us in a manner that is clearly protective.

"What's wrong?" I ask.

"Please don't approach my client."

"I was going to sit down."

"You can sit if my client agrees, but you will not get within arm's length of him. Please don't make any sudden movements, Ms. Lurie, or I will be forced to escort you out."

She looks at my father, and he nods. It is okay for me to sit down.

I slide slowly into place at the table, trying to keep my movements as un-sudden as possible.

"I brought the things you asked for." I take out the rest of the cigarettes and the money and slide them across the table. I glance at the guard, but he is staring over our heads.

My father is happy with the cigarettes, but disappointed with the money. "Is that all?"

"It's all I have. I should get paid later this month, and then I can bring more."

"I won't be here later in the month," he says with a look at his lawyer. "I'll be out of here on Tuesday."

Abigail Nkabinde's face urges caution. "One way or another," she says.

"What do you mean?" My father's face falls. The whole superstructure of his cheeks, lips and chin sags downwards. It is the look of a baby processing its disappointment and about to cry.

"You will either be released on bail or you will be taken to join the awaiting-trial population at Table Bay Prison. I already explained this, Mr. Lurie."

"If you do your job properly, I'll be released on bail. You will do your job properly, won't you, Ms. Nkabinde?"

"I will, but it'll be up to the magistrate to decide. There is always that element of unpredictability in any court proceeding."

"But they'll listen to you, won't they? A black woman, I mean. They know you wouldn't argue something unless you really believed it."

"Mr. Lurie, I will represent you to the very best of my ability because that is my duty to you as my client. My personal beliefs don't enter into the matter. They are irrelevant."

"Okay, but for you as a black woman to stand up and defend a white man . . . well, it looks good, doesn't it? It looks like I can't be such a bad guy after all if I've got this black woman representing me."

The lawyer's mask of professional courtesy disintegrates for a second and I glimpse the frustration beneath. She composes herself.

"I promise to do my very best for you, Mr. Lurie. You can count on it."

My father seems satisfied with that.

I turn towards him. "Where are they keeping you?"

Again, Ms. Nkabinde moves to body-block me. "Please keep your distance from my client, Ms. Lurie."

"I'm not going to hurt him."

My father subjects my face to a long and anxious scrutiny. Then he laughs. "You don't have to worry about the girl," he says. "She doesn't want to hurt me. You can let her stay there—she won't do anything to me. I told you she would understand."

The look on Ms. Nkabinde's face indicates that he told her the exact opposite. And now I understand where this fear comes from—this belief that my father has to be shielded from me lest I attack him physically. It comes from him. He asked the lawyer to protect him from me. Now that he feels safe again, he is withdrawing that request and painting her as the anxious one.

He is light-headed with relief. "Didn't I say she would understand? She knows what's what, this girl."

CHAPTER 16

My father is denied bail.

One of the police officers at Mowbray police station testifies that my father tried to bribe him to fetch his passport from the apartment. The state uses this as evidence that my father is a flight risk. The magistrate agrees, and my father is sent to join the awaiting-trial population at Table Bay Prison.

I don't attend the bail hearing, but I read about it on every news site in the country. Interest is not quite at Oscar Pistorius levels, but it is higher than it was for the Monster of Modimolle trial. This case ticks all the boxes. The protagonists are white, middle-class and English-speaking. In media terms, that is the perfect trifecta.

When the protagonists in a crime are black, the matter is believed to be of interest to the black community only. When the protagonists are white and Afrikaans-speaking, it will be covered by the Afrikaans press, with limited spill-over to other media. But when they are white, middle-class and English-speaking, the matter is presumed to be of interest to everyone, and will receive blanket coverage. If there is a celebrity angle, or salacious sexual details, the international media will also take an interest.

The international media is taking an interest.

I receive interview requests from CBS, ABC and the *Independent* of London. I take my phone off the hook, block their domains on email, and screen all calls on my mobile phone.

I puzzle over why my father didn't ask me to fetch his passport for him. Did he think of it only after I had already brought him the cigarettes and money? Was he afraid I would say no? That I would rat on him? Did he trust a chance-met security guard more than his own daughter?

What would I have done if he'd asked me? Probably agreed, going on past form. My track record of turning down morally dubious requests from my father is not good. Inflate the value of home furnishings in order to defraud the insurance company? Sure. Pretend we owned items that we didn't? Of course. Slip him his passport so he can flee the country to avoid prosecution before the court requires him to hand it over? Why not?

But he didn't ask me, so the question doesn't arise. My father has been denied bail, and it is through no act or omission of mine. The drama will play itself out without me.

I settle down to work. I have someone's PhD thesis to copyedit. It pays a pittance, but will keep me in white bread and peaches next month. Or possibly the month after that, depending on when the client pays. My rent for next month is already taken care of. A series of Geography textbooks I edited saw to that.

I manage to concentrate for forty-five minutes before my phone beeps to alert me to an incoming email. It is another interview request. But instead of deleting this one, I stare at it for a long time.

Ms. Lurie,
Jacob here from the Journal of Literature of the African Diaspora. If you have time, we would like to interview you about how your real-life narrative has diverged from that of John Coetzee in his celebrated novel, Disgrace.
It is for our special issue on "Fiction and faction: how real-world

narratives inform fiction streams in the diaspora."
If you would be interested in participating in this project,
please contact me on 093 678 9876.

Two thoughts spring to mind. The first is that I might persuade them to pay me for this. When journals bring out a special edition, they often have a budget for doing so. This is only disbursed when someone asks for it. The money is there. You just have to refuse to work for free.

If I only get paid for the PhD thesis the month after next, I will need rent money for next month. The *Journal of Literature of the African Diaspora* could provide that. Yes, I would probably get a better payment from CBS News, but I have more chance of controlling the story in this forum.

My second thought is that this could be the platform I've been looking for to talk about precisely how my real-life narrative has always diverged from Coetzee's fictional version. This could be what I've been waiting for.

I decide to reply.

> *Lucy: For R8000, I will give you an exclusive interview about what happened that night, along with access to inside information about my father's trial. Regards, Lucy Lurie*

He has either stepped away from his phone or he is thinking about it, because ten minutes pass with no reply.

> *Jacob: Our other interviewees are not being paid for their contributions. They are doing it for the exposure and for the chance of being part of something historic.*

I've heard this nonsense before and know how to deal with it.

Lucy: Exposure is something you die of. If you want my story, the fee is R8000.

Silence again. I'm not worried. If these people turn me down, I will go to CBS after all. But this time, I will ask for five figures, not four, and I will ask for them in US dollars.

Jacob: I need to speak to my editor.

I smile. My rent for next month is as good as paid.

Lucy: You do that. And remember to tell him or her not to kid a kidder. I know you have a budget for this project, so no pleading poverty.

There is a brief pause, and then:

Jacob: Give me twelve hours.

* * *

Unlikely as it seems, I have another date with Eugene.

I have my father to thank for this. If he hadn't been arrested for conspiracy to commit rape, sexual assault, and common assault—thereby making national and international head-lines—I doubt I would ever have heard from Eugene again.

We are meeting for coffee. He suggests the vegan café on Kloof Nek Road. I suggest Starbucks. I feel no urge to apolo-gise for my global capitalist tendencies. I have something he wants, so it is time for him to accommodate me.

I order a double-shot caramel macchiato with extra whipped cream. Eugene orders black coffee after quizzing the barista about whether it is fair trade and ethically sourced.

Each time I am about to see him I wonder if my memory

has exaggerated his beauty. It doesn't seem possible that a real person could be as flawless as the Eugene who lives in my memory, but invariably he is. Today it is warm, and he is wearing a tight, white T-shirt and a pair of knee-length khaki shorts. The T-shirt is obviously an old favourite because it has been washed as thin as paper and as soft as down.

I watch his skin rippling over the muscles in his arms. It takes a while, but I finally recognise what I am feeling. It is lust.

My libido is stirring into life after more than two years of dormancy. I was starting to think it would never happen in the daytime.

I have a window of opportunity here, but I'm not sure how long it will remain open. Will the trial be enough to keep Eugene coming back to me? Or will he get his fill from news reports and social media, and not feel the need to stay connected to me? Perhaps this is the last chance I will get.

"When does the trial start?"

It seems he is thinking along similar lines.

"In four months," I say. "The prosecution has been working on this for a long time. They say they are ready to go, but the defence team has asked for more time. My father has chosen to waive his right to a speedy trial."

"Four months? That's a long time to wait."

I agree. It is a long time. Especially when it is quite likely that Eugene will have moved on. He will probably be in a relationship by then. I don't want to take the chance.

"What are you doing after this?" I ask.

"I need to go back to work. I'm on a team that's busy with a big design project, and our deadline is next week."

This might be true, or it might not. Even if it were true, he would offer to blow off work if he really liked me. Or he would suggest meeting up later, or tomorrow. But I already know that he doesn't really like me, so this revelation is no great, ego-damaging shock.

On balance, I believe I could get him to sleep with me, but the moment would have to be propitious. He would have to have absolutely nothing better to do. That moment is not now.

Instead of trying to steer him towards my place or his, I answer his questions about my father's trial.

"Will you be testifying?" he asks.

"Testifying?" This hadn't occurred to me. "For which side?"

"Either?"

"I don't think so. No one has asked me to."

He seems incredulous. "I don't see how the trial can go ahead without your testimony."

I don't want to think about this. It kills my burgeoning libido, and makes me want to get as far away from him as possible.

* * *

A week passes.

It is enough time for me push the uncomfortable thoughts away. Then my father phones me.

A stranger's voice asks if I am Lucy Lurie. When I concede that I am, she asks if I will accept a reverse-charges call from Mr. David Lurie in Table Bay Prison.

"Yes, okay."

There is a long pause. I feel as though I am in a period film, set before the invention of mobile phones.

"Are you there, girl? Can you hear me?"

"I can hear you."

"You must go to a meeting with the lawyers tomorrow. They will tell you what to do."

"Must I go to the head office of Claasen, Nkabinde and Marriot?"

"No. You must go to see the advocate in Queen Victoria

Street. His name is Imraan Deshen, and he works in Huguenot Chambers."

"What time?"

"Nine o'clock."

"Okay."

It feels as though Eugene has conjured this into being by asking me about it. If he had just kept quiet, the lawyers might have forgotten about me. I battle cross-town traffic the next morning. At least my car is being used more often these days.

I announce myself to a receptionist. A clerk comes to take me upstairs to Advocate Deshen's chambers. Abigail Nkabinde is waiting there for me. She introduces me to two colleagues from her firm, as well as the advocate, his pupil, and the clerk who brought me here.

We sit down around an oval conference table. It seems Advocate Deshen and Gregory Marriot from the law firm have different ideas on strategy. They were arguing when I walked in, and they are still arguing.

"Diminished capacity is a non-starter," says Deshen. "I'll be laughed out of court. Maybe if he had done it himself rather than hiring a proxy, we'd have something to work with. But as it is . . ."

"Imraan, I respect your judgement, I really do, but I don't think you're familiar with the PTSD suffered by white farmers in this country. There is a lot of literature on it. I'll get my secretary to email some of it to you. Just because there is the distance of time and place to separate him from the act, doesn't mean he couldn't have snapped. For him, the act of snapping was calling the proxy."

"He has never been attacked in his life. How could he be suffering from PTSD? PTSD from what? Living a life of unassailable ease?"

"There are studies to show that white farmers suffer from PTSD even if they haven't been attacked themselves. They are affected by the long history of violence against their peers. It's a real, documented syndrome, suffered by thousands of farmers due to . . ."

"If you use the words 'white genocide,' I swear to God I am going to . . ."

Abigail calls them to order. "Gregory . . . Imraan . . . with respect, I think we should confine this consultation to matters that affect Ms. Lurie. We can discuss strategy once she has concluded her business with us." This is accompanied by a significant look.

"You're right," says Advocate Deshen. "Of course."

Marriot opens his briefcase and takes out a case file loosely tied up with green tape. When he opens it, I see my name and my father's name. He tilts the file, so I can't read the words.

"Now, Miss Lurie, we've been over the statement you originally gave to the police on the morning after your attack, and I have to say, well done. It has been of great help to us in building your father's defence strategy. There are just a few matters we want to go over with you."

"You want me to go over that night again?" I say. "I suppose I can if I have to. The first thing I remember is . . ."

"No!" Advocate Deshen almost shouts.

"Stop!" says Marriot.

I recoil.

"You have to understand that we can't unhear anything you may choose to say to us," explains Abigail. "As a member of the bar, Advocate Deshen has an obligation to disclose any relevant evidence he may come across that might assist the court in making its finding. Even if that evidence goes against us."

"You don't want me blurting out anything that might hurt my father's case?"

"Yes." She looks relieved by my understanding. "It would be best if we were to ask you questions and you were to confine yourself to the briefest possible responses. Then we will put it all into an affidavit for you to sign."

"If we do a good enough job, this might not even go to trial," Deshen says. "The state will see that they don't have a winnable case here, and either offer a deal or drop charges altogether."

"Then fire away."

Everyone in the room is smiling now, pleased by my co-operative attitude. Before the rape, I prided myself on being easy to deal with. I was afraid of being labelled "difficult," so I made sure I was the very opposite. Since the rape, I have tried to regain that easiness. It hasn't always worked that well.

There are parts of me that are thornier than they were. And parts that are stickier. Where previously I was smooth, now I am abrasive. But I keep trying.

"Would you agree," says Advocate Deshen. "That you saw no communication pass between your attackers and your father that made you think they were in league with each other?"

"Yes, I would agree with that. I had no idea at the time."

"And do you stand by your earlier statement that you did not recognise these men at all? You had never seen them in your father's company, for instance?"

"No, never. I didn't recognise any of them."

"Excellent. Good. And would you say that after the attack your father behaved in a solicitous manner towards you, leading you to think he was concerned for your welfare?"

"After the attack? Yes, I suppose he did. He brought me a blanket and offered to run me a bath. But then the fire started, and he helped me get out of the house."

A frisson zips around the room at my use of the word "bath." Glances pass from one lawyer to another like a rapid-fire game of pass-the-parcel.

"And finally, Miss Lurie, would you concede that the sexual assault you suffered was in no way necessary for the kind of insurance fraud that the prosecution is alleging?"

"Yes. Only the fire was necessary for that."

Advocate Deshen puts down the pen he has been making notes with. "Thank you so much, Miss Lurie. I think that is all we need at the . . ."

"I have a question," Gregory Marriot interrupts. "Miss Lurie, would you agree that your relationship with your father was not antagonistic before the incident, and has remained that way subsequently?"

"Not antagonistic? Yes, that is correct. It was not and is not antagonistic."

"Fantastic. Then if we're all happy?" He glances around the table, collecting nods. "Great. I think we're done here. Miss Lurie, we'll just pop this into the form of an affidavit for you to sign tomorrow. Do you think you could stop by and sign it in the morning? Would that be convenient?"

It would be extremely inconvenient, but I agree like a woman who is not difficult. Then I accept handshakes and thanks from everyone. The mood in the room is buoyant, as though some obstacle has been cleared. I suppose the obstacle was me. They have leaped effortlessly over any difficulty I may have caused them, and now they are giddy with relief.

Being helpful is supposed to make one feel warm and uplifted. Am I warm and uplifted? Possibly. Am I relieved that it is over? Yes.

* * *

Later that day, I am afforded another opportunity to be helpful.

It arrives at my door in the form of two prosecutors from the NPA—the National Prosecuting Authority. Their names are Advocate Meintjies and Advocate Ndlovu. They are accompanied by a young woman whom they introduce as a student who is doing work experience in their office. I am told that her name is Itumeleng. I am not told her surname. I invite them into my house, but don't offer them anything to drink. They ask me if it is true that I am testifying for the defence.

"How did you hear about that?"

"You were seen going into Huguenot Chambers this morning," says Ndlovu. "It was an obvious conclusion to reach."

"They took a statement from me. They haven't said anything about testifying."

"But you're on their witness list."

"I had no idea."

"The thing is," says Meintjies. "We want you to testify for us."

"Against my father, you mean?"

"That is correct."

"You must see how awkward that would be. I don't think I'd be able to do it."

Advocate Ndlovu frowns. "If we subpoena you, you won't have a choice."

I think about this as I play with the crocheted blanket next to me on the chair. I like to stick my fingers through the holes and enlarge them by pulling and fiddling with the wool. My knowledge of legal matters is rudimentary, gleaned from movies and television. I don't know exactly what a subpoena is, but I have an idea it is something that will compel me to show up in court on a particular day and answer questions in the course of a trial.

"You can do that," I say. "But you can't force me to say what you want me to say."

"Perjury is against the law, Miss Lurie," says Advocate Meintjies. "If you are found to have lied to the court, you could go to jail."

I have five fingers stuck into the blanket now. I am twisting and turning them, flexing my knuckles to make the holes bigger.

"There's a difference between lying to the court and being a hostile witness. You can punish me for doing the former, but you can't stop me from being the latter. You also can't force me to go over my testimony with you in advance. So think about what you really want."

"We can force you to appear in court and tell the truth," says Advocate Ndlovu. "That's all we need."

"You will have no idea what I'm going to say. You can ask me questions, but you won't know what answers I'll give. Isn't that the first rule—never ask a question to which you don't know the answer? I'm the only one who knows what happened to me, and what I saw that night."

The men are angry. Their voices are raised and their postures bullish. The tang of testosterone hangs in the air like ozone after a lightning strike. I am a little afraid of them, but my urge to taunt is stronger than my fear.

"We don't need you to co-operate," says Meintjies. "We just want the judge to hear what happened to you. We need that to be on the record. And all the reporters in the courtroom will hear it too. Your testimony will be on the front page of every newspaper. It will be the lead story of every news bulletin."

I almost laugh. "Do you think that scares me? Public exposure? My rape was turned into a bestselling book. *Disgrace* is the most talked-about novel of the last two years. It won major international prizes. People all over the world have read about my rape. I don't care about adding a few more South Africans to their number."

"I think you'll change your mind when it happens."

"What are you trying to do here? I thought you were persuading me to testify for you. Now you're saying I won't be able to handle the invasion of privacy."

Meintjies pulls himself together. "I'm sorry. I lost my temper. We do want you to testify for the prosecution. We do."

"But you must understand how difficult it will be. He's my father."

Meintjies and Ndlovu look stumped. The student I know

only as Itumeleng starts to speak, then stops. Meintjies turns to look at her. He frowns and shakes his head, as though it is not her place to speak in this forum.

"What is it?" I ask.

"I don't understand you, Ms. Lurie," she says. "You keep saying how difficult and awkward it would be to testify against your father, but did he ever stop to think how difficult it would be for you to be raped? How awkward it would be for you to have him there watching? I don't understand why you feel you owe him any filial duty after that."

"He is still my father."

"Was he your father when he hired six men to rape you?"

"That hasn't been proven yet."

"And it never will be without your testimony."

"That's circular logic," I say. "You're saying I must testify against him because he is guilty, but then you say he can't be proven guilty unless I testify against him. You can't have it both ways."

"But that's the thing, Ms. Lurie. I think you already know he's guilty. Everyone in this room knows he's guilty. Even the defence team knows he's guilty. You were there. You saw how he reacted. Was he surprised and horrified when those men broke into his house? Was he shattered when they assaulted you? Did he plead with them to stop? Did he do anything— anything at all—to try to stop them?"

"He was in fear of his life."

"Really? Is that how he seemed to you? Afraid?"

"He rushed at them and they stopped."

"They stopped because a single, unarmed man rushed at them?"

I nod.

"Then answer me this," she says. "When you heard he'd been arrested for conspiracy to commit sexual assault, were you surprised?"

"Surprised? Of course I was."

"Or did everything seem to click into place at that moment? All your unanswered questions, your lingering doubts? Did everything begin to make sense for the first time since your assault?"

"No. That didn't happen."

"I don't believe you. You have that look in your eye. The one that says you know the man in your life is guilty, but you're choosing to protect him anyway. You're the enabler that every abusive man needs in order to keep on doing what he does."

I don't like this woman. She is rude and meddlesome. She makes me want to do the exact opposite of what she says.

I get to my feet.

"I want you all to leave now. The defence lawyers are drawing up an affidavit for me to sign this afternoon. You can subpoena me if you like, but the answers I give won't help your case."

The advocates start speaking, but Itumeleng rolls over them.

"You're not helping your own case by living in denial," she says. "You need to get over whatever Stockholm syndrome you've got going on in your head. Wake up and smell the patriarchy. You won't heal until you do."

I point to the door. "Leave. Now."

The men are displeased by the disruption Itumeleng has caused. I can imagine the scene in the car on the way back to the office. They will berate her for speaking up and blame her for my lack of co-operation. She may even lose her place on their work-experience programme.

Good.

CHAPTER 17

IN THE HIGH COURT OF SOUTH AFRICA
(WESTERN CAPE DIVISION)

CASE NUMBER: 05/201901

In the matter between:

THE STATE

and

DAVID LURIE

AFFIDAVIT

I, the undersigned

LUCY LURIE
hereby make oath and state as follows:

1. The facts deposed to in this affidavit are within my personal knowledge and are true and correct.
2. I am the daughter of the defendant, David Lurie, currently residing in Sea Point, Cape Town.
3. I have always enjoyed an excellent relationship with my

father and have found him to be responsible and loving in the discharge of his duties towards me.

4. My mother passed away eight years ago, and since then my father has been a conscientious single parent.

5. On the night of 3 April two years ago I was visiting my father at his farmhouse in Worcester. We were having dinner together. At approximately 20.00, six men broke into the house. They were carrying weapons. All six men assaulted me sexually. My father appeared deeply distressed by these events but was unable to assist because the men were holding a knife to his throat.

6. At no time, did I see any signs of recognition between my father and the men. No communication of any kind passed between them.

7. When the men left, they set fire to the house. As soon as my father became aware of the fire, he helped me to escape and called the emergency services.

8. Ever since that night, my father and I have continued to enjoy an excellent relationship.

9. I am not financially dependent on my father in any way.

LUCY LURIE

I CERTIFY THAT THE DEPONENT ACKNOWLEDGED TO ME THAT SHE KNOWS AND UNDERSTANDS THE CONTENT OF THIS DECLARATION, THAT SHE HAS NO OBJECTION TO TAKING THIS PRESCRIBED OATH AND CONSIDERS IT TO BE BINDING ON HER CONSCIENCE.

THUS SIGNED AND SWORN TO BEFORE ME AT CAPE TOWN ON THIS DAY OF ___

COMMISSIONER OF OATHS

I am back at the offices of Claasen, Nkabinde & Marriot.

I am here to sign the affidavit they have drawn up on my behalf, based on the statement I gave them yesterday. I am allowed to read it before signing it.

I read over it in the manner of one scanning the terms and conditions of the user agreement for their new mobile phone. My eyes flit across the page, looking only for the place to sign. I spot the signature line and pick up my pen.

My eyes are drawn back to a word further up the page.

"Distressed," it says.

My father was "deeply distressed" by "these events."

I kept my eyes closed during the rapes because every time I opened them, I saw my father watching. His face was calm, perhaps even a little curious. His eyes met mine without embarrassment. This was his new favourite show and he wasn't about to miss a minute of it.

My eyes get stuck on other words. "Responsible and loving." "A conscientious single parent."

Abigail Nkabinde taps the signature line. "Please sign there, Ms. Lurie."

I grip the pen and bend over the document.

More words. "Excellent relationship." "Holding a knife to his throat."

"We have a consultation starting in five minutes, Ms. Lurie. Please sign the document so we can lodge it with the court before five o'clock."

"Unable to assist me."

"Ms. Lurie, we're all very busy. I have to insist that you sign."

I sign on the allocated line.

When I straighten up, everyone is smiling. The attorney Gregory Marriot looks delighted. I understand for the first time how important my testimony is to their case, and how relieved they are to have it.

They shake my hand one by one and thank me for my contribution.

"This will probably be the end of it, but we'll let you know if the state wants to take it any further," says Abigail Nkabinde as she walks me to the lift.

It is only as the lift doors are about to close that I hear sounds of consternation from the consultation room.

"Mickey Mouse. It says Mickey Mouse."

"Jesus Christ."

"She didn't sign it properly."

"Get her back in here."

* * *

L. BASCOMBE: You signed a sworn affidavit as Mickey Mouse rather than admit that you weren't comfortable signing it.

ME: I didn't plan it. Right up until the moment my pen touched paper, I believed I was going to sign my name.

L. BASCOMBE: And then?

ME: I don't know what happened. I found myself writing Mickey Mouse. It was as though someone had taken over my body.

L. BASCOMBE: Automatism is a myth perpetuated by people who are too weak to take responsibility for their own actions.

ME: Right.

L. BASCOMBE: You made a conscious decision to ruin the defence's case. Own it, Lucy. Accept responsibility for your actions. And then explain to me why you would do such a thing to your own father. He was counting on you to make a statement that helped his case.

ME: I know he was. And I still haven't done anything to hinder his case. The net effect of my actions is zero. All that has happened is that I've made no statement at all.

L. BASCOMBE: In a case like this, that is just as bad as making a statement against him. He needs your testimony.

The absence of it is the equivalent of an accusation against him. In fact, it's worse. At least if you made a statement against him, his lawyers could cross-examine you on it. They could poke holes in your testimony and expose its weaknesses. Now you're leaving them with nothing to attack. I call that unfair.

ME: I'm a bad daughter, I know.

L. BASCOMBE: After everything your father has done for you.

ME: I know.

L. BASCOMBE: Don't sit there bleating, "I know." You need to put this right. Go to the lawyers and tell them you're prepared to sign the affidavit. It's the only way to make amends.

ME: I don't want to.

L. BASCOMBE: What? Why not?

ME: What if he did it? What if he hired those men to rape me? Does he deserve my loyalty?

L. BASCOMBE: There is a maxim in our law that states that a man is innocent until proven guilty. Your father is innocent of these accusations, Lucy. Until such time as a court of law convicts him, he is innocent.

ME: If he is innocent, my testimony can't hurt him.

L. BASCOMBE: But if he did it, your testimony could put him in prison for life. How would you live with yourself if that happened? Imagine being responsible for putting your own father in jail. How will you deal with that?

ME: I wonder how he has managed to live all this time knowing what he did to me. And not only live, but thrive. He seems happier now than he has ever been.

L. BASCOMBE: Would you take that from him? Would you dash the cup of happiness from his lips?

ME: What about my lips and my cup of happiness?

L. BASCOMBE: Tell me, Lucy—were you a difficult child?

ME: What do you mean?

L. BASCOMBE: It's not a trick question. Were you or were you
    not a difficult child? Did your parents find you chal-
    lenging to deal with? Was parenting you a chore for
    them?

ME: My mother loved me. She didn't find me difficult. She
    enjoyed being my parent.

L. BASCOMBE: Your mother is dead. What about your
    father?

ME: He seemed to resent me. My mother and I annoyed
    him. The farm annoyed him. He complained a lot.

L. BASCOMBE: Now we're getting to the crux of it. You were
    a burden on your father, Lucy. Your very existence was
    an annoyance. Can you blame him for arranging to have
    you raped?

ME: Are you really saying this? Are you thinking it?

L. BASCOMBE: I don't know, Lucy. Am I?

* * *

Lucy: You were right. They asked me to testify.

My text messages to Eugene often go unanswered for
hours. Sometimes days. Today, the answer arrives in less than a
minute.

Eugene: Which side asked you to testify?

I consider making him wait for an answer, but I don't have
the patience.

Lucy: Both.

Eugene: I see. And which one are you going to choose?

Lucy: I haven't decided yet.

Eugene: Would you like to talk about it?

Lucy: Yes, please.

And that's how it comes about that I have one last date with Eugene. He thinks he is coming over to help me wrestle with the thorny question of which side I should throw my weight behind in my father's trial. I think he is coming over so I can have sex with him. We'll see which one of us is right.

On the off chance that it is me, I make an effort to tidy my cottage. The crocheted blanket goes under the bed, along with a pile of clothes and underwear. I open the door and all the windows to air the place out. I splash detergent around in the bathroom. I open a black bin bag and throw many things into it. Then I wash the dishes, wipe the counters and put things out of sight in the kitchen.

The place looks better. It is now merely shabby, rather than dirty. I buy vegetables, cut them up and serve them on a plate with hummus for dipping. I can offer him coffee, but it is instant, so he might decline.

The hardest part is stripping off my suit of armour. I refuse to greet Eugene in a long skirt over tights and cycling shorts, paired with a high-necked blouse and a cardigan. But without my uniform I feel exposed and naked, like a white grub flailing in the light when you lift a rock off its back.

I put on a pair of jeans and a long-sleeved top. They feel inadequate. I have to remind myself that I am not trying to keep everyone out today. There is someone I want to allow in.

Or do I?

I am struggling to access that surge of libido I felt a few weeks ago. Eugene will be arriving shortly, and I'm not ready. Perhaps seeing him in all his physical perfection will do the trick. But it's not really about him. It's about me. The engine of my libido is self-propelled. If I can't get it to fire, this will be just another insipid conversation over coffee that reminds us both that we don't get along.

I close my eyes and try to locate my inner heat. I am Shadrach, Mesach and Abednego preparing to enter the fiery furnace. But when I crank the door open, I find only cold, dead ashes. I keep seeing my father's eyes colliding with mine over the shoulders of my attackers. It's ruining the mood.

Is the human libido like a car battery? If you don't use it, do you lose it? Do the power cells become depleted until they are impossible to recharge, and the whole battery is an inert lump? At least you can replace a car battery. You can take out the old one, throw it away, and replace it with a powerful new version.

I imagine myself lifting my old libido out of my pelvis. It is chilly and covered in dust. There are cobwebs hanging from its sides like tattered curtains. I discard it on the dust heap of things unremembered and unregretted. Then I fit myself with a shiny new libido. It is warm to the touch and hums with stored energy. My pelvis feels cosier already, and a gentle warmth starts to thaw the neglected parts of my body.

I open my eyes and smile.

It's working.

Eugene presents himself at my door at the prearranged time of four o'clock. It is a Saturday afternoon, and he has once again told me he has to work this evening. He wants a reason to leave early if conversation starts to flag. I don't mind.

Today he is wearing a pair of faded jeans and a checked shirt. His Instagram page is full of hipster friends of both sexes. I am glad he doesn't personally affect the Edwardian beard or manbun of his fellows. The checked shirt is enough of a nod in that direction. His hair is short, but not militarily so. There are flyaway bits and suggestions of a curl that hint at the luxurious mass that would burst forth from his head if he allowed it to grow unchecked.

One advantage of the hipster plague sweeping Cape Town is that it makes my protective clothing look like a fashion choice rather than an iteration of fear.

"You look different today," he says as I let him into the cottage.

"I felt like a change."

His eyes sweep incuriously around the room, absorbing nothing. I wasted my time clearing up. He wouldn't have noticed the signs of dysfunction.

As with many physically gifted individuals, Eugene doesn't have to try very hard in social situations. He holds himself to a lower standard when it comes to interacting with others. His manner doesn't have to be as ingratiating or his conversation as engaging as those of less strikingly beautiful individuals.

This probably extends to sex as well. I don't mind that, either.

I put the vegetables and dip on the table and offer him coffee, which he accepts. As I prepare it, he asks whether I've decided what to do about testifying.

"Not yet. What do you think I should do?"

"I think you should say what happened. Whether it ends up hurting or helping your father, it's the truth and it needs to be said out loud in open court."

I take a carrot stick and dip it in flavoured mayonnaise. When I put it in my mouth, it assaults my tongue with barbaric flavours. I shudder and force myself to chew and swallow. I sip water, reassured by its blandness. My palate has become habituated to my meagre diet. Anything else feels like an invasion.

I wonder what Eugene will taste like. Will my mouth reject him too? Will his tongue taste acrid against my tongue? Will his skin leave a trail of salt on my lips? Perhaps my body will reject him like it rejected the carrot stick. I might have to smear him in tinned peach juice to make him acceptable.

Of course, it is possible to have sex without involving the mouth, but some humans don't favour that option. I remember one of the men who attacked me planting wet, open-mouth kisses on every inch of me he could reach—my shoulder, my ear, my chin. I scrubbed for days to eliminate the sense-memory of his saliva on my skin.

When Eugene has finished his coffee, I take the cup out of his hand and lay it on the table. I move the vegetables and dip out of his reach.

He looks at me enquiringly. It is clear that my actions are not casual. I am initiating something, but he doesn't know what.

"I want to have sex with you. Just once. It will be the first time since I was attacked." My observation of Eugene has led me to conclude that this approach is the most likely to succeed. If I could have traded on his overwhelming physical attraction to me, I would have, but it is clear that the chemistry between us is tepid at best.

He can choose to believe that his magical penis has the power to fix me, if he likes, but I will know the truth—that I am taking a step towards fixing myself.

I have taken him by surprise. He looks at me with his mouth slightly open as he struggles to process my request.

"I am going to take my top off now," I say. "If you don't want me to do that, just put your hand on my arm and I'll stop."

I cross my arms over my body and take hold of my T-shirt at the hem. Then I pull it up, up, up very slowly, giving him all the time in the world to touch my arm.

He will do it now, I think as the T-shirt covers my face, blinding me and causing my breath to blow back at me. Now. He will do it now.

The T-shirt is off. The air in the cottage stirs against my skin, raising goose flesh on my arms and mottling my shoulders pink and white and purple. I expect him to avert his eyes, but he doesn't. I allow myself to feel a man's gaze stinging my body for the first time in two years. Panic threatens to rise, but I breathe it back down.

Eugene stands up and takes my hand, pulling me to my feet. He reaches behind my back and touches the clasp of my bra.

"May I?"

I nod.

He unfastens it and draws the straps over my shoulders and down my arms until it falls to the floor. He rubs my shoulders with his hands, trying to warm me up. It is the gesture of an adult to a child. I don't want to be the child in this interaction.

I invite him to follow me to my bedroom. The air is heavier in here than it was in the kitchen. It is weighed down by the nights I have spent in this bed—the dreams I have dreamed. I take off the rest of my clothes and ask Eugene to do the same.

When we are both naked, I look at him for a long time. His body is even more beautiful without clothes. It is a great privilege for me to have access to all this perfection, but I can't allow myself to feel grateful. The last time I had sexual intercourse there was an imbalance of power. This time I am determined that there shouldn't be. Besides, gratitude is not sexy.

I am thinking too much.

I close my eyes and think about the furnace again—about lighting a spark and rekindling that furnace. About heating up the cold, dead ashes. About a warm glow and a slowly rising heat. About quickening and swelling and lengthening and expanding.

Sexual energy is a tangible force. When I open my eyes, I know Eugene can feel it in the room with us. He is becoming aroused. I move towards him and let the energy take over. Touching, tasting, stroking, licking. Our movements become clumsy and urgent. I want this to last, but I also want it over quickly.

The needs driving me are exigent, bold, powerful. But they are also fragile, weak, ephemeral. One wrong word, one impatient look, could banish them forever. The longer this takes, the more likely it is that something will go wrong.

I push the pace along, driving us forward with a momentum that won't be denied. I want the moment of penetration to be frantic and mindless. I want to be out of my head and in my body when it happens. I don't want to think about what it means.

Pressure is building inside me, a wave of tension that begs for release. I look down the length of my body and see that it has already happened. Penetration has occurred, and Eugene is inside me.

Disequilibrium strikes. All is fear and force. Seawater rushes in and extinguishes the furnace in a wave of disappointment. The ashes are not merely cold now, they are a swill—rainwater in an ashtray on a damp Sunday afternoon.

Eugene stops moving. He breathes, and I breathe, but he doesn't withdraw. I tighten the ring of my vaginal muscles around his rubber-sheathed penis, feeling the three-dimensionality of it. It doesn't hurt. I am hugging it into my body rather than being stabbed by it. Carefully, deliberately, I welcome it into me. I am the genial hostess, not the terrified victim of a home invasion.

The cold seawater ebbs away. The pilot light dries out. The tinder crackles with dry potential. Now the furnace is alight again, and Shadrach, Mesach and Abednego face imminent immolation. The fire roars through my body in a cleansing sheet of flame, reducing me to cinders.

* * *

Eugene behaves well afterwards. He lies with me without speaking after dropping the condom into my waste basket. He doesn't check the time. He doesn't allow restlessness to twitch at his limbs. He holds me in a way that mimics affection. I am the one who breaks the spell by sitting up. When I come back from the bathroom, he hasn't moved. Perhaps he is dead.

"I think it might rain later."

Not dead, then.

"Maybe," I say.

"The air smells like rain. And I thought I heard a rumble of thunder."

Cape Town is traumatised by the memory of a drought. People who normally don't talk about the weather are obsessed with the will-it-or-won't-it of precipitation.

"Goodness knows we need it," I say, according to the accepted formula.

I start putting my clothes back on, which Eugene takes as his cue to do the same.

"Have you made up your mind yet?" he asks.

"About what?"

"About whether you are going to testify, and for which side."

"Oh, that."

I forgot that I used that dilemma as a pretext for luring him here.

"Yes," I say. "I've decided. I know what I'm going to do."

He glances at me, but I don't elaborate. I have decided, and that is enough.

CHAPTER 18

J acob of the Journal of African Literature of the Diaspora has been pestering me to commit to a time when he can interview me for his special edition.

I flirt with the idea of insisting that I will write the paper myself, rather than be interviewed for it. It would be a foot in the door if I ever wanted to return to academia. The problem is, I'm not sure I remember how to write like an academic. It is a particular discourse that you lose if you don't use it for a few years. It's like becoming rusty in a foreign language, and I am very rusty indeed.

Two years ago, I could not only understand phrases like "heuristic meta-analysis," "empiricism of hubris," and "collective locus of agency," but use them correctly. Now I fear I would confuse my logocentric assumptions with my epistemic violence.

I could take the time to brush up on some of the most used catchphrases, but time is what I don't have. The deadline for submission is rushing towards me, and hurrying is something I've become bad at. Perhaps it would be easier to submit to the process of interview.

I message Jacob and let him know I am available to be interviewed. My phone rings almost immediately.

"Would you really count John Coetzee as an African writer of the diaspora?" I ask as we get underway. I know he is supposed to be interviewing me, but I have questions.

"Well, yes. He was born and raised in South Africa, and now lives in Adelaide. That's the very definition of diaspora."

"You know he doesn't refer to himself as a South African any more, never mind an African? He calls himself an Australian. He has taken citizenship of that country and refers to himself and his fellow antipodeans as 'We Australians.'"

"Yes, I've heard that. But it doesn't negate the reality of his origins. He lived the first sixty-two years of his life in Africa, and only the last several months in Australia. That doesn't make him an Australian, whatever he may claim."

This is exactly what I think. It is wonderful to hear that someone agrees with me. Some of the stress of my furious internal argument abates.

You are not an Australian, Prof. Coetzee, you are not. And you cannot wish yourself into being one.

"This special edition we are working on deals with the disjuncture between real-life narratives and the fictionalised versions of them. And while we acknowledge that turning any experience into narrative necessarily involves a form of fictionalising, we are interested in exploring that tense and contested space between what we may loosely term fiction and what we may even more loosely term reality."

I make assenting noises. So far so predictable.

"Your name came up because of recent revelations in the press about your assault. The narrative that appears in Coetzee's book has been replaced, as it were, by a new narrative. We are no longer dealing with a standard farm-violence scenario a stranger-danger, cross-racial sexual assault. It now appears that the whole incident was masterminded by a white man, your father. That changes the complexion of the thing, doesn't it?"

I agree that it does.

"Which is not to say, of course, that Coetzee's narrative has been invalidated. It remains an iconic novel of massive importance and resonance. But our knowledge of what really happened changes the lens through which we view *Disgrace*. We might, for example, start to question Coetzee's automatic and uncritical acceptance of the stranger-rape scenario, mightn't we?"

"Well . . ."

"But let me not get stuck in lecturer mode." He chuckles. "The point of today's exercise is to make room for your narrative. How do you interpret this new dialogue between what 'really' happened and what Coetzee wrote about? It must have added new layers of interest for you."

"Interest doesn't quite capture it."

"I'm all ears."

Now that I have an audience hanging on my words, anxious to hear about these issues that have preoccupied me for the last two years, I hardly know where to begin. I feel my tongue cleave to the roof of my mouth. I ask myself if this is really happening, if I will allow it to happen. Will I really blow my chance to be understood, to express everything that has been boiling inside my brain?

"I never accepted Coetzee's narrative in the first place," I say. I hear scratching sounds as Jacob takes notes. "I was never that woman—fiction-Lucy. I was never her. I don't believe any woman is her. She is the product of male fantasy. The angelic victim who accepts her rape as a natural part of the order of things. Who takes the punishment for colonialism upon her own body and happily bears the child that results from it. Who chooses to live amid her assailants and share her life with them."

Jacob makes interested noises.

"If the message of atonement and reconciliation had been framed in any other way, I could have accepted it. If it had been represented in any other way besides the rape of a woman. That's what places it beyond the pale. And the fact that he used my own rape as his template for this message makes it even worse. No woman's rape should be appropriated and used as a metaphor. It's completely unacceptable."

"A valid argument," mutters Jacob. "And yet Coetzee's book has been well received, hasn't it? It has gained considerable traction as the final word on the reconciliation narrative. It is unlikely that there will be another text of sufficient stature to replace it. It straddles our literature like a colossus."

"I like to think my own narrative has the power to unseat it. Especially now that the waters have been muddied with evidence of my father's involvement in the rape. It has become just another incident of family violence. I think when people see that Coetzee got the whole story wrong, it will undermine his credibility."

There is a sound like air being squeezed out of a cushion. It is Jacob laughing. "I'm afraid I can't see that happening. If you want your own rape to become the dominant narrative, you will have to tell it yourself. And in such a way that it eclipses his. That's not very likely, is it?"

"It has to happen. It has to. I will make it happen."

"What do you want from John Coetzee, Ms. Lurie? Really, when you come right down to it, what do you want from him?"

"I want him to sit opposite me while I explain why he shouldn't have used my rape in his book. Then I want him to look me in the eye while he apologises and acknowledges that he was wrong."

More air wheezing out of a cushion. "How will you achieve this face-to-face meeting? Will you pursue him to the ends of the earth? Will you go all the way to Adelaide?"

"If I have to."

"So you are Ahab and he is your white whale."

"You're not the first to make that observation."

"You will never unseat or even unsettle Coetzee's narrative because he is canonical, and you are fringe. He is the English literature degree, and you are the gender studies module. He is the default and you are the outlier. You don't have the power to replace his version with your own."

"You are probably right, but I won't stop trying."

"We at the *Journal of African Literature of the Diaspora* are happy to do what we can to give you a platform. This interview will serve as your first public challenge to Coetzee. If he still moves in academic circles, he will hear of it. Of course, it will be framed in such a way as to make it clear that you are the hyena snapping and whining at the heels of a lion, hoping for scraps of its meal. The most dignified course for Coetzee will be to ignore it."

I am not sure whether he says these last words out loud or not.

TRACY WHITEGIRL'S LEGAL BLOG ON THE INTERNET

Today is the day. In the matter of the State v David Lurie, the defendant's daughter Lucy Lurie is expected to testify for the state. Public interest is running high and the courtroom will be packed with journalists from all over the world.

The state is represented by Bheki Khumalo who will lead Ms. Lurie as she presents her evidence of what happened on that fateful evening when she was assaulted in her father's presence by six men who had broken into the house.

Mr. Lurie is accused of having planned and orchestrated the attack. It is the state's case that he hired the six men to make the break-in look like a random home invasion. His motive is believed to have been the money paid out by the insurance company after his farmhouse was torched by the men. Police sources say they might never have looked more closely at the case if they hadn't been tipped off by the insurance company.

Insurance assessors became suspicious when Mr. Lurie

tried to inflate the value of his property and possessions as the claim dragged on over two years. Had he not drawn attention to himself in this way, the alleged fraud might never have been discovered.

The judge, Mohale Mkhwane, has entered the court-room and invited the state to call its next witness. Lucy Lurie is sworn in and settles herself in the witness box. She looks pale but composed, glancing only occasionally at the table where the defendant's team sits. Her father is there, flanked by high-priced lawyers, and looking sober and respectable in a three-piece suit.

Advocate Khumalo thanks Ms. Lurie for her presence here today and expresses sympathy for her ongoing ordeal. He does so at such length that Judge Mkhwane invites him to move matters along.

KHUMALO SC: Miss Lurie, could you describe for us what happened on the night of the third of April when you had dinner with your father?

MS. LURIE: Certainly, Advocate Khumalo.

MKHWANE J: Please address your responses to me, Ms. Lurie. Not to counsel for the state.

MS. LURIE: Right, yes. Sorry, M'Lady. On the evening in question, I arrived at my father's house at about five o'clock in the afternoon.

KHUMALO SC: Were you expected?

MS. LURIE: Yes, it was a long-standing arrangement, and one we had confirmed by text message as recently as that morning.

KHUMALO SC: If it please the court, I would like to enter into evidence these transcripts taken from the defendant's phone and the witness's phone, showing that the arrangement had been discussed between them several times over the preceding weeks.

MKHWANE J: Hand them to the bailiff. Continue, Ms. Lurie.

MS. LURIE: Yes, M'Lady. I had been at my father's house for nearly three hours when the front door burst open and six men streamed into the house. They were armed with knives. One of them took my father away to make him reveal the whereabouts of the safe, and the other five attacked me. They held knives to my throat and made me take off my jeans and pants. Then they raped me one by one.

KHUMALO SC: Did they discuss it among themselves first?

MS. LURIE: They seemed to. They mimed the action. I assumed they were discussing whether there was enough time for them all to rape me. Then they just got on with it.

KHUMALO SC: Did they all have erections?

MS. LURIE: Yes, M'Lady.

KHUMALO SC: Did they all penetrate your vagina with their penises?

MS. LURIE: Yes, they did, M'Lady.

KHUMALO SC: Did any of them make use of condoms?

MS. LURIE: No, M'Lady.

KHUMALO SC: Did they all ejaculate?

MS. LURIE: I can't be sure of that, M'Lady. I lost track. Some of them raped me more than once. I know the doctor who examined me and performed the rape kit retrieved several samples of semen.

KHUMALO SC: Where was your father during all this?

MS. LURIE: As far as I knew, he was being forced to open his safe by the sixth man. But then the sixth man was in the room too. The others stood back and let him take his turn raping me. I was numb and exhausted by then. I had been in that position for so long that I couldn't feel much any more. That was when I opened my eyes and saw my father looking at me, at what was happening to me.

KHUMALO SC: And what did you see in his eyes, Miss Lurie?

DESHEN SC: Objection, M'Lady. Counsel is asking the witness to speculate about the significance of the defendant's facial expressions. That is well beyond the scope of the witness's expertise.

MKHWANE J: Your objection is sustained, Mr. Deshen. Mr. Khumalo, kindly limit your questioning to matters within the direct scope of this witness's knowledge.

KHUMALO SC: As your ladyship pleases. Miss Lurie, what was your father doing while you were being assaulted?

MS. LURIE: I used to think he was staring in horror at what was happening to me—that his inaction was caused by the paralysis of shock. But in recent months I have come to realise that he was simply . . . watching.

DESHEN SC: Objection, M'Lady. Counsel has sneaked this speculation into the record under the guise of legitimate observation. It is entirely groundless. The witness has no way of knowing what the defendant was thinking or feeling during this terrible assault.

MKHWANE J: Sustained again, Mr. Deshen. The witness's testimony with regard to what the defendant was doing during the rape will be struck from the record.

If Lucy Lurie thought she had a tough time during Advocate Khumalo's examination-in-chief, she soon discovered what a tough time really meant when counsel for the defence, Advocate Imraan Deshen, began his cross-examination of her. Examination-in-chief is a much friendlier and more rule-bound process. There are strict limits on how counsel may phrase his or her questions, and the extent to which he or she may put words in the witness's mouth.

Examination-in-chief is to cross-examination as a civilised tea party is to the Wild West. During cross-examination, almost anything goes. Counsel can be as hostile as he likes. He can interrupt the witness, badger her, put words in her mouth, express disbelief at what she is saying, and call her a straight-up liar if he wants. This was the part where the prosecution's legal team should have taken great care in preparing Ms. Lurie for what was to come. Perhaps they did, but it was difficult anyway. No amount of preparation can steel you for the process of having your integrity, your character, your very being flayed alive in open court.

DESHEN SC: What were you wearing to have dinner with your father, Miss Lurie?

MS. LURIE: What was I wearing? Gosh, it must be on record somewhere. Jeans, I think, and . . .

DESHEN SC: Low-rise skinny jeans, according to police records, Miss Lurie, and a skimpy low-cut top. M'Lady, the defence would like to submit into evidence this artist's impression of the clothing Miss Lurie was wearing on the night in question. As you can see, Miss Lurie, the jeans you were wearing were skin-tight, and the top was cut so low as to reveal a portion of your breasts. I put it to you, Miss Lurie, that no decent young woman would wear such an outfit to have dinner at her father's house.

MS. LURIE: No, I assure you, there was nothing at all unusual about that outfit. It was very much in fashion two years ago. . .

DESHEN SC: And now, Miss Lurie? And now? Do you still wear such harlot's garb?

MS. LURIE: Well, no. Not any more. But that's because of the trauma I experienced which made me believe, incorrectly as it turned out, that I was somehow responsible. . .

DESHEN SC: Shame, Miss Lurie. That would be a good word for what you experienced, wouldn't it? Shame, for the inappropriately sexual clothes you chose to flaunt your body in under your father's roof. Shame, for the lack of decorum that let you visit your own father dressed like a temptress—like the Whore of Babylon herself.

MS. LURIE: No, you've got it all wrong. Those clothes are normal street wear for a woman in her twenties, or of any age for that matter.

DESHEN SC: Then why have you stopped wearing them, Miss Lurie? Why do you now drape yourself like a woman of decency and propriety, if not because you have realised the error of your ways? If not because you have acknowledged to yourself, if to no one else, that you brought your rape upon yourself by dressing like a sexual object? If you clothe yourself as a sexual object, how can you blame the rest of the world when it treats you as such? The world takes you at your own valuation, and you valued yourself as a common tramp. Of course, you got raped. How could it have been otherwise?

KHUMALO SC: Objection, M'Lady. Counsel is badgering the witness.

MKHWANE J: Yes, indeed. Mr. Deshen, I think you've made your point.

In every criminal case, the defence team has one crucial decision to make—whether to put the defendant on the stand or not. The correct decision is almost always to keep the defendant as far from testifying as possible. Many defendants are champing at the bit to get their moment in court, convinced that all the judge or jury needs to find in their favour is a few well-chosen words from them. They are nearly always wrong.

The problem with defendants is that they are usually

guilty, which means that the only contribution they can make to their own case on the witness stand is to sink it. It's all very well for the defendant to present his version of events to the court. Sometimes this can even be helpful. The trouble starts during cross-examination when prosecuting counsel has carte blanche to rip the defendant's testimony to pieces, to tie him up in knots, and to expose him as the liar he (very often) is.

Analysts are watching the David Lurie trial with interest to see which way the defence team will jump. David Lurie has been on their witness list from the beginning, but that was understood to be no more than an exercise in keeping their options open. The question is: will they actually call him to the stand?

Pundits have also speculated about whether Lucy Lurie will be in court to watch her father's testimony if he does take the stand. Will she want to hear his version of events, or will she choose to absent herself? And will Lurie himself speak more freely with his daughter out of the courtroom than if she is in it? Surely her physical presence watching and listening as he gives his testimony will inhibit him in some way?

DESHEN SC: Good morning, Mr. Lurie. Please accept the thanks of the court for being willing to assist us in this matter.

DAVID LURIE: It's a pleasure. I know Your Ladyship's time is valuable, and mine is too. I'm sure we can sort this out quickly enough if we put our minds to it.

DESHEN SC: I'm sure we can, Mr. Lurie. Would you please explain to this court what you were hoping to achieve when you hired those men to break into your house?

DAVID LURIE: Certainly, M'Lady. You must understand that the farmhouse in Worcester was originally the property of my wife's parents. They gave it to her when we got married, and she in turn left it to me when she died.

DESHEN SC: I see. A mixed blessing, perhaps?

DAVID LURIE: Precisely. I was left with a millstone around my neck, with most of my capital tied up in it. I'm an urban creature, M'Lady, happiest when I am close to the shops, the theatre, my golf club. The farmhouse offered a rural existence far from these creature comforts, and it was stifling me. I admit it freely, M'Lady. Stifling me.

DESHEN SC: Very understandable, I'm sure.

DAVID LURIE: I longed to sell the farmhouse, but it was such a bad time. Two years ago, the property market was at its nadir. It was a buyer's market, and nothing was moving. Properties were spending months, if not years, on the market, with no takers unless the owners dropped the price to such an extent that they were virtually giving it away.

DESHEN SC: I hate to play the devil's advocate here, but could you not have waited it out? The property market has recovered well in the last year, after all.

DAVID LURIE: Look, I suppose I could have, but Your Ladyship must understand that I was getting impatient. I had lived in that farmhouse for nearly twenty-five years. I didn't know if the property market would ever recover enough for me to get a decent amount of money for the house. And I'd been faithfully paying my insurance premiums for all that time. Was it really so unreasonable of me to want something back?

MKHWANE J: Insurance companies! Don't get me started. They are the worst. You pay and pay and pay for years, but as soon as you want them to pay you, they have a thousand reasons not to.

DAVID LURIE: Exactly, M'Lady. It occurred to me that the house was worth more on paper than it was on the market, and that the quickest way for me to access that money was via my insurance policy.

DESHEN SC: Mr. Lurie, it is my duty as an officer of this court to remind you at this time that you have accepted a deal from the prosecution whereby you will testify fully and frankly to the events of the night in question in return for leniency with regard to insurance fraud. Do you understand the terms of this arrangement?

DAVID LURIE: I do.

DESHEN SC: You have testified by affidavit to the fact that you hired these men to set fire to your farmhouse so that you could claim the insurance money on it. But now the court needs to know why you also asked them to rape your daughter. It seems extraneous. Did you have a grudge against her?

DAVID LURIE: Goodness, no, M'Lady. Not at all. I have no objection in the world to the girl. It was just for authenticity. It had to look like a real break-in, you see, but I didn't want them to steal anything of real value. I was going to take the valuables—the electronics, a few bits of jewellery—out with me in a backpack, and everything else was supposed to burn in the fire. So what could the motivation for the break-in be if not robbery? I immediately thought of rape. My daughter is an attractive girl, or at least she was. You might not think so to look at her now, but she used to be pretty. No one would question that as a motive. They broke in to rape her. It made sense.

DESHEN SC: Forgive me, Mr. Lurie, but I have to ask. Did you have no qualms about making this decision? Did it not trouble you to think about the ordeal your daughter would undergo?

DAVID LURIE: Of course it did, M'Lady. I'm not a monster. I thought about it long and hard before I made this decision. But the fact is, my daughter and I have never been close. She was much closer to her mother than to me. And she was part of the problem. She was very attached to the farmhouse and didn't want to sell it. Her mother left it to both of us, but it was insured in my name only. I thought that after the rape, she would be too disoriented to look closely at the title deeds and start demanding half of the money. And I was right. She didn't give it a second thought.

DESHEN SC: I see. Yes, I see. I think I speak for this court as a whole when I say that you had no choice. You did what you had to do.

DAVID LURIE: I knew if I had the opportunity to stand up and tell my story that you would see it my way. I'm a reasonable man, M'Lady. And this is a court full of reasonable men. Mutatis mutandis, of course, M'Lady. We are all reasonable men.

In a stunning twist in the case of the State v David Lurie, the accused, Mr. David Lurie, seemed to talk the court around to his way of thinking this morning.

Before today, commentators were adamant in their belief that the defence was making a serious misstep in putting Mr. Lurie on the stand at all. They believed he could accomplish nothing beyond giving the state more ammunition to hammer him on in cross-examination.

Mr. Lurie proved the naysayers wrong in his evidence-in-chief today. The lawyers, the audience in court, and the judge seemed to be eating out of his hand. Even this journalist has to own herself convinced. When David Lurie got the bit between his teeth and explained why he'd had no choice but to order the gang rape of his own daughter, you could have heard a pin drop.

What a triumph for the defence. When we look back on

this case and talk about the moment at which the momentum of the trial swung away from the prosecution and towards the defence, this is what we will be discussing. Today was a black day for the prosecution, a black day indeed. I don't see how they can recover from this. David Lurie has dealt a stunning blow to the state's case, and most pundits can't see the prosecution coming back from it.

CHAPTER 19

T he trial hasn't started. While I was trying to make up my mind about whom to testify for, my psychologist—Lydia Bascombe—presented me with a thought experiment. She told me to walk myself through two possible scenarios for the trial in my mind: one in which I testified for the prosecution, and one in which I testified for the defence. She told me to imagine the best- and worst-case scenarios for both options, and to think them through. She believed that would help me decide which choice I could live with.

The scenario I came up with was a kind of mixture of both options. In that sense, I didn't fulfil the brief she gave me. But it helped me to realise one thing—this trial cannot be good for me. Participating in it will damage me in ways I can't begin to imagine. Even watching it or following the proceedings in the media will hurt me.

I don't know what my father will say if he takes the stand. I don't know what the defence's case will be, but I do know that I don't want to hear it. Whether he denies the charges completely and claims that my assailants acted on their own, or pleads guilty to everything and accepts full responsibility, none of it will make me feel good.

The tiny fragments of mental health I have managed to claw back over the past few months will be scattered by this trial. I may never get them back. This trial is the depth charge that will undo me.

And so I have made up my mind not to testify for either

side. I will also not attend the trial, or follow it in the media. I will make myself not care whether my father is convicted or acquitted. My peace of mind cannot be allowed to depend on these events over which I have no control. It can also not be allowed to depend on the illusion of control.

If I testify for or against my father, I might start believing I have control over the outcome. If things don't go the way I want, I will always believe that I could have done something differently, that it is my fault things turned out the way they did. And so, I am removing myself from this circus. It will continue without me, and I without it.

Lydia Bascombe is impressed with my capacity to make decisions that are good for me.

L. BASCOMBE: You are starting to practise self-care. This is an excellent development. I applaud your willingness to remove yourself from situations that are hurting you.

ME: Do you? Or do you think I'm letting my father down by not testifying for him?

L. BASCOMBE: I never thought that. That was a belief you imposed on me, fuelled by your own guilt and self-doubt.

ME: Would it not be better for the sake of closure to see the trial through?

L. BASCOMBE: Sometimes, in seeking closure, we merely open more unresolved issues for ourselves to stew over.

ME: So, I would hear things that would bother me more than I am already bothered?

L. BASCOMBE: Precisely. The only thing that concerns me is whether you will spend the rest of your life wondering why your father did what he did. Might it not be better to hear the truth once, so you can start processing it?

ME: Would he tell the truth?

L. BASCOMBE: I don't know. Possibly not.

ME: Besides, I think I know why he did it. He wanted the housebreaking to look authentic, but he didn't want the men to take anything valuable. And he found it exciting to engineer my rape. For years, I believed it was shock and grief I saw on his face as he watched me being raped, but a part of me always recognised it as excitement. It was thrilling for him to witness my violation. I don't think he knew himself how he would react until it happened. He is not a good man. My mother was a good woman, but my father is not a good man.

L. BASCOMBE: And what are you?

ME: I am human, and therefore fallible. I am middle class, and have therefore not had my goodness tested much. I am broken by what has been done to me. A broken thing isn't capable of meaningful moral choices.

L. BASCOMBE: Are you ready to give up your obsession with John Coetzee?

ME: No.

* * *

The *Journal of Literature of the African Diaspora* has been out for several weeks now. When an invitation to join a panel discussion lands in my inbox, I am excited for a few seconds, believing that John Coetzee will be one of the panellists. He won't, of course. There will be two men and two women, including me. The other three people on the panel are academics. I will be embarrassingly out of place. Or rather, I will be the hamster and they will be the scientists. All four belong in the laboratory, but not on equal terms.

The discussion will be held at a SAPIENS conference at Constantia University. SAPIENS stands for something like the South African Parastatal for Industrial, Economic and Natural Sciences. It makes for a nice acronym—one that suggests wisdom on the part of the members, without overtly making any such claim.

They are holding a symposium based on the articles in the journal, all of which have generated considerable interest in the public sphere. While academics take their own work very seriously, they are not accustomed to anyone else doing so. The fact that this edition of the journal has been tweeted about, blogged about, and even discussed on television, has come as a pleasant surprise to the contributors.

The truth is that Constantia University is in disarray. It is riven by factions that loathe each other with an intensity that permits no middle ground. You have the black radicals who believe that the sight of a white person should come with a trigger warning. They disrupt university events, demanding that nothing may proceed until all white people have been cleared from the room. When invited speakers in the form of Black Consciousness icons object to this policy, they are condemned as Uncle Toms who have lost their edge and relevance.

Then you have white students from Sandton and Newlands who chose Constantia University precisely because there weren't all that many black students there. These white students vote for the DA and support a person they refer to as Moosie. Imagine their surprise when the black students who do go to Constantia turn out to be more militant than their most fevered dreams could have imagined.

And finally, you have the vegans. This tiny but vocal minority disrupts staff meetings to protest the presence of doughnuts made with palm oil on the menu. When management points out that it is sustainable palm oil, they say there is no such thing. They equate factory farming with #BlackLivesMatter and the Holocaust. Of the three factions, the vegans are the smallest, but the least reasonable.

The hope is that this SAPIENS conference will have a unifying effect on the faculty and student body. I am sceptical, but have agreed to participate. The latest rumour is that John Coetzee may join the conference via video link from Adelaide. This is enough to ensure my attendance. Berating John Coetzee over video link may be less satisfying than in person, but it remains a strong incentive.

The morning starts out well, with the first session of the day proceeding in a haze of self-congratulation. It is about African literature in translation. The panel of translators speak about the challenges facing them in transcribing local vernacular expressions into European languages, and about the drive to produce more literature in African languages. It is a subject everyone can agree on. The only enemy in the room is the straw man of monoglot neo-colonialism, and he is easily defeated.

Then comes tea time, and the miasma of goodwill is threatened by the vegans. The snacks are strictly vegan, with no palm oil in sight, but it has come to someone's attention that the syrupy filling inside some of the Danish pastries is not syrup at all, but honey. The vegans threaten to mobilise and disrupt the pre-lunch session. The omnivores say this is ridiculous and that we are all "bending over backwards" for the vegans. The vegans wave photographs of murdered calves in their faces, and the omnivores ask what the fuck calves have got to do with honey. The vegans accuse the omnivores of species-ism because the lives of insects are as valuable as the lives of mammals.

Then it is confirmed that the Danish pastries are made with syrup, not honey, and the panic is over.

The pre-lunch session is about the perception that literature produced by writers living outside of Africa is somehow more valuable than that written by writers living in Africa. The preponderance of diaspora literature on literary-award longlists is wheeled out as an undeniable statistic. Things get testy when a speaker from the floor launches into a long comment during question time. Another speaker puts up her hand and points out that white people have been allowed to attend this session on sufferance only, and that they should be respectful and not speak. Black voices have been silenced and suppressed for long enough, so it is time for white people to be quiet and listen.

The white commenter says this is ridiculous and that we are all "bending over backwards" for the radicals. He accuses the second speaker of "racism" and invites everyone to agree that "Madiba" would not support this. Then he stomps out in protest, as do his companions.

This brings the number of white people in the room down to one. I disclaim any desire to ask a question, and the session proceeds peacefully.

Lunch is an orgy of lentils, chickpeas and egg-free, dairy-free, gluten-free pasta. The vegans remark on how delicious everything looks. The radicals complain about how oppressed they feel at having their traditional foods banned from the menu because of a few bourgeois crackpots.

One of the vegans comments that anyone who supports #BlackLivesMatter should surely support animal rights too. One of the radicals comments that the vegan appears to be drawing an equivalence between black people and animals. The vegan accuses the radical of wilfully misunderstanding her, and says that we will one day look back in horror at this period of human history when it was legal to kill animals to eat their flesh. She reminds us that slavery used to be legal too. The radical comments that it now sounds as though the vegan is drawing an equivalence between meat-eating and slavery. A lively debate ensues, and the food gets cold.

Before actual blows can be exchanged, someone suggests adjourning to a nearby Nando's for lunch. This idea is hailed with enthusiasm by the black radicals, the white DA-supporters (who have returned for lunch), the administrative staff, the catering staff, and a guy who came into the wrong room by mistake. The vegans are left to enjoy their lentils in peace.

We file back into the conference venue. The delegates take their seats and sink into a post-prandial stupor. I trudge up to the stage, with a strong sense of impostor syndrome, to take my place among the panellists. This is the session that goes to the heart of the special issue of the journal. It is the one called "Fiction and faction: how real-world narratives inform fiction streams in the diaspora."

John Coetzee has reached a point in his career where whole conferences are dedicated to this single book of his. His life's work is contained between the covers of a single novel, but it is enough. People will never stop talking about what he has achieved. Even if he never publishes another thing, which seems increasingly likely, his immortality is assured.

All the other writers whose books were featured in the journal were discussed in previous sessions. John Coetzee has a session to himself. None of the others has the weight, the heft, the gravitas of this man who made my assault the basis for his book.

I notice a flat-screen TV mounted on the wall next to us. It is tilted slightly to face the audience. If John Coetzee appears today, it will be on that screen. I glance at my watch. It is two in the afternoon. That means it is nine in the evening in Adelaide. What are the chances that he will appear there, broadcast from the other side of the world? What are the chances that I will be able to challenge him on his appropriation of my life for fictional purposes?

The session gets underway. The moderator invites us to introduce ourselves. The first panellist is a Coetzee scholar. That is how he describes himself. Like it's a legitimate speciality. What did he do for the first four decades of his career, I wonder? He could hardly have been a "Coetzee scholar" before the book came out.

There is a sociologist who is conducting research on memoir as a site of healing. Then there is a literary theorist who writes about post-structuralism.

We start off with the three academics batting around some ideas about reality being a text, fiction being a text, and the relationship between the two being an intertextual conversation. It is, to put it mildly, an argument I have heard before. The literary theorist asks whether we can claim ownership over the events of our own life—the story of our life. Do we have any claim to understand that story better than anyone else, or even to tell it better?

A murmur of agreement ripples around the venue. The consensus seems to be that people have no special claim to the stories of their own lives. They don't have sole rights to it, and they don't have the power to withhold it from anyone else who wishes to tell it, modify it, exaggerate it, or change it completely.

"Then why does the law give us some measure of protection against those who tell falsehoods about our lives?" I ask.

"It's a limited protection," says the sociologist. "It applies only if you can prove that you have suffered harm as a direct consequence of the falsehood that has been told about you. Quantifiable, material harm."

"Okay, then. Are those who appropriate our stories and use them for their own ends ethically wrong to do so?" I am determined that John Coetzee shall be publicly judged for taking and using my story, even if only by this tiny and limited forum.

"Do you believe that John Coetzee was ethically wrong to take the story of your rape and turn it into a book?" asks the sociologist.

"I do."

"Who owns the rights to that story? You?"

"Yes, me."

"Were you ever going to use it? Were you going to write a book of your own about what happened to you?"

"Possibly not. But I would have been happy for a sympathetic feminist writer to write it—someone who wasn't going to portray my rape as a seminal, transformative experience for South Africa."

"You wanted quality control over the telling of your story? You wanted it to be told in a way that accords more closely with your world view than John Coetzee's version did?"

"It sounds untenable when you put it like that."

"Well, actually," says the Coetzee scholar, "I think you'll find that rape is a pretty universal experience. When women experience rape, they usually feel some measure of shame after the fact. They often blame themselves. It's only natural, considering that there is such a fine line between consent and the lack of consent these days. But there is nothing unique about rape. It's pretty much experienced in the same way by most women. If you think about it carefully, you'll realise that John Coetzee was taking the universal experience of rape and using it metaphorically for his literary purposes. You must try not to take it personally."

"You must also recognise and acknowledge that Coetzee is writing fiction," says the post-structuralist. "The world will be in a parlous state when fiction writers can no longer draw on real-world experiences—either their own or those of others— to inspire their stories. They must be able to write without fear or favour. They have to."

"I'm not proposing a worldwide ban against fiction writers," I say. "I am merely stating the fact that John Coetzee's book caused harm—both to me personally, and to the fight against rape culture in general. He set my healing back and retraumatised me. And he made respectable the notion that the rape of a woman can be used as an extended metaphor for the cathartic violence that black South Africans need to inflict on white South Africans in order for the country to move forward to a new, multiracial future. The Lucy in the book consents after the fact to her rape having been a vital and transformative process. She becomes the vessel through which the new world order will be born, in the person of her brown child."

"How is your personal journey of healing going now?" asks the sociologist.

"Better, thank you. It's now more than two years since the attack. I've had therapy, which has helped a little. I've learned to practise better self-care. I've learned to avoid situations that are damaging to me. I think I've made progress."

She looks as though she has bitten into something unpleasant-tasting.

"Your self-care is better, is it? You've learned how to help yourself heal? You have the luxury of choosing to walk away from situations that will damage you. Do you even hear how privileged you sound?"

The temptation to feel sorry for myself is very strong.

"I went through a hard time," I say.

"No harder than thousands of black women in this country. Women who have to see their abusers every day—perhaps live with them, cook for them, sleep with them. Women who don't have the space to avoid situations that retraumatise them. Women who don't get retraumatised by a book, but by a second assault, or a third, or a fourth. This was a once-in-a-lifetime occurrence for you. For many black women, it may happen several times. And then they watch it happen to their daughters."

"Yes, but . . . you can't quantify pain, can you? You can't really compare what different women are feeling . . ."

"Yes, you can. You can understand that racism and poverty make everything worse. When you suffer PTSD as a result of what happened to you, you have access to medicine and a therapist. Most black women have no access to any kind of support. Nothing. It is never even acknowledged that their pain exists. Try suffering from a mental illness in a poor and marginalised community. There are no words to articulate your pain. You go through it alone and have no name for it."

"I understand that, but . . ."

"That's why the doctrine of self-help, self-care and so on, is so dangerous. It places the burden of care for mental health on the individual, instead of on the system—where it belongs. And when individuals like yourselves—white, middle-class women—begin to heal, you give the credit to self-care rather than to the systemic privilege that gives you access to medication, counselling, exercise, and good nutrition. It makes it seem as if black women are responsible for their own misery. Like, if only they were better at self-care, they would cope better."

I feel hurt and misunderstood and attacked. Tears threaten to well up in my eyes. The tears of my white fragility. I have said all these things to myself before, but they had no power to hurt me then. Now, coming from the mouth of a black woman, they cut deep. Part of me wants to fight these ideas, to defeat them as you would an invading army. I can feel them threatening the very core of my being. Worse, I can feel them threatening my privilege. If I don't have my privilege, what is left?

Life is hard enough. How can I face it without my privilege? Why would anyone voluntarily give up their comfort and security? Would anyone benefit if I did? It's not that I want my privilege to be exclusive. I am happy for others to have privilege. I just don't want to give up mine so that they can also have some.

I have a capitalist soul. I believe there is enough to go around, especially if you make more. Not enough water for everyone? Just make more. Not enough oxygen to go around? Make more. Not enough food to feed everyone? Grow more. Not enough planet to house us all? Find another one.

I cannot bring myself to see these resources as finite, as having to be shared. The notion that I am wrong about this disturbs me in a very deep place—the heart of the child who hears that monsters are real after all. I thought I had faced all my monsters when I realised that my father organised my rape. I thought the world held no further terrors for me. I was wrong. It turns out that the prospect of losing one's privilege is the biggest terror of all.

I can feel the impulse to ridicule what this woman is saying, to call it absurd and dangerous. It rises in me like the urge to vomit. She is wrong. She must be wrong, because it is inconvenient for me if she is right. I force the impulse down. I make myself stop trying to raise objections, to exceptionalise myself, to legitimise my pain. I stop talking altogether, and listen. This is not something I am good at. I have spent so much time trying to make my voice heard that my ears are out of practice.

The sociologist continues talking about what it is like to be a poor black woman who has survived sexual assault in South Africa, and I try to listen even as the information batters my brain with unwelcome sensations.

"Don't look at me like that," she says. "I am not your path to self-awareness. I am not Spike Lee's 'Magical Negro' who will lead you to enlightenment. But I couldn't bear to listen to you speak about self-care another minute."

Then the large flat-screen monitor on the wall flickers and buzzes, and we fall silent.

"This is it!" says the moderator, not even trying to hide her excitement. "The moment we have all been waiting for. John Coetzee is joining us live from Adelaide. Let's give John a warm Constantia U welcome, everyone."

The audience claps and whistles and stamps, as though a Hollywood celebrity were visiting, rather than a man who taught here for over thirty unremarkable years.

I can't help it. I too am craning towards the screen like a flower seeking sunlight. But the face that resolves on the screen is not that of John Coetzee. It is a young woman with tight skin over her jawline and a sleek blow-dry. She introduces herself as John Coetzee's Australian publicist.

"Good afternoon to you. Professor Coetzee offers his compliments and apologises for not being able to make it today. He is busy writing. I think we can all agree that a new John Coetzee novel is worth sacrificing a panel discussion for." She smiles to show that this is humour, and a chuckle scampers around the room. "He did send a message, however, based on the journal papers that were sent to him in preparation for this session."

I almost fall out of my chair in my attempt to get closer to the screen—to miss not one single word of whatever may be coming now.

"He suggests that you stop making use of such dubious lenses for literary criticism as race, class and gender, and rather focus on a close analytical reading of the text itself. He is sure you would find that much more rewarding."

I glance around the room, looking for any suggestion of the eye-rolling that would have greeted this statement if John Coetzee had made it in his lecturing days. This is not a guess on my part: there were times I was physically present when Coetzee stated that any form of criticism besides that of the traditional New Critical close reading was invalid. On those occasions, he was derided as a dinosaur.

Today, everyone is nodding respectfully, as though he has supplied an insight none of us could have guessed at before.

"Professor Coetzee would also like to say that he doesn't consider himself to be part of the African diaspora. He is an Australian. Furthermore, Professor Coetzee would like to address himself to one person among you in particular . . ."

I lean forward hungrily, hoping to catch my name.

"Jacob Edelstein, the editor of this journal: Professor Coetzee wishes you could understand how peripheral Africa is to world culture. Now that he has moved to the centre of things, he has acquired insight into the marginality of Africa as a cultural entity. He wishes you would stop focusing on this artistic backwater and concentrate your energies rather on the Anglo-American world, where they would be relevant and appreciated."

There will be more, I am convinced of it. John Coetzee will have a message for me. Just for me. Some acknowledgement of my existence. A tribute to the contribution that my real-life circumstances made to this stunning change in his fortunes. If I hadn't been raped, he would not now be a global superstar. Surely that is worth a nod on his part?

"Professor Coetzee wishes you all the best with this conference and looks forward to reading the papers you sent him at some time in the future. Good afternoon to you."

The screen goes blank, and I stare at it with my Ahab eyes. The whale has escaped again. He hasn't read my interview, and probably never will. We break for tea, and there is a general movement towards the lounge where vegan biscuits and almond milk are being served.

I stay in my seat watching the screen. I have my harpoon in my hand, but the whale swims free. I can see his tail flicking into the air as he dives, and sounds. Then he rises up and blows spray into the air. He swims under water for hundreds of metres, then leaps into the air and falls back with a mighty splash. There is something joyful about his whaleness. He is living his best whale life, freer and more fulfilled than at any other time in his existence.

I wander through to the lounge and pour myself a cup of tea. I become aware of someone standing close to me. It is the sociologist—the black woman who brought my white tears up from a place deep inside and almost caused them to fall. I wonder if she intends to apologise. Perhaps she realises she hurt me, and wants to say sorry. Perhaps she wants to acknowledge that I am not like those other white people, the ones who are unconscious of their privilege. I am the exception. My exceptionalism shines through in everything I do, and perhaps she wants me to know that she is aware of that.

I smile at her, waiting for her to apologise.

"Your story is less interesting than you think."

It is going to be a long wait.

"But it is my story," I say. "And I should be the one to tell it."

"Then tell it."

"I do. In forums like this conference, and in journal articles like the diaspora collection."

"I'm talking about a novel."

This makes no sense, and I say so.

"You don't like the narrative John Coetzee has created out of your experience, so set up a competing narrative. Write your own novel. Tell your own story."

"Oh, no. I couldn't do that. It would make people uncomfortable. No one would want to read it. Coetzee's story would stand head and shoulders above it. His story is a clean, coherent narrative. It is powerful and iconic. Mine is an uncontrolled emotion dump, lacking in structure and framework. If John Coetzee's story is fountain pen on vellum, mine is menstrual blood on toilet paper."

"You have a problem with the way he framed your story, with the way he imagined your thoughts and reactions. So write your own novel. It will set up a tension between the two works. Your story will always exist in intertextual conversation with Coetzee's story."

"But it will be female and angry and incoherent and messy and ugly and raw."

"Then let it be so."